Undone

Double D Ranch
Book 1

Jeanne St. James

Jeanne
ST. JAMES

**Sign up for my newsletter for insider information, author news, and new releases:
https://www.authorjeannestjames.com/**

Double D Ranch Series

Undone (Book 1)
Unbridled (Book 2)
Unrestrained (Book 3)
Undeniable (Book 4)
Unexpected (Book 5)
Uninhibited (Book 6)

Chapter One

"I didn't expect us to be back here so soon," Dylan murmured, staring at the house in front of them.

The last time all three of them were home, it was for their father's funeral six months prior.

"We couldn't put it off any longer. Mom can't handle this place herself," Dayne said.

Dylan glanced at his younger brother. Younger by a mere six minutes. "Hell, she doesn't want to, either."

"Can you blame her?" their younger sister, Danica, spouted. Younger than them by five years.

"No," both he and his identical twin answered at the same time.

"We could sell it. It would be the easiest solution," Dayne suggested. His hands were planted on his hips and his hazel eyes narrowed on the old two-story farmhouse. "I certainly don't want to raise dairy cows and deal with all the bullshit that goes along with that."

Dani giggled. "Literally."

"Apparently, neither does Mom," Dylan added.

"Splattering cow pies, the relentless flies, and ornery heifers trying to kick you into next week are the whole reason I left as soon as I could." Dayne elbowed him. "Just like you did."

Their sister, standing between him and Dayne, exclaimed, "And I had to watch you two speed away with dirt kicking off those spinning tires. You two left me in the dust!"

"The hell if I was taking you with me and raising a smart-mouthed tween," Dayne informed her. "Did you forget we were only eighteen? Anyway, do you think Mom and Dad would've let you leave at thirteen?"

Dylan snorted. "And just think how messed up you would've been if Dayne raised you."

Dani elbowed him in the ribs. "You could've taken me in, Dylan. You were always the more responsible one."

"At least that stick up your ass is one thing we don't share," Dayne told him.

"I don't have a stick up my ass," Dylan grumbled.

Both of his siblings laughed. Louder than necessary.

They'd find out soon enough how untrue that was. Then he'd have the last laugh.

He shook his head. "Well, our choices are to either sell it or do something else with it." He wasn't sure if his siblings would go for his idea since it was unorthodox. Since their father willed the three-hundred-acre property to his two sons, Dayne would have to agree first.

"Sell," Dayne and Dani said at the same time.

"Or..." Dylan started.

His siblings turned to stare at him.

"Or what?" Dayne prodded and narrowed his eyes again, this time on Dylan.

Dani groaned. "I see those wheels spinning, Dayne. He's about to come up with some cockamamie idea."

Dayne *mmm*'d and scowled in his direction.

"I have good ideas sometimes," Dylan murmured.

Dani rolled her eyes. "They're few and far between."

"Too bad Dad didn't want to raise horses instead of Holsteins. I might have stayed," Dayne said next. "We could always trade the cows in for horses."

Dylan could've lived with raising and training horses, too, but their father had a dislike for them. He preferred riding his utility task vehicle to chase down a calf or travel to the far end of the three-hundred-acre farm. Unlike an ATV, his UTV had a roll cage, could fit more passengers and was less likely to tip. Plus, it had a larger tow capacity than a regular four-wheeler.

To Dad, a horse was unpredictable, but he never met a cow he didn't like. Dayne and Dylan felt the opposite.

Dayne went on, "Mom already found a smaller place in town. I don't think she'll care whether we keep or sell it."

"I don't think that's true," Dylan murmured. "She would love for us to take it over and keep it in the family since this farm was everything to him."

"Everything?" their sister exclaimed. "What are we? Chopped liver?"

"Don't twist what I'm saying. Of course we were important to him, but so was this farm. Even so, she told me she's leaving it up to us to decide what to do with it."

"You mean you two," Dani corrected, "since he didn't pass it on to me. Only you two boneheads."

Their sister must have a short memory. "Since you constantly complained about having to do chores around here, he didn't think you'd want anything to do with it."

"The value of the property? Sure I would. Squeezing cow nipples twice a day? No way."

A snort exploded from Dayne. "Automated milkers are used for that, sis."

"Even so, he named the damn farm Double D, instead of Triple D. That proves I'm always the forgotten one," their sister bitched.

"You weren't forgotten." Dylan reminder her, "You were born after they bought the farm."

"Yeah, you were a mistake," Dayne teased. With a grunt, he folded in half when she whacked his gut with the back of her hand. "You know what I mean."

"Not a mistake," Dylan clarified, "unexpected."

"I guess Mom and Dad humped like rabbits," Dani said.

Dylan groaned. "Please don't take us back to all the times we overheard it."

"Or accidentally walked in on them," Dayne added.

"Shut your face!" Dani yelled. "Just the thought of that is causing me emotional damage!"

"Join the damn club!" Dayne exclaimed. "But thanks to you being *unexpected*, I think they gave it a break afterward. At least you were good for something."

"They were probably too tired between running the farm and wrangling three kids to keep up their bedroom antics," Dylan murmured.

"Stop," Dani groaned.

"We're getting off track. What's this cockamamie idea, brother?" Dayne asked.

He needed to ease them into it. "First, let's discuss the farm name... We'll change it from Double D Farm to Double D Ranch."

Dani sighed. "See? Once again, I'm the forgotten one."

"We're not calling it Triple D Ranch. That doesn't sound as catchy. Anyway, who cares what the hell it's called? The point is to make this place profitable."

Dayne's brow dipped low. "Why 'ranch?' And didn't we just outvote you two to one on the decision to sell?"

"Maybe you'll reconsider your vote once I explain my idea."

"We're waiting," Dayne said dryly.

Dylan pulled in a breath. It was now or never. "I want to turn this place into a ranch resort. I'm calling it that because 'farm resort' doesn't make sense. We won't be making money off livestock or breeding horses. We'll make money off people looking for an escape, hence the resort part of the name. Dad constantly busted his ass and struggled to financially survive raising dairy cows and selling milk. We can make this property more profitable by turning it into a lucrative business."

"An escape," Dani echoed, then shook her head. "I'm confused. And it seems like you already have your plan mapped out before even clearing it with us."

"It's called a *business proposal,* so of course it's mapped out."

"I want to hear this so-called business proposal, sis." Dayne turned to Dylan. "You've got my attention. What does this so-called lucrative business entail?"

"What sells?" Dylan asked them.

All he got from his siblings were confused looks.

"Come on!" He impatiently threw up his hands. "Sex! Sex sells! Pleasure. Pampering. Peace and quiet. Or even the opposite. Parties. Mixers. Whatever."

Dani stared at him with wide hazel eyes and a gaping mouth. "What the hell are you talking about?"

It was time to let them know everything that had been swirling around in his head since their father died. Share the ideas that kept him up at night. The plans he'd been fleshing out for months. The business he'd been researching.

"Think about it. There are all-inclusive resorts on beautiful islands that cater to swingers. Around the world you can find plenty of BDSM clubs, strip clubs, sex clubs, sex shops and massage parlors. Why not do something along those lines, but different? Something unique. We can turn this farm into a resort for adults to relax or a place to play. Or both. A place to fulfill their desires with zero judgement. Guests can explore the ranch, as well as other guests. Want to go on a trail ride? Great. You want to ride the cock you spotted at the bonfire while making s'mores? That's perfectly acceptable, too. Anything goes as long as the participants are consenting."

"It doesn't sound like you're talking about some family-style dude ranch," Dayne huffed.

"No. Plenty of those are readily available. Some even have adults-only weekends but not like what I'm thinking. We need to do something unique to corner a specific market. We'll offer an escape no one else offers. A place where you're free to do whatever with whomever and not be judged for your choices or your kinks. As long as they're legal, of course."

"You mean free to do whatever sexually," Dayne summarized with a raised eyebrow.

"Sure."

"No holds barred?" His brother's eyes now held a spark.

Dylan figured out of his two siblings, his twin would be the one to see some value in his idea. "As long as whoever you're doing it with consents. That's one rule that cannot and will not be broken." They'd have zero tolerance for that. "I want all the guests to feel safe."

Dani, still appearing shell-shocked, lifted a palm. "Hold on. You want to turn *Dad's* farm into a sexual playground?"

"An all-inclusive, adults-only resort. Where the guests' fantasies will be at their fingertips." Dylan turned toward the lake and the spot he planned on putting up the main lodge.

He swept his hands out saying, "Welcome to Double D Ranch, the adults-only ranch resort where your fantasies become reality. Unpack, unwind and get uninhibited."

"Oh my God," Dani whispered, pressing her fingers to her lips, "he already has a slogan."

"Of course I do. I wouldn't propose this idea to you two without it being thoroughly thought out first. Again, it's a business *proposal.*"

Dani rolled her eyes at that.

"There's that stick I thought went missing," Dayne grumbled. "I figured it only disappeared farther up your ass."

"I never expected this from you, Dylan. Dayne, maybe, but not you. Have you had a fever recently that fried your brain?" Dani asked.

"No, just a seed of an idea that took root and began to grow."

"I have to agree with Danica. This idea of yours is totally unexpected, Dyl."

"Maybe you don't really know me," he suggested.

"I'm your damn twin. I don't know anyone better than you. We think alike..." Dayne's eyes widened when he repeated in a whisper, "We think alike. That means..."

Dylan tipped his head to the side but said nothing.

His brother's eyebrows shot up his forehead. "Oh, you dirty, *dirty* boy. You've been hiding this from us."

"I'm not hiding anything. It's simply no one's business. Not even my twin's."

One side of Dayne's mouth pulled up, and a gleam filled his eyes. "I think we need to compare notes."

Dylan shook his head. "No, we don't. You keep your dirty ideas in your head, and I'll keep mine."

"*Umm.* You're not keeping them in your head, brother, if you want to turn your dirty thoughts into a business," Dani said. "But, *eeeewww*. I don't really want to know what kind of perverted thoughts either of my brothers have in their pea brains. Wait. I'm out if you two are going to be letting it all hang free. I don't want to see your manhood in any form." She visibly shuddered.

Dayne frowned. "*Any form?*"

"Yes, you know," she flapped a hand around, "bored or excited."

"I hate to break it to you, sis, but we don't want to see you naked, either. How about we make sure that *never* happens?"

Dani turned to Dylan next. "Are the guests allowed to be naked?"

"There will be no rules against it. Clothing will be optional. This will be a place for adults to live out their fantasies and be uninhibited. If that means being naked..." Dylan shrugged.

"Except for employees, right?" Dani asked. "You can't have someone prepping food or cooking naked. That would be a health code violation. And if it isn't, it should be."

"That's why, sis, if we take this on, we need you to be involved. We need to divide and conquer this place."

"*We*," Dayne huffed. "Neither of us have said yes to this proposal."

Dani's brow scrunched low. "How involved?"

"One hundred percent," Dylan answered. "I can't do it alone."

"You're asking a lot," she muttered.

"We're asking for everything."

"There's that *we* again," Dayne mumbled.

Their sister continued like Dayne never spoke. "In case you've forgotten, I already have a career. And I'm good at catering. My boss loves me."

"I know you're good. I've eaten your food. That's why

your skills will be needed here. Just think of it… You'd be your own boss. You can design your dream commercial kitchen. You can set up the restaurant however you'd like. You can plan the menus, cater events… And,"—Dylan lifted a single finger—"you'll have a place to live so you can give up your current shit hole."

"I don't live in a shit hole."

Dayne raised an eyebrow at their sister's exclamation, making her mouth flatten.

Danica lived in a dump outside of Scranton, but it was what she could afford. Both he and Dayne, as well as their mother, worried about her. Moving her back to the farm would be so much better and safer for her. It would also make their mom happy.

"Sis, you majored in culinary arts and minored in hospitality. What you do can't be any more perfect for this resort. We'll throw events, like weddings and themed parties. Have a café for snacks. A dining hall for meals. You can hire the staff to help you plan menus, buy supplies and cook. Having a baker on site is a possibility, too. The food has to be good. No, it has to be stellar for what I want to charge guests. I'm confident you can pull it off."

"Damn, you have some lofty goals," she whispered.

"Aim high and dream big, right? That's why Dad bought this property in the first place," Dylan reminded her.

"Sure. Unless your idea crashes and burns. You could lose the farm and end up in debt, maybe even bankrupt."

Before Dylan could respond to his sister, Dayne surprised him with, "Then, we make sure that doesn't happen. We'll hire a PR company. We'll do social media blasts. Maybe hire some influencers. We'll do whatever we need to do."

It sounded like his twin was okay with the resort idea. "Are you in?" Dylan asked him, just to be sure.

Dayne's answering smile was blinding. "Hell yes! I'm only pissed I didn't come up with the idea myself."

Dylan shoved his brother playfully. "Good to have you onboard, brother."

Dayne shoved him back. "You know I could never pass up a good time."

Chapter Two

Having Dayne involved was certainly a relief. Now it was two *for* the idea, instead of the opposite.

Technically, they didn't need Danica to agree. The property hadn't been willed to her, but that didn't mean Dylan didn't want her to be a part of the business. He wanted it to benefit her, as well as their mother. If the three of them joined forces and made enough money, they could make sure their mother's future was secure. Her portion of their father's life insurance policy wouldn't last forever.

Plus, it would be good for her to have her children nearby to help her as she got older.

Now, Dylan only needed to convince his sister. "Like I said, it'll be the perfect opportunity to put that expensive degree to use."

"I already do with my current job."

"You work for someone else," Dylan reminded her needlessly. "Don't you want to work for yourself and have all the control?"

"I wouldn't be working for you two? You'd have no say in how I run my corner of the world?"

"Well..." Dylan started.

Dani rolled her eyes. "See? No."

"Could we make suggestions, at least?" he asked.

"You could, but it doesn't mean I'll take them."

"Sis..."

"If you want me to be a part of this crazy, very risky idea, not to mention, quit my job and give up my apartment, then you let me do what I know best."

"How to annoy your brothers?" Dayne teased.

"That would be a perk," she murmured. "Even so, all of this will take a lot of money, boys. I can see that already without even sitting down to go over all the finer details. What you're planning will take all kinds of staff and ranch workers, not to mention the cost of construction with all the buildings needed to make it a resort. Like you know, rooms for people to sleep and apparently... do other things." She grimaced. "Where's that money coming from?"

"Well, we each got a chunk from Dad's huge life insurance policy. We can also sell off the herd, except for one or two of the calmer heifers. Sell all that expensive milking equipment. Keep some of the other livestock as part of the 'ranch' experience. And... Dayne and I can sell our homes, since we'll be living here."

"Did you even ask Dayne if he wanted to sell his place?" their sister asked.

"No, he didn't," Dayne answered. "As much as I love this concept, the thought of moving back to Pennsylvania and having to deal with the humidity, mosquitoes, freezing cold weather and snow..." He groaned. "I don't miss any of that."

Dylan agreed. "You and me both, brother, but we have

three hundred acres to work with here. Acreage that's ours free and clear."

Dani raised an eyebrow. "And what about the rest of the money needed to create this sexual paradise?"

"We'll have to borrow against the farm," Dylan answered. "The real estate is worth a small fortune. The equity on this property alone should give us plenty to play with."

"We would need to borrow that right out of the gate," Dayne said. "We shouldn't open the doors until this place is ready to go. As much as I hate to admit it, our baby sis is correct. To do it right, we'll need a lot of cash. We'll also need a good PR firm from the start. We don't want to do this half-assed. The experience needs to be exceptional and memorable from day one."

Dylan liked what he was hearing. "Once we get rolling, we need to start interviewing employees and maybe even hiring some before construction is complete. Plus, we need to find a good general contractor to start building."

His to-do list was long.

"Being an architect, I'm assuming you already have the plans drawn up," Dayne said.

"I do." He'd spent many sleepless nights drawing, designing, and tweaking. "Since I can work from anywhere, I can continue to do freelance design work to keep some money flowing in during construction."

Dayne sucked on his teeth. "How long have you been thinking about this?"

"Since Dad died. I knew we'd have to do something with the property."

"We could lose everything," Dani repeated. "Dad's dream, Mom's money, our money. All of it. Do you have a backup plan?"

"Let's hope that doesn't happen. But I'm confident this

business will be successful. Like Dayne said, we shouldn't open until we have most of what's in the business proposal in place."

"The man's got a business plan, drawings, even a damn slogan," Dani muttered.

"Well, I didn't want to present a half-cocked idea."

Dayne snorted. "Half-cocked."

"So... Are you in, sis?" Dylan asked.

"To work with you two boneheads? No. To help secure mom's future? Yes. To keep the farm Dad loved so much in the family?" She pulled in a long breath, then released a long, loud sigh of resignation. "Before I agree, I need a guarantee that I'll have full control of hiring the food service staff, planning the meals and handling the catering."

"You have my guarantee."

Dani threw her hands up. "Then, how can I say no?"

With a smile, Dylan pulled his sister in for a hug.

She shoved him away. "Yuck. Now I'm wondering where those hands have been."

He laughed and shook his head.

"Forget what I said about having a stick up your ass. Now I'm wondering what else you've had up there, kinky boy," Dayne ribbed.

"I'm not wondering, so please don't tell us." Dani glanced around the farm and released another long sigh. "From an innocent, humble dairy farm to a pervert's paradise."

"We can use that in the advertising." Dayne joked, then slapped Dylan on the back. "Okay, who's breaking the news to Mom?"

———

THE WORK NEEDED to get the resort up and running seemed endless. A lot of it included major construction, so he hired a general contractor to oversee it all.

The contractor they hired, Ford Harris, was well known in the area for quality work, as well as having a great work ethic. That was exactly what they needed.

The sooner they could get everything done, the sooner they could open and start making back some of the money they were investing. Dylan had sold his home in Virginia and moved into their parents' farmhouse while Dayne was in the middle of selling his house in North Carolina.

Once Ford finished the two new wings on the farmhouse —one for him and one for his brother—the contractor would begin updating the original house where Danica would eventually reside. Besides sharing the original kitchen, she'd have her privacy for the most part, as would they.

Their sister was currently living with their mother in town until Dylan could move out of the main house and into his wing. They were not only updating the farmhouse's interior; they were completely changing the exterior to match the soon-to-be-built lodge.

With everything going on, Dylan was overwhelmed but it was satisfying to see his project and their future business all coming together with only minor hiccups.

Since he was already in town to cross more things off his insanely long to-do list, his sister had asked him to stop at the butcher and see if they'd be willing to provide all the meat for the resort.

Dani wanted as much locally sourced food as possible. Fruits, veggies, meats, baked goods... Dylan agreed and also wanted to keep as much money in the community as possible. The town of Fisher Falls had about six thousand residents, but, for the most part, it was a close community.

As expected, the local butcher was thrilled. He had connections with farmers in the area to get whatever the resort needed, including game meats like rabbit, venison, bison and wild boar.

The bell above the door jingled when he stepped out of the shop and onto the sidewalk. When the afternoon sun blinded him, he squinted and automatically reached for the sunglasses on top of his head, then froze.

His chin jerked back and he blinked.

Then blinked again at the woman walking in his direction to make sure he was seeing who he was seeing.

The second she spotted him, her steps stuttered before she stopped and stared.

He knew he'd eventually run into her.

Only, he didn't expect it to be today.

Dropping his shades into place to help cover his reaction, he wasn't sure if he should simply ignore her and head back to the ranch, or stay and say hello.

His first instinct was to avoid her. Of course, that reaction pissed him off, so he forced himself to stand his ground and wait.

With a head twitch and a set jaw, she began walking again. Unfortunately, toward him and not in the opposite direction.

"Dylan?" she asked in a damn wispy voice that made his chest tighten. She had an uncanny knack for telling him apart from Daync—despite his twin trying to trick her many times —but it had been a long time since she'd seen either of them.

"Erin," he greeted after prying apart his clenched teeth.

She ran her gaze up and down him, making him tense even more. "You look good."

If she expected a return compliment, she would be waiting a while. But she did look good. Too good.

Of course, that pissed him off, too.

Her long dark brown hair hung loosely around her bare shoulders. She wore a yellow sundress that showed off her tan, with a wide leather belt cinched around her narrow waist. Of course, she wore cowboy boots with her skirt.

Her looks and her "all-American" girl style hadn't changed a damn bit.

She was the same as he remembered but also different. She clearly embraced her thirties. Her maturity fit her even better than her youth. Not that—he did some quick figuring in his head—thirty-three was close to being old.

But thirty-three was a long way from when they dated back in high school.

"I ran into your mother at the grocery store the other day. She mentioned you were back in town. How long are you here for? We should grab a coffee or something."

Coffee? Was she kidding? Like they were long-lost friends who needed to catch up? "I'm here for good."

She hid her surprise at that news well. "I thought she said you were only here to sell your family farm?"

"That was the original plan. But..."

"Plans change," she finished softly. "We know that only too well, don't we?"

"Yeah, Erin, we do. Dayne and I decided to keep the farm." She didn't need to know why.

"Well... I'm sure your mom is thrilled that you and Dayne have come home."

"Danica, too, since we'll be running it as a family. We're doing this for Mom. Dad, too. He wanted us to take care of her and that was a huge factor in our decision to come home. How about you?"

"How about me, what? I never left," she murmured. "You know that."

"I meant, are you thrilled I'm home?" he asked more sharply than he should. But the long-buried bitterness was bubbling to the surface.

She pinned her lips together. "I have to go. It was good seeing you, Dylan." She turned and strode away.

"Talk about whiplash, Erin," he called out. "You're all open and welcoming when you think I'm only home for a minute, then as soon as you find out I'm here to stay, your reaction changes. Are you no longer up for coffee and small talk?"

She stopped abruptly and spun on her boot heel. "Do you want the truth, Dylan?"

No. "Always."

"Because it's easy to fake it for a short bit of time. It's too much work to do it forever."

Damn. "Then don't. I'll be busy out at the farm turning it into a resort. I don't have time to play those types of games, either."

She nodded. "Welcome home, Dylan." She turned and began walking again.

"Good to see you, too, Erin. Tell your husband I said hello," he yelled, no longer bothering to hide the jealousy in his tone. He was done pretending.

She stopped dead in her tracks, then stood there for far too long.

She didn't bother to face him when she finally responded, "Next time I visit his grave, I'll pass along the message." With that, she strode away.

He was so focused on her and what she said, he jumped when Dayne came out of nowhere and bumped a shoulder into his. "Who's the hot piece of ass?"

Dylan pulled in a sharp breath through his nostrils. When he finally managed to loosen his jaw, he muttered,

"Erin."

"No way!" burst from his brother.

"Yeah."

"Well, hot damn! Too bad she ditched you and married that Kyle guy."

She didn't ditch him and apparently, she was no longer married. "He's dead."

Dayne ripped the baseball cap off his head and slapped it against his thigh with a *thwap*. "Sounds like she's available, then."

Normally, he'd think Dayne was being heartless about Erin losing her husband, but his brother had been pissed at Kyle Hart when he married her not long after Dylan left.

"Not to you," Dylan informed him.

"All's fair in love and war, brother. I figured you learned that when Kyle stole her away."

Dylan gritted his teeth. "He didn't steal her."

Dayne chuckled, knowing the truth. "No? Then why doesn't she have your ring on her finger and your babies right now?"

Erin was the reason no woman had his ring on their finger, and he didn't have any children. "She didn't want to leave, and I never wanted to stay. Apparently, that no longer made me a viable option."

Dayne elbowed him. "Well, now you have your chance."

"That ship has sailed," he mumbled.

"Ships don't only sail in one direction, Dyl Pickle."

Dayne using a stupid childhood nickname wasn't helping his mood. "She's probably dating someone."

"So?"

He turned to face his brother and shook his head. "Really?"

Dayne shrugged.

"Anyway, I'm surprised Mom didn't tell me that Hart died." She had to have known but decided to keep it from him. Her children might be in their thirties, but she still protected them like they were children.

It was both endearing and annoying at the same time.

"What did he die from?"

"How the hell do I know? I certainly wasn't asking his widow how it happened, jackass. I wonder about you sometimes."

"I wonder about you all the time," Dayne responded on a laugh. "Wanna grab some lunch while in town?"

"At Mom's?"

"No, at Patsy's Diner, Dyl Weed."

"Are you five, Great Dayne?"

Dayne chuckled. "God, I miss making up names for each other."

"Again, are you five?"

"Oh, good to see that stick is back in place... Lodged up your tight ass."

"At least I can say my ass is tight. I'm sure as hammered as yours is—" Dylan shook his head. "Why am I letting you drag me down to your level?"

"Because deep down we're the same, brother. You might not want to admit it, but it's true. You coming up with the idea of an adult amusement park proved that."

"It's not an..." He grimaced. "I'm not sure I want to sit across from you at the diner. You'll probably give me indigestion."

Dayne threw an arm around Dylan's shoulders and steered him in the direction of Patsy's. "I'm buying. And you're in luck, I have a roll of antacids in my pocket in case you need them."

Chapter Three

Erin wasn't surprised to see the paved parking lots packed since the Lyons children coming home to turn their parents' farm into an adult-only ranch resort was the talk of the town.

And had been for the last eight months.

Erin tried to stay away from all the gossip and rumors. She managed to avoid Dylan and Dayne Lyons whenever they came into town.

But here she was anyway.

At the Double D Ranch's open house.

Some folks were happy since this new endeavor created a whole lot of jobs for area residents. The Lyons family was also helping local businesses by using their services.

Some folks weren't happy at all.

Not because the resort's guests would pump more money into the community—something badly needed—but because there were rumors floating around on *why* the ranch resort was adults-only.

And to find out that reason was why almost everyone from town and the surrounding area were here being nosy.

Including her.

She came to see if some of the whispers she heard in passing were true.

Not because she wanted to see Dylan again.

Not because after running into him a few months ago, she hadn't stopped thinking about him.

Not because the bitterness in his tone had made her heart ache.

To this day, she regretted hurting him even though that hadn't been her intention. At the time, she thought they had both moved on.

He'd been in a rush to leave Fisher Falls, to go off to college, to make a life elsewhere. While she wanted to remain in the town where she grew up, surrounded by family and people she knew. This community was where she wanted to raise her children.

The children she never had. Kyle's unexpected death changed her future's trajectory.

She glanced around the property, at least what she could see of the three-hundred-acre resort. She didn't even recognize it. The only thing remaining somewhat the same was the lake. But even that now had a small dock, as well as a few kayaks, canoes and paddleboats pulled up on shore. On the opposite side, she could see a half dozen brand-spanking new cabins.

Also facing the lake was a huge lodge made of logs, mountain stone and massive two-story high windows to give the guests a beautiful view of not only the lake but the surrounding mountains.

A small pop-up tent being used as an information booth caught her eye. As she approached, Erin was greeted with a huge smile. "Hi, Erin! Welcome to Double D Ranch! We have a pamphlet that includes a property map, the schedule of today's events and demos, as well as a coupon for a free adult beverage."

She accepted the pamphlet without a glance. "Hi, Cherise. I didn't know you got a job here."

"Today I'm the greeter but they hired me full-time as part of the cleaning staff. I'll be cleaning the guest areas."

"Like the cabins?"

"I think our team will be rotating between the lodge rooms, the cabins and cleaning the common areas."

Erin gave the twenty-something single mother a smile. "I'm glad you finally found employment, Cher."

"With benefits!" she chirped. "It'll be a lifesaver for me and the kids."

Erin flipped open the pamphlet. "What kind of demos are they doing?"

When she glanced up, she saw that Cherise's cheeks were a bit pink when the girl whispered, "Not any of those."

Not any of those?

"Only things like—"

Erin read the list and read a couple of things off, "Horse-shoeing. Cow milking..."

"They wanted the open house to..."

Erin didn't want her to feel uncomfortable having to explain. "I understand." She lifted the pamphlet. "Thanks for this."

"Free refreshments are available in the lodge. They're taking people out on ATV and trail rides. You're welcome to take a kayak out on the lake, too. Feel free to look around. And don't miss the big bonfire tonight! They'll be having a band."

She wouldn't be doing any of that today. Most likely never.

"Nowhere is off-limits," Cherise continued. "Except for the second floor of The Mane Event Hall. That's currently closed."

"What's on the second floor?"

That pink in her cheeks turned bright red. "I... I'm not sure. It might still be under construction."

That was funny. The last time she talked to Ford, he told her all the projects needed to be finished before the open house. He had even worked longer-than-normal hours seven days a week with a large crew to get everything done on time.

She had hardly seen him in town once Dylan hired him to head all of the construction. And the few times she did see him, he looked exhausted.

"Today's open house is to get in good with the locals, I see," Erin murmured.

"I haven't heard too many complaints because a lot of residents are benefitting. Even the county government."

"*Mmm hmm.* Well, I guess I'll wander around a little. This place sure has changed."

Cherise's smile widened. "It sure has. For the better."

Erin would hold her opinion on that until she knew if it was true or not. She was sure, if the rumors were correct, that not all the town folks would be thrilled when they actually found out what kind of "resort" Double D Ranch was, at least, according to the rumors.

It might look family-friendly on the surface today, but there was a good reason why it was an adults-only resort.

She decided to head to the lodge first. From the outside it was gorgeous and fit into the landscape well. She couldn't wait to see the inside.

On her trek to the lodge, she recognized just about everyone wandering around and exploring. She said endless hellos, waved to people she knew and kept a sharp eye out for Dylan or Dayne.

She planned on changing direction if she spotted either twin.

Instead, she ran into their mother, Evelyn.

"Erin! So good to see you," she gushed, giving Erin a big hug.

Evelyn was one of the kindest women she knew. She never held it against Erin what happened between her and the woman's son. Though, she wasn't sure of how much Dylan told his mother.

"The lodge is gorgeous! And I didn't even recognize this as your farm, Evelyn!"

"I know. Dylan had such a vision, and it turned out beautifully. He was lucky that Ford was available and able to gather a large enough crew to get it done in time."

"Will you miss the dairy cows?"

Evelyn squeezed her arm. "I'm just thrilled the property is staying in the family. David would be so happy. He loved this land and his cows. I appreciated the land and loved their dad with all my heart and soul, but, truthfully, I did not love those damn fly-drawing, shit machines."

Erin laughed. "I was never a big fan, either." She tipped her head to the side and considered the older woman. "How do you feel about them turning this into an adults-only resort?"

She wondered if Evelyn knew the details yet.

"Honestly, I think it's a hoot. If this is how the kids want to handle running the farm, then more power to them. I've never been a prude and what happens in someone's bedroom is their business, not mine."

"Do you think what happens here will be confined to the bedrooms?" she asked cautiously.

Evelyn shrugged. "Well, since you have to be over twenty-one to be a guest, my guess is, anything goes."

Anything goes.

Dylan's mother laughed. "When I was young, I actually considered running away and joining a nudist colony."

Erin didn't think a nudist colony was even close to what Dylan had planned for this property. Again, according to the rumors. But the more she heard, the more she had a feeling it was truth and not speculation.

Actually, it really surprised her Dylan was the one to come up with the idea. She would expect Dayne to be the instigator. He'd always been the wilder one of the two.

Of course, people tend to change after they've graduated high school or college and matured. But still...

This was not the direction she'd ever guess Dylan would head.

Evelyn clapped her hands sharply together once. "Well, I have to run. I hope to see you again soon, Erin. Don't be a stranger!"

"Same, Evelyn."

As his mother walked away, she tossed over her shoulder, "Make sure to check out the old farmhouse before you leave. I'm not sure you'll recognize that, either!"

"Is it open to the public?"

"You're not just anyone, Erin. I've always considered you family."

She doubted Dylan and Dayne did. "I'll check it out." She probably wouldn't. "Have a great day, Evelyn!"

Dylan's mother waved a hand over her shoulder and kept moving.

The woman was in amazing shape for being in her early

sixties. She was also in good spirits, even after losing the love of her life over a year ago.

Maybe it was true that time healed all wounds. She only wished it applied to Dylan, too. As well as herself.

She shook herself mentally. She needed to continue looking forward and not live in the past.

But one thing was for sure, if she and Dylan would once again be living in the same town, they needed to settle some things between them. This way, every time they ran into each other, it wouldn't be uncomfortable for either of them.

They were immature kids back then. They were mature adults now. They needed to act like it.

She could if he could.

The second she stepped inside the lodge; she lost her breath. It was absolutely stunning. She was proud of Ford for taking Dylan's vision and making it a reality.

The main area of the lodge—what she would consider the "lobby" if it had been a normal hotel—was full of people milling around, snacking on hors d'oeuvres, carrying around drinks—including champagne flutes—while chatting and laughing.

She spotted a high school friend standing at the back of the room near the impressive two-story stone fireplace. It was flanked by propped-open French doors since the day was beautiful.

They sure lucked out with the weather today.

As she headed in that direction to say hello, a man stepped in front of her and blocked her path.

"Hey," came the deep greeting as she glanced up.

She smiled. "Hi, Ford."

He grabbed her elbow, leaned in and pressed a kiss to her cheek.

Even such a simple show of affection from Ford made her

heart flutter. The man was criminally handsome, and had a rocking hot body as well.

With one side of his mouth pulled up, he asked, "How have you been?"

"Surviving. I'm glad to see that you are, too,"—she swept a hand around—"after working your magic."

"I appreciate the work the Lyons brothers threw my way."

His head tipped down as hers tipped up to search his face. She cupped his bearded cheek. "You look exhausted."

Ford pulled in a breath. "I am. I had a hard deadline, and I busted my ass to make it."

"Well, you pulled it off. So, now what? Do you have another job lined up?"

"Now, I sleep for the next week." He dragged the rough pad of his thumb over her lower lip. "Do you want to join me?"

"Sleeping? No. You snore."

Ford chuckled. "I figured if I tired you out enough that you'd sleep right through the sound of a chainsaw."

"You are always good at tiring me out, but no one can sleep through that, except you."

He gripped her hips and pulled her tight against him in what appeared to others as a friendly "hug." With heat filling his dark brown eyes, he dropped his voice an octave, as well as the volume. "It's been a while."

"It has."

"Why?"

"Obviously, you've been a bit busy."

"True. But I should never be so busy that I ignore you."

"We have our own lives, Ford. You don't owe me anything."

One dark eyebrow cocked. "A few orgasms?"

"Those are great and all but not required for us to be friends."

He jerked his chin into his neck. "Erin Hart, have you just friend-zoned me?"

She laughed softly. "I'd like to think we've always been friends."

He squeezed her hips. "Normal friends don't do what we do."

He was right.

"Mr. Harris, are you getting hard right here and now?" she asked under her breath, so no one nearby heard her.

"I'm exhausted but not dead. Though, you could still give a dead man an erection." He squeezed his eyes shut and shook his head. "Sorry."

She placed a hand on his chest. "It's been ten years, Ford. I think I can handle a joke, and I know you weren't referring to Kyle."

When he leaned in and pressed his warm lips to her forehead, his short, dark beard scratched her skin. It had been too long since she'd felt the same on her inner thighs.

Her pussy clenched with the memory of the last time they were together. Maybe she did need to do a sleepover with him again soon. She'd simply have to pack some ear plugs in her overnight bag.

Or leave before he fell asleep.

"Have you seen the rest of the property yet?" Ford asked.

"No, this is as far as I got."

He released her and jutted out his elbow in invitation. "Well, let the guy who knows this place inside and out show you around."

She placed her hand in the crook of his arm. "Do you happen to have access to the second floor of the event hall?"

He dug into his jeans and pulled out a set of what looked like shiny new keys. He held them up with a gleam in his eyes and a wicked smile. "I certainly do."

"Then, I'd love a tour."

Chapter Four

Since nothing was currently happening at The Mane Event Hall, Ford decided it was the perfect time to show it to Erin and get her reaction.

He was actually surprised she showed up at the resort at all. Especially after finding out she and Dylan Lyons dated back in high school. Not because she mentioned it, but because someone else had told him a while ago in passing.

From what Ford found out, when Dylan graduated, he was eighteen and Erin only sixteen and they had dated for two years. The second Dylan graduated, he booked it out of Fisher Falls as fast as he could, while Erin stayed to finish high school.

She had always made it clear she wanted to stay in Fisher Falls and didn't have any plans to follow him. Not long after Dylan left, Erin began dating Kyle Hart, Dylan's classmate. At barely twenty years old, she married him, ready to settle down and start a family.

Once Ford moved to the area, he ended up hiring Kyle for his fledgling construction company and that was when he first met Erin. He and Kyle also became fast friends. Erin's late husband was a good man, a reliable worker and a great friend.

Then, he died while on a job.

Of course, that turned Erin's life upside down.

While it was a freak accident and nobody's fault, Ford still felt guilty and also responsible for the young widow. That led to him checking in with her often, helping her out when he could, and causing them to become close. Initially, they remained friends and nothing more.

He always thought she was smoking hot but remained hands off until she was ready to move on. Once she was, he moved in to take his shot.

Their relationship started out casual, and for the next few years, it remained that way. Mostly because he worked long hours growing his business and she didn't seem interested in anything serious.

He didn't have an issue with keeping what they had together loose and free. Mostly because they lived in Fisher Falls, where the likelihood of her meeting another man worthy of her attention was slim to none.

Until now, anyway, since Dylan and his twin Dayne were back in town for good.

At this point, Ford needed to decide if Dylan was a threat to the relationship he and Erin had. And if he was, what Ford would do about it.

If anything.

Seeing her today reminded him that he didn't want her to slip away and into someone else's arms. Or another man's bed on a permanent basis.

She might act like a typical "small-town girl" on the surface, but in reality, deep down, she was far from that. Where she got her wild sexual appetite, he didn't know.

Not that he was complaining since he encouraged it and benefitted from it, too.

Too many times to count.

The only issue he'd have was if she shared that certain particular appetite with others. At least without him taking part in that "sharing."

Not that he had much say in what she did.

Maybe he needed to change that. Make more of an effort. Ask her to make more of one, too.

Their personalities didn't clash. They had unmistakable chemistry. They had the best sex he ever had in his life. The woman was beautiful inside and out. Kind, giving, intelligent...

The list was long.

So, why weren't they a couple?

Not only were neither in a rush to commit, Ford had some tastes he had not shared with her.

Fisher Falls tended to lean more toward the traditional side. Most residents graduated high school, got married, had babies, grew old, doted on their grandbabies, sat in a rocker on the porch, then died. It seemed to be the town's circle of life.

They liked life simple. Though, that kind of simple sounded boring to Ford.

This resort, once it was revealed for what it truly was, would turn this area on its ear.

The Lyons brothers were smart to have this open house. They wanted everyone to see how it would impact the area financially first before they found out how that money was made later.

This was no ordinary resort.

Unlike most of his neighbors, he was all for everything this ranch would bring.

He squeezed Erin's hand as they approached the stairs on the east side of the event hall. He was sure Erin would be fine with what happened at the resort, too.

When she tugged on his hand, he stopped and saw her pointing at the small sign at the bottom of the steps. A little arrow directed guests up to the second floor.

Her expression was both curious and amused as she read the sign. "Stairway to Heaven?"

"It's appropriate," he answered.

A twinkle lit up her brown eyes. "I thought the second floor wasn't finished?"

"That's what everyone is being told today. Let's go." He encouraged her to take the stairs first—like the gentleman he was—mostly because he wanted to watch her ass rock and roll and maybe get a peek of her smooth legs under her sundress as she climbed.

As she did so, she asked, "Why are the steps to the second floor outside and not inside?"

"For the same reason I built them on the side opposite The Mane Lodge, darlin'. Guests might want to sneak away for playtime and not be seen." They expected the first floor of the event hall to be a busy place since it would be used for various events and even weddings.

"Playtime," she repeated in a murmur. When she reached the top landing, she read the sign above the window-less door. "Welcome to Heaven." She turned and faced him. "You said playtime. That tells me the rumors are true."

"I'm not sure what you heard, but I promise you this: The reality is so much better than the rumors."

With a husky voice, she urged, "Then, hurry up and unlock the door."

"Are you impatient?"

"Well, you explained why the stairs are on this side of the

building. Maybe I don't want us to get caught heading into Heaven. Especially since the second floor is 'still under construction' and technically, we shouldn't be here."

"*Ah*, but I'm the general contractor. I'm just checking my crew's work."

She laughed. "Smart."

But being the general contractor didn't mean he'd be allowed to use one of the playrooms, so they still needed to be cautious.

From his front pocket, he dug out the master key he carried. It opened every door on the property, except for the farmhouse. Only Dayne, Danica and Dylan had the keys to their residence.

As he turned the key in the lock, Erin drew her fingers down his spine and caressed his ass.

Jesus, he missed her touch.

He missed touching her.

He'd been stupid to let it go far too long.

The whole point of working hard, long hours was so he could enjoy life when he wasn't working. He needed to start doing that again.

His business was doing well. The money he earned from this project put him in a very safe financial position and Dayne had hinted about keeping him on full-time on the ranch as the facilities manager.

If they gave him a hefty salary, along with retirement and health benefits, he might actually consider it. Working a job with normal hours would free him up to enjoy that life he'd been working toward.

If he really wanted to, he could keep his crew on and simply hire a foreman to oversee the construction jobs. But the possibility of no longer being responsible for payroll, taxes, insurance, benefits and everything else that went along with running a business was tempting.

As soon as he opened the door, she stepped over the threshold and waited since the interior was pitch black. Especially without any windows for natural light. He followed her inside and hit the main light switch by the door.

"*Oh*," she breathed as the second floor lit up.

If that was her reaction simply to the long hallway, he couldn't wait to show her one of the rooms.

She started down the hallway. "How many playrooms are up here?"

"Eight."

She paused in front of room number two. "They all have windows so people can watch?"

"They do. But they also all have blinds for those preferring privacy."

Since he followed closely on her heels, when she continued, he could feel the energy buzzing from her. But then, knowing exactly what was beyond the locked doors did the same for him.

In fact, every time he'd been up here to check on his guys or to help carry up equipment, he pictured a naked Erin in every one of the themed rooms.

One fantasy included her locking herself in a room while she left the blinds open and played with herself until she came. Of course, he'd be on the other side of the window, watching and incapable of doing anything about it.

His cock was already getting hard at the thought of watching her finger her slick pink pussy to the point of orgasm. Maybe even using some toys on herself, too.

Anal beads, vibrators, a pussy clamp, nipple clamps... The list of toys could be endless and bring her multiple orgasms. To the point she'd be dripping on the floor.

When she was done, she'd unlock the door, crook a finger at him, then point to the puddle, demanding he drop to his hands and knees and clean it up with his tongue.

Fuuuuuck.

He might have to run that scenario by her, despite the fact he was the dominant one out of the two. But for that specific fantasy, he certainly wouldn't mind switching things up.

"Are there cameras up here?"

That question pulled him out of his head.

His cock was now so damn hard, it was uncomfortable. "There are, but they don't record." Normally, anyway. The Lyons planned on hiring staff to watch the cameras around the property, only to make sure everything was consensual. However, no cameras were allowed in the actual playrooms or guest rooms, only in common or public areas. The only time staff were allowed to push the record button would be if they needed proof of an active incident happening.

It would protect both the resort and the guests.

"Will that be disclosed?"

"Yes." He pointed to a sign she missed. "They will only record any kind of questionable incident. By the way, all staff will be signing NDAs."

"Smart."

He had to sign one prior to being hired as the general contractor. All his guys did, too. The Lyons brothers didn't want to risk a contractor or an employee blackmailing any of their guests. That would quickly destroy their business and reputation. If that happened, they'd fall into bankruptcy with all the money they invested in getting the resort up and running.

Ford could only imagine how much it was. His labor charges alone were astronomical. Mind-blowing, actually, and he had no idea where that money came from. He guessed the majority came from the equity on the three-hundred-acre property, the land itself was worth a small fortune.

After David Lyons passed, his wife Evelyn was approached by several developers offering her the world. However, since the property had been willed to her sons, she wanted them to decide the dairy farm's fate. She had trusted her sons to make the right choice.

Ford stopped in front of room number six and slipped the master key into the lock.

He stepped inside and flipped the switch, lighting up the room.

When he heard her sharp intake of breath behind him, he turned to see her eyes wide as she took in the whole room.

"Holy crap," she whispered as she glanced around. "This is insane."

"A good kind of insanity, right?"

"Oh yes," she breathed. "It's amazing, Ford. I had no idea that Dylan had any of these kinds of thoughts in his head."

That was certainly not what he wanted to hear. "He might not have had these tastes back in high school, Erin. As we mature sexually, our desires can change or develop. We figure out what we want, what we need, what we can't do without to make sex both exciting, as well as satisfying."

She glanced at him. "True."

"Did you two have sex back then?"

She shook her head. "We did normal teenage stuff—you know, kissing, touching and the rest—but we never went all the way. I didn't lose my virginity until Kyle."

"You never told me that."

"No reason to bring it up," she said simply.

That was true. Honestly, he didn't care who took her virginity. It didn't matter, nor was it his business.

As she wandered around the room, she checked everything out. "Are all the rooms outfitted the same?"

While she was distracted, he locked the closed door and shut the blinds to the viewing window.

When he turned, he realized she'd been watching him.

A slight flush filled her cheeks, and the outlines of her nipples were now visible through the light fabric of her sundress. "Ford?"

That was right, she had asked him a question. "No. Each room has its own theme."

She brushed her fingers across the spanking bench. The base was black and the vinyl padding red. More importantly, he was itching to use it. "And the theme to this room?"

"It's set up for impact play."

"And the others?" She inspected the custom-made, padded St. Andrew's cross securely attached to the wall next.

Another piece of equipment he couldn't wait to use. "I'd rather they be a surprise."

She shot a quick glance over her shoulder at him. "When you show them to me today?"

"No. When we use them in the future."

Her breath hitched and she turned to face him. "Will that be allowed? We won't be guests of the resort."

He shrugged slightly. "Perks of the job."

"But isn't your job finished? Are you sure it's okay that we're in here right now?"

He didn't want to tell her yet about Dayne's hinting at hiring him. He'd wait until the job was offered and he decided whether he'd accept or not.

He would not be making any rash decisions, especially if it meant giving up or selling the business he worked so hard to build.

Circling her slowly, he inspected her from the top of her

dark head to the tips of her pink-painted toes. "No one will be up here today."

"I know but..."

"We won't use the equipment." Today, anyway. If he *was* allowed access to the rooms in the future, he'd make sure to take full advantage of everything they offered.

He had so many damn plans.

As he closed in on her, she moved away and headed right toward the basket found in every room. It was full of single-use lube packets, condoms, dental dams and the like.

She picked up one of the small packets of lube at the same time he grabbed her hair, fisting it into a tight ponytail. She gasped when he used it to spin her to face him.

"On. Your. Knees."

Chapter Five

"ARE you sure we won't get caught?" her question had a tremor to it.

"Do you care if we do?"

Something in her expression changed. Did she have a sudden realization?

"Actually today, yes. The farm"—she shook her head and corrected—"*ranch* is full of locals. If it was full of guests with the same mindset, I'd say no."

Good call.

Today's guests were people they both knew. Some were even his customers.

He'd leave the blinds shut and the door locked, then. "You're still standing."

With a slight smile, she locked gazes with him, grabbed his hips for balance and lowered herself to her knees.

He brushed a lock of hair off her forehead. "It's been far too long, darlin'."

With a lick of her lips, she said softly, "I agree, Sir."

He loved the fact they could easily slip into their roles of Dom and sub, even after months of not seeing each other.

He dragged the pad of his thumb across her bottom lip, then tucked it into her mouth, encouraging her to open it. "Have you missed my cock?"

She nodded. The hungry look in her eyes made that same cock jump in his jeans.

She sucked on his thumb as he pumped it in and out of her mouth. "You know what to do," he murmured. "I suggest you hurry up if you don't want to get caught."

She wasted no time sliding her hands from his hips to his belt buckle. As soon as it was undone, she popped open the button on his jeans and worked them down enough, along with his boxer briefs, to give her access.

"Take out my cock."

She reached in and wrapped her fingers around the root, making him bite back a groan.

When she started stroking it, he ordered sharply, "Stop! I didn't give you permission to do that. Hands behind your back and keep them there until I tell you otherwise."

He was on the edge of covering her face in his cum as it was. That was not where he wanted to put it. He had other plans.

As soon as she did as she was told, he whispered, "Good girl."

Having her hands invisibly bound behind her back pushed out her chest, tempting him to fuck her tits instead of her mouth.

So many damn options, so little time. Today proved they needed to make more of it. They just wouldn't get it right now. Today would be more of a sprint than a marathon.

The last time they spent all night together, he tied her to his bed naked. He had played with her until she was about to come, then stopped, leaving her hanging and also left the room.

He edged her for hours and when he finally let her orgasm, she came so hard, she said she almost blacked out.

That was a *very* good night. He'd also love to repeat it sometime soon.

Ford tugged on her chin. "Open. That's it," he whispered. "Stick out your tongue."

He fisted his cock and dragged the tip down her tongue to clean off the beading precum.

"Wider."

Her brown eyes met his as he fed her his cock.

"That's it, darlin'. Take it all in. Now close your lips around me. Don't do anything more than that," he warned. "If you don't follow my instructions, you'll be punished, and not in the ways you prefer."

Since he was the first man to play with her like this, they experimented a lot. Some she liked, some she didn't. He respected that and didn't push her to do things she didn't enjoy or wouldn't get her off.

This wasn't only about him. It was about her, too.

Watching Erin come was one of the biggest rewards next to his own release.

He got a better grip on her by using both of his hands to hold her long, dark hair in two pigtails, an effective way to control the action.

He started slow, sliding his cock in and out of her mouth. Not taking it super deep... yet. He let her get used to his size first.

After a few more normal thrusts, he asked, "Ready, darlin'?"

She made a sound around his hard cock when he paused with the tip pressing against the back of her throat. He kept it there for a few seconds before he moved again.

Using her hair as handles to keep her head in place, he began to fuck her mouth. He knew her limits and didn't push past any of those.

He closed his eyes and threw his head back for a moment, blowing out a breath to rein in the urge to come within seconds. But once he felt her body shift, he opened his eyes to make sure she wasn't trying to tap out.

She wasn't.

"That's a good girl. Milk my cock with your mouth. Take it all. The whole thing. I want your lips wrapped around the base. I know you can do it." He released one handful of hair to stroke her throat. "Relax and swallow me whole, darlin'.'"

She was doing her best to take him deeper but couldn't quite swallow him to the root. She reached her limit.

So did he.

With a set jaw, he listened to the wet sucking sounds of her taking him hard and deep. His cock was throbbing, his balls pulled tight. Right now, it was mind over matter to keep from coming. He'd have to throw in the white flag unless he wanted to come down her throat.

Normally he would. Today, he had other plans.

Using the grip on her hair, he yanked her head back. "Don't release it. Keep it in your mouth, but don't move. Don't do anything."

He took in how beautiful she looked on her knees with his erection in her mouth. With flushed cheeks. With a sheen in her eyes. With spit clinging to the corners of her lips.

"You like sucking my cock, darlin'?"

Since he ordered her not to move, she couldn't answer or even nod her head. That didn't mean he couldn't see it in her face. Plus, he knew from the last few years that she did.

As much as he enjoyed eating her pussy.

Reluctantly, he pulled out his cock, slippery from her saliva. "God, I want to fuck you," he murmured, combing his fingers through her silky hair.

She pulled in a shuddered breath.

"Are you wet, darlin'?"

"Yes, Sir," she breathed.

When she accepted his offered hand, he helped her to her feet. For a second, her knees wobbled, and he waited to release her until she was steady. Once she was, he took her mouth, kissing her long and deep, causing her to fist his shirt and a groan to bubble up her throat.

He *really* missed this. Missed her. He was a dumbass for being too focused on his business to spend time with her.

A mistake that wouldn't happen again. If the ranch hired him on full-time, he hoped it would give him even more free time in the near future.

But the future was just that and he needed to remain in the here and now.

With the woman wearing a sundress.

She loved to wear them, and he loved when she did. They gave him easy access for quickies. Like today. "Are you wearing panties?"

She nodded. "Yes, Sir." She cleared her throat when her voice caught on that very simple answer.

"Give them to me."

She reached under her sundress and shimmied out of her panties, then held them out to him.

She wasn't lying. They were soaked. Simply from her giving him head.

He held them up to his nose and inhaled deeply. "I'm keeping these," he announced, tucking them into the front pocket of his jeans. "Since we're not supposed to be up here, I can't spend the time needed to turn your ass a cherry red before fucking you. I can't spend the time making a proper meal out of your cunt. So, I'll fill it, instead. For the rest of the ranch tour, I want your pussy full of me. I want my cum making your inner thighs so slick, they slide together easily when you walk."

With any other woman, he'd don a condom, especially with so many in the basket within reach, but Erin was on birth control. They had stopped using condoms a few months after they began to hook up.

Even though they weren't officially exclusive, they both agreed that if either had sex with anyone else, they would use protection.

He trusted her to keep their word. She did the same.

Whether she had sex with anyone else in the last few years, he didn't know. He also didn't ask since it wasn't his business.

He couldn't be possessive if they weren't exclusive. If he demanded that from her, she could demand the same from him.

Again, he had certain tastes she couldn't satisfy, even if she wanted to.

"Bend over the spanking bench, pull up your skirt and show me how wet you are."

Without hesitation, she immediately bent over the bench and flipped her skirt up and over her back, exposing her perfectly shaped ass and her shaved cunt.

The dark pink center glistened and called to him.

He shoved his jeans down even further and with each stroke of his cock, he squeezed out another drop of precum. Within two steps, he was behind her, dragging the crown between her plump, smooth lips. "Want me to fill you with my cock, darlin'?"

"Yes, Sir," she breathed.

"Want me to fill you with my cum?"

"Yes, Sir," she repeated, her nails digging into the vinyl padding of the spanking bench.

He slapped his cock against her clit a couple of times before lining up the slick, blunt tip and pressing forward.

She stretched around him, easily accommodating his girth and length within her silky heat. Her pussy clenched around him in an attempt to draw him even deeper.

He obliged.

"Give me access to your tits," he ordered.

With her palms planted on the bench, she lifted her torso. He slipped the straps of her sundress off her shoulders, reached around and snagged both nipples between his fingers, twisting as hard as he could.

It was no surprise that she wore no bra. Her tits were perky because they were on the smaller side. But they fit her petite frame perfectly.

Truthfully, he didn't care how big they were. He didn't discriminate. Large and heavy or just a handful. He loved them all.

"Sir," she cried out, squeezing his cock planted deep inside her.

He twisted them again, making her toss back her head, pelting him with her long hair.

He drove his cock fast and deep, at the same time tugging on her hard nipples. If he had been thinking straight, he would've put her on her back so he could wrap his lips around them and sink his teeth deep into her soft flesh.

Next time.

"Sir," she groaned over the sharp slapping of their skin.

"That's it, darlin'. Take every inch of me. Do you want it harder?"

"Yes, Sir," she hissed.

"Deeper?"

"Yes, Sir... *please.*"

With gritted teeth, he abandoned her tits to grab her hair again with one hand and her hip with the other, so he could slam into her as hard as he could.

He was pleased that the custom-made spanking bench was holding up against the pounding. Maybe that should be his job on the ranch: equipment tester.

He grinned but quickly lost it when the tiny ripples grew in intensity, telling him she was close.

The second she came, he would quickly follow.

They needed to hurry before they did get caught. Not only did he not want to blow a potential job opportunity by selfishly using a playroom without permission, but fucking the woman Dylan used to date—no matter how long ago it was—could potentially cause issues.

He also wasn't sure how Erin would feel if their relationship was exposed.

While they never kept it a secret, they certainly didn't do anything as a couple, like go out on dates. Because of that, most people in town thought they were close friends, rather than lovers.

And if anyone asked, they didn't confirm. They left it a mystery.

Basically, because it was no one's business.

However, now that the Lyons brothers were back in town... He had no idea if Dylan would try to rekindle their past.

Ford had choices to make.

But not at this very minute.

Erin began to meet him thrust for thrust, jamming her ass against him every time he drove deep. Her little whimpers were hard to ignore.

"Please, Sir," she begged.

"Please what?"

"Make me come... Sir."

"I'm not stopping you." But he also hadn't given her permission, either.

"I'm allowed, Sir?"

Ah, yes. She was being a good girl. "Yes, darlin', come for me."

Dropping her forehead to the padding, she pushed out a ragged breath. Relief was what it sounded like to him.

Maybe edging her for as long as he had last time hadn't been a good idea. "Come, darlin', soak my cock."

On a groan, she arched her back and clenched her pussy tightly around him. The little pulses grew more intense by the second.

"I'm going to come, Sir."

That was music to his ears.

Erin could get loud when she orgasmed, so he quickly covered her mouth with his hand. Her teeth sinking into his palm made him wince but at least her scream was muffled as she impaled herself on his cock.

A climax ripped through her, taking him with her. He came deep inside her and stilled, riding out the aftershocks. "I'm planting my seed deep, darlin'. I want it to stay inside you as long as possible. When it slides down your thighs, I want you to think of no one but me for the rest of the day."

She shuddered at those instructions.

"Are you good with that?"

"Yes, Sir," she breathed.

He regretted that he couldn't stay inside her any longer, but they needed to clean up and get out of the room.

"Good girl." He slowly pulled out. "Cover your tits but stay bending over the bench for a moment."

Of course, she did as she was told, but then, she always did. She enjoyed him giving her orders during sex and only during sex.

He dug for the panties he had tucked in his pocket and used them to wipe off his cock. Once he was finished, he tucked them back away. He was taking those home with him. A reminder, even a trophy of sorts.

He secured his jeans and belt, then drew a finger through her slit. "I'll be inside you the rest of the day." Then he placed a kiss on her ass cheek and pulled her dress back into place before helping her to stand straight.

With a hand curled around the back of her neck, he turned her to face him and dipped his head to meet her eyes. Her expression was soft from satisfaction.

"If you want to call me Sir for the rest of the day, I won't hate it, but I wouldn't suggest it," he teased.

She grinned and shrugged. "Some people would only think I forgot your name."

"And some others would know the meaning." Especially at a resort designed for sexual encounters. "We didn't have enough time for me to eat your cunt. Can I make it up to you later?"

He wanted to make up for the last eight months of not seeing her, except for a few moments here and there around town.

She reached up and cupped his cheek. "It doesn't have to be *quid pro quo,* Ford. You know that. It's never been like that with us."

"But I want to bury my face between your thighs."

She gave him a sly smile and wiggled her eyebrows. "Before or after I clean myself out?"

She might not know all of his tastes, but she knew enough. "Whatever you prefer."

He definitely had decisions to make when it came to this woman. He didn't want to lose her to anyone else.

She tapped his cheek and laughed softly. "You're a naughty boy, Ford Harris."

One side of his mouth pulled up. "And that's why you keep coming back for more."

Chapter Six

Dylan stood in front of the newly renovated farmhouse, surrounded by a half dozen residents of Fisher Falls. They were talking excitedly about what the resort would bring to the town and surrounding areas.

He only hoped they continued to hold that same excitement when the resort officially opened next weekend, and their first guests arrived. And once they found out that the resort was open to a special type of clientele. Of course, Double D Ranch wouldn't discriminate, and guests didn't have to participate in any activities. They could simply use the ranch as an escape from their stressful lives. The only requirements were to be accepting of everyone else, have an open mind and not be prudes.

If they couldn't handle nudity or sexuality—or anything that went along with that—this would not be the vacation spot for them.

The PR company his brother hired had done a great job of spreading the word to the right audience. He was relieved that every room and cabin was now booked for the grand opening week. The money that would bring in was sorely needed.

Just like today, he and his siblings needed to make sure everything went smoothly all next week. The first week could possibly make or break the resort. They needed to start out strong and remain flexible enough to make changes, if necessary, even if on the fly.

One day he hoped to be busy enough they wouldn't have to pay a PR company at all and could rely on only word of mouth advertising. Realistically though, he knew that might take a while. A year or maybe even two.

The PR company also found a few social media influencers to bring in for the opening week and recommended to comp their stay. He agreed with the hope it would pay off.

A movement out of the corner of his eye had him glancing toward the spa building located behind the event hall.

He narrowed his eyes on the tall, dark and very handsome man with an arm thrown over the shoulders of the woman in a bright yellow sundress, walking hip to hip with him.

Ford Harris and Erin Hart.

His chest tightened. He did not expect to see her here today. But here she was, wearing a sexy sundress, her signature cowboy boots and a blinding smile as she stared up at Ford.

For fuck's sake.

He'd appear like a deer caught in headlights if anyone asked him a question right now. He'd lost track of what the group was discussing because Ford and Erin were now heading their way. They probably didn't realize he was in the group. Or maybe they did and simply didn't care.

But to his eyes, as he watched the exchange between his

ex-girlfriend and his general contractor, they looked like a couple.

"Excuse me," he muttered, leaving the group.

"It's crazy. I don't even recognize this farm anymore," he heard her say as he got closer.

He stepped into their path, blocking it. "That was the point."

They both stopped abruptly. Ford dropped his arm from around her shoulders and his expression closed up while hers became guarded.

That couldn't be a sign of guilt, could it? Had they been hiding their relationship from him?

He waved a finger between the two. "I didn't realize you two knew each other." Or were close enough friends to be touching like they had been.

Ford wasn't born in Fisher Falls like Erin and Dylan. From what he knew, the contractor moved to the area about fifteen years ago to start his business.

Why in Fisher Falls, Dylan had no idea, but he'd been grateful to find someone local to pull off what Ford did in a short amount of time.

Erin's cheeks became flushed. "We... uh..."

"Dated," Ford volunteered.

Dylan's eyes narrowed on his contractor. "Before, during or after her marriage to Hart?"

Erin sucked in a breath.

Ford's tense jaw shifted. "Unnecessary."

It was, and Dylan's unfiltered question made him sound like a jealous asshole. Since it was too late to take it back, he moved on. "Dated. As in past tense?"

"We enjoy each other's company," Ford answered between clenched teeth. He turned to Erin. "Sorry, darlin',

I'm tired. I'm going to head out. Do you want me to walk you to your car?"

Her face dropped. "I thought you were going to finish showing me around?"

Ford's gaze sliced from her to Dylan and back in an unspoken message.

Before he could answer, Dylan offered, "I can finish giving her the tour if you need to leave."

After a slight hesitation, Ford asked Erin, "Are you okay with that?"

Her mouth gaped open for a second before she answered, "Sure."

To Dylan's ears, she didn't sound so sure.

For a moment, the two again seemed to communicate silently—proof they were more than only friends—before Ford gave her a single nod. "I'll catch up with you later. Hopefully, the gift I gave you will last a while."

When her head snapped toward Dylan, her cheeks appeared a bit darker. She said nothing as Ford shot him a sloppy two finger salute and took long, stiff strides in the direction of his truck.

Dylan turned his attention back to Erin and cocked an eyebrow. "Gift?"

"Ford is always generous."

Great. "Not enough to share that you dated," Dylan murmured. Or were still dating. He wasn't quite clear on it.

"I asked him not to."

Dylan frowned. "Why?"

"Because, like he said, we enjoy each other's company on occasion, and I didn't want you to punish him because of me."

"How and why would I do that?"

"You could've pulled him off the job. And the why..."

"He didn't steal you from under my nose, Erin."

"Kyle didn't, either."

Dylan tipped his head to the side. "Debatable."

"I'm not in the mood to debate, Dylan. It's a beautiful day and you should be celebrating the success of your open house."

She was right. He was being an ass for no reason other than unreasonable jealousy.

If Dylan had wanted to keep Erin, all he had to do was stay in Fisher Falls. At least until she graduated. Then maybe he could've convinced her to leave with him. But no, he left the area like his ass was on fire. He'd been more than ready to see the world. Or at least the world outside of a small town in very rural central Pennsylvania.

"It *has* been a very successful day." He needed to stop being miserable and petty when it came to the unforgettable woman before him. He was better than that. "How much of the property have you seen so far?"

"Only the spa, some of the lodge and the event hall."

"That's it?"

"Yes. I would love to see the rest. Especially the updates to the farmhouse. But you don't have to be my guide, Dylan. I can check it out on my own."

That would not be happening on his watch. Especially now that he knew she was a widow and apparently, not in any kind of "committed" relationship. That was how he took Ford and Erin seeing each other "occasionally."

What surprised him was that he found himself still attracted to her the same as he'd been when they first started dating way back when. But then, he shouldn't be surprised. She had left a mark on him despite them being both so young at the time.

Since leaving Fisher Falls, his tastes in women might not

have changed, but they did expand. He left as an eighteen-year-old virgin and returned as a sexually well-rounded thirty-five–year old.

His eyes and mind might not be as open as they were now if he hadn't left. Throughout the years, he tried things he never wanted to do again but also discovered what he wanted and needed in his life.

The truth was, if they had stayed together or even if he stayed in Fisher Falls, his life would be totally different.

The only regret he had when it came to leaving was... her.

Also, not being around when his father died since he would've liked the chance to tell his father goodbye and that he loved him one last time.

Loss was difficult and he needed to get it through his thick head that Erin suffered a big one, too. It cost nothing to be a kind or decent human being. He needed to be the example and not the exception. "I'm sorry about your loss, Erin."

Her brown eyes widened. "Are you?"

He shouldn't be surprised by her reaction after he'd been a dick. "I'm sure it was devastating."

Her tension seemed to dissipate a little. "It was. I'm sure the same as your father's loss was to you."

"We expect to outlive our parents, but not our spouses. Or our children." He scraped a hand through his hair. "Erin, can we start over?"

Her head twitched. "What do you mean 'start over?'"

"Can we forget the past and move forward from here? Like two adults?"

"I already did, Dylan. I moved on not long after you left Fisher Falls. You just didn't like that fact. And despite what you might think, I was not seeing Kyle while we were together. I was in love with you. If you had stayed, I would've married you, if you had asked."

Despite already knowing that, hearing her say it stabbed him in the heart. "We were only kids."

"We also turned into the adults we are now."

"We are the adults we are now because of the paths we took," he explained.

"You're saying you'd be different if you hadn't left?"

"Absolutely," he answered. "And you'd be different if you had."

She chewed on her bottom lip while she considered that. "That may be true. But at the time, we *were* young, and I was also in no position to leave with you. I was only sixteen and still in high school. You know that."

"You also insisted you'd never leave Fisher Falls." He raised his eyebrows. "That turned out to be true, didn't it?"

"Absolutely," she echoed.

"Do you have any regrets?"

She tipped her head to the side and countered, "Do you?"

Only of leaving you behind. "No."

"I don't, either."

Were they both lying to each other? "Well, there you go. We both lived the lives we were meant to live." It might have crossed his lips, but he didn't fully believe that.

"We're only in our thirties, Dylan. We still have a lot of living to do."

He jerked his head toward the farmhouse. "Then, come on, we should go do that. I'll finish showing you around."

"Before we do, I'll answer your question... Yes, I would love to start over. I've only ever wished you success and happiness, Dylan."

"I'm working on it." He waved his arm toward the farmhouse, and they began walking that way.

"You never got married or had children?" she asked as they approached the door to the main portion of the farmhouse.

He unlocked and opened it, then waited for her to cross the threshold before him. "I figured you'd already know that."

"I never asked."

Since gossip was considered an Olympic sport in Fisher Falls, she wouldn't have to ask. Maybe she just didn't care enough to listen.

He followed her inside and locked the door behind them. Being their private residence, the farmhouse wasn't open for tours or to the public. "You didn't care enough to know?"

"I figured it wasn't my business."

He watched her carefully as she glanced around and took in the changes.

"It's so different than what I remembered. It was a gorgeous house before but now, it seems more updated."

"It is. New floors, paint, wiring, new appliances. Dayne and I will share the kitchen with Dani but we each have our own wing, so we all have privacy. Her rooms are upstairs."

"I remember your room," she said with a soft smile. "The posters, the baseball and football trophies, your drawings... They were so detailed. It's no surprise that you became an architect."

He remembered her being in his room. Of course, his parents insisted they keep the door open while they were up there. However, that didn't stop them from fooling around. They just didn't do it in his room. A three-hundred-acre farm had plenty of hiding spots.

They never went as far as intercourse, though, since he wanted to wait until she was eighteen. Unfortunately, he had left town before then.

No doubt Kyle Hart was the one who finally took her virginity. Something that should have belonged to him.

Maybe it was for the best since his first time was a complete disaster. His second time, too. It took hooking up with more experienced partners before he had a good handle on how to please them. Or to know what he needed from them.

"Do you want to go upstairs and see the changes?"

She shook her head. "If that's Dani's space, I don't want to intrude."

"I doubt she'd mind."

She walked through the dining area, the living area and circled back to the kitchen. "I'd rather hear that from her."

The original farmhouse had been a four bedroom with only one full bathroom on the second floor and a half bath on the first. Ford had his crew turn two bedrooms into one large primary suite with its own full bathroom.

Dani loved it. She also loved that she wouldn't have to share her space with her twin brothers.

Dylan pointed toward the living room. "Over there is Dayne's wing. It mirrors mine, so there's no point in showing you both."

"Again, I wouldn't want to intrude in his personal space without his permission anyway." She met his eyes. "And unlike Dani, Dayne might mind."

"But I don't," he murmured.

She tipped her head to the side. "Then, I'd love to see it."

Chapter Seven

By ADDING the two single-story wings on either side of the original farmhouse, they just about tripled the size. But it still surprised Erin that all three siblings would want to share a residence, even with how it was laid out.

"Ford did all of this?" she asked, entering Dylan's private area.

"I drew up the plans and he executed them."

"Of course," she murmured. "From what I've seen so far—the event hall, the lodge, this house—your work is impressive, Dylan. Changing a simple dairy farm into a stunning resort couldn't have been an easy feat."

"Thank you," she heard from directly behind her. Not even a foot away. With her heart beating wildly, she spun to face him.

Was she more attracted to him now that he was a man and not the boy from back when they dated?

She casually took him in, trying not to be too obvious.

His short, dark blond hair was cut close on the sides and left a bit longer on top. It used to be so much lighter in high school and most likely darkened with age. Plus, back then it was sun-kissed since he was always outside, whether doing farm chores, swimming in the lake, or riding his dirt bike and ATV.

Both Dylan and Dayne always had a love for the outdoors.

In fact, he was a lot tanner now than when she ran into him in town all those months ago. Being out in the sun on the ranch, instead of locked up in an office all day, agreed with him.

The closely trimmed beard covering his face was new, too. It was as short as Ford's but much lighter in color, fitting his complexion.

She continued comparing the two men.

Ford was thirty-seven with dark hair and beard, deep brown eyes and darker skin tone from years of working construction.

Dylan, only two years younger, had dirty blond hair and beard, along with hazel eyes.

Their height was similar, with Dylan maybe being shorter by an inch, if that.

Both were ridiculously handsome. Fit. And downright sexy.

Dylan had looked good standing outside of the butcher shop. He looked even better now. Coming home seemed to agree with him, despite the hard work and stress from building a business from the ground up.

Her heart ached when she realized where they might've been if he had stayed. Possibly married with kids. Maybe even living on the dairy farm, surrounded by the mountains and cows.

Instead, she was a childless widow. And he was... She had no idea. "Did you ever get married?" she asked again since he never answered the last time. Just because he seemed to be single now, didn't mean he was always that way.

"No."

Her head snapped back. "Really?"

He nodded.

Now she had so many questions, even though the answers were none of her business. "No children, either?"

"No children. Apparently, I fail at picking partners on the same page as me."

Shots fired. "I never said I would leave," she reminded him.

"I never said I would stay," he countered.

"And that's why we are where we are right now."

"True." He exhaled loudly. "Let me show you around before someone sends out a search party for me."

"Please. I'd love to see the rest."

"It's pretty basic." He waved an arm around. "We're standing in the living room, of course."

"I was wondering. Thanks for clarifying that," she teased, hoping he still had a sense of humor.

Unfortunately, he didn't even crack a smile.

His wing of the house was decked out in rustic furniture with a "ranch" type of feel to it. Two large sepia-toned photos of cattle hung on the walls. Using the reddish-brown coloring gave the photos a more artistic and country feel than the typical black and white. "Were those photos taken here on the farm?" The landscape behind the herd of Holsteins looked familiar.

Again, he moved to stand directly behind her. So close, it would only take a slight shift for them to be touching. "They were. My father took them. I had them blown up and framed so I'd never forget the resort's humble beginnings."

"I doubt you could ever forget since you were raised here." She looked closer. "He had a great eye."

"I didn't know that about him until I found a few of his photos going through his stuff after he died. It was actually difficult to pick which ones I wanted for myself. I had some others of the amazing photos he took around the area, including town, hung in the lodge and cabins. A few I had framed for my mother's new place."

"Our parents always end up being more complex people than we expect. Why are we so surprised when we find out these sorts of things about them?"

His hands landed on her shoulders, and he gave them a gentle squeeze. "We see them solely as our parents and not as others see them? I don't know. On that note, how are yours?"

She turned, dislodging his touch, since it was increasing her heart rate. For a reason she didn't want to admit. She just had sex with Ford, another man shouldn't be getting her worked up, even if it *was* Dylan. "Great. They are loving the warmer weather in Georgia."

"So, they left Fisher Falls," he murmured.

She was surprised he didn't know that, either, especially with the town being as small as it was. However, he'd been busy building the resort ever since he returned. And if he didn't know Kyle died, or that her parents moved, then her best guess was he'd been avoiding any news or gossip from town. "They did. Not long after Dad retired. They didn't want to deal with the snow and freezing temps anymore."

"Good for them."

"It turns out the move *was* good for them." Though, she dearly missed them. Especially around the holidays. To see her parents, she either needed to fly south or they needed to travel north. It would've been the same for Dylan, since he had moved south, as well, after college. "Didn't you come back for visits?"

"I stayed out of town when I did."

Him not leaving the farm during his visits home would also explain why she hadn't seen him in the last seventeen years. Otherwise, it would've been difficult to not run into each other.

"To avoid me?" she asked.

Him evading her question was her answer. Even so, they were supposed to be moving forward, so maybe it was for the best he didn't answer.

The spacious living room included a big, comfortable-looking couch, an overstuffed recliner, an enormous TV hanging on the wall with a gas fireplace under it and a "live edge" wood coffee table. "That table is gorgeous. Did Callum make it?"

Callum was a woodworker and artist that lived right outside of town and made stunning custom furniture and decor from local trees. His stuff was pricy but worth every cent since each piece took him weeks, some even months, to handcraft. Anything he made would last forever and could be handed down through generations.

"He did. He also made my bedroom furniture. I bought some of his pieces for the lodge, too."

"That had to set you back."

Dylan nodded. "It did, but the man is a true artist and craftsman. He was happy I bought almost everything he had stored in his barn, and I was happy to support another local business. With the amount I purchased, he won't have any problem paying his bills for a while."

After that, Dylan might. But Erin was sure Callum was ecstatic to have spare cash in his pocket. "That's great. Can I see it?"

"Sure. I was planning on giving you the whole tour, anyway. This way..." He headed toward a closed door off the living room.

She thought it would be his bedroom. Instead, they entered a huge bathroom.

She blinked as she took it all in.

It was a bathroom she could only dream about. The huge glass shower stall had multiple shower heads. She wondered why he had two metal handrails attached to the walls since she was damn sure Dylan didn't need help keeping his balance while showering. It also was equipped with a built-in bench he could use if, for some reason, he had a difficult time standing while sudsing up.

Dylan was fit and healthy. He wasn't an eighty-year-old needing assistance in the shower. That meant those extra features had other purposes.

"Do you plan on having a party in there?"

"You never know."

She glanced over her shoulder to find him staring at her with his expression locked down.

It hit her then...

Dylan was the architect that designed the whole ranch. *He* designed the playrooms on the second floor of the event hall. *He* designed this space.

"Dylan..." she started.

"Whatever you're about to ask, I'd prefer you didn't."

She would respect that. "I guess I'll make my own conclusions."

"You would, whether I answered or not. It's human nature."

"It's also human nature to be curious."

In front of the only window in the room was a simply designed but beautiful free-standing tub large enough for two adults. As she inspected it, she trailed her fingers along the curved porcelain edge. When she noticed the jets, she realized it was more than a typical soaking tub. "I would kill for this tub. The shower. Actually, the whole bathroom."

"No reason for murder. I could design one for you. You only need to ask."

Again, zero humor in his tone. "While that's very generous of you, I couldn't afford to build it, even if you designed one for me for free."

"I'm sure Ford could help."

She *mmm*'d. She didn't want to get dragged back into a conversation about her relationship with Ford. Instead, she drifted toward a partially opened door. This one most likely led into his bedroom. She pointed at it. "This way next?"

"Yes."

As she walked in that direction, she asked, "You only have one bathroom?"

"It's all I need. If I need to entertain a bunch of guests, I have the whole resort at my fingertips."

"True." After pushing the door open wider, she stepped through, and her feet stuttered to a stop.

If she thought the bathroom was impressive, the bedroom...

Holy smokes. It was clearly meant for more than only sleeping.

She recognized the tantric chaise occupying one corner. Ford had a similar one in his bedroom, and they had used it often.

The enormous wood-framed bed, wider than a king, had thick, sturdy hand-crafted posts and headboard. Nothing looked delicate about it. Not only was it masculine and fit the updated look of the farmhouse, but...

Immediately, Erin saw it for what it was. A bed that could be turned into a sexual playground. She scanned it for hooks or eyebolts, but if the bed had any, they were hidden well.

The room also had a whole wall of built-in cabinets. Cabinets that could be used for storing clothes, shoes or other objects. Or for hiding secrets. Like toys.

"I love the built-ins."

"They're convenient," was all he said.

She bet they were. To the average eye, Dylan's bedroom looked very masculine and very bachelor-ish, since even an ounce of feminine touch was missing from the decor.

When she turned, he was once again close. And once again, her heart began to beat rapidly. Not due to fear, but the opposite.

She lost her train of thought as he stepped even closer. She had space to escape, if needed, but was surprised to find she didn't want to. Truthfully, she was thrown off by how her body was reacting to his being only inches away.

"You look good, Erin," he murmured, with his serious face tipped down to hers.

"You already said that."

"Worth repeating." He fingered one of the straps on her sundress. Doing so caused him to make contact with her skin, in turn, causing goosebumps. "The sundress fits you perfectly. At first glance you look wholesome, but I have a feeling that could be the farthest from the truth."

What did that mean? What did he know? Ford said there weren't any cameras in the playrooms. Was that false and some were hidden? Had Dylan watched them? And if he did, why didn't it bother her?

He skimmed the back of his knuckles down her cheek. "Your nipples are hard."

There was no denying that fact. They ached and it was no longer from Ford twisting them less than a half hour ago.

This wasn't good. Her attraction to Dylan was fighting its way back from where she buried it so long ago. After he left, she tried to forget him.

Clearly, she failed.

She shouldn't desire two different men, should she? Did that make her a bad person?

Why was society so determined to shove people into boxes? And if someone didn't fit neatly into their perceived box, they were judged. Sometimes harshly.

That fear was why she and Ford weren't open about their relationship. They pretended to be friends, not lovers. If anyone in town knew their true relationship, they'd be constantly pressured to get engaged, married and have children.

Because that was what was expected in Fisher Falls.

She tried to force herself into a box when she married Kyle. The universe had different ideas.

Chapter Eight

"WHY, ERIN?"

Why? Why what? She shook herself mentally, pulling herself back to the present.

Oh, that's right... Her nipples decided to make a bold statement.

"It's far from cold in here," he continued.

He wanted her to admit she still wanted him. Even seventeen years later. Practically a lifetime ago. "What do you want me to say, Dylan?"

"Are you afraid of me?"

"Absolutely not."

"Then, why is there a tremble in your voice? If it's not fear, what is it?"

She pulled in a breath, trying to stop her body from going haywire. "You know what it is."

He leaned in even closer and whispered, "Tell me."

She didn't want to admit it out loud. If she did, it would feel more real. She shouldn't have agreed for him to give her a tour.

She tried to convince herself that she wanted to avoid running into him today. However, if that was true, she shouldn't have showed up for the open house at all.

But she had.

If she searched deep down, he was the reason why. She hadn't stopped thinking about him since running into him in town, even though she tried her damnedest to do so.

"Erin..."

The way he whispered her name shot a shiver down her spine. Again, not from fear. Not even close.

Wanting him so soon after having sex with Ford couldn't be normal, could it?

"Do you feel what I feel?"

"Wh—" She cleared her throat when the words got caught. "What do you feel?"

"The chemistry we always had."

"Is that what that is?" she asked. Again, ignoring the truth.

"What would you call it?"

Foolishness. He'd blamed Kyle for stealing her away when that wasn't close to being true. It was only sour grapes, plain and simple.

But they had both grown up a lot since then.

Looking at Dylan, she couldn't ignore the fact that he had *definitely* grown up. He looked so damn good, it gave him an unfair advantage.

Keep your wits about you, Erin. Don't fall for him all over again. You might not survive if he rips out your heart a second time.

When she was sixteen, she thought the world was about to end when he left. At thirty-three she knew better, but that didn't mean he wasn't capable of causing emotional damage.

If he could leave his family, his friends and his girlfriend so easily the first time, what would stop him a second time?

She glanced around.

The ranch resort.

He was planting roots so deeply in this place, only a tornado could rip him free.

But, she reminded herself, tornadoes did exist. She didn't want to be the victim of one.

"Erin."

When she glanced up, their eyes locked. "*Hmm?*"

"You didn't answer my question."

"I don't have an answer. This was all so unexpected."

"What was? Me coming home to stay, building the resort, or our attraction reigniting?"

"All of it," she admitted.

His mouth turned slightly up at the corners at the same time he closed the small gap between them and said softly, "So, you do admit you're still attracted to me."

"Why are you doing this, Dylan?"

"Because I saw you with Ford and, honestly, it bothered me."

"It shouldn't."

"You were supposed to be mine, Erin."

Ditto. "You made a choice that changed that."

"And now I'm making another choice."

"To cause issues between me and Ford?"

"The way you two explained earlier, it sounded as if he has no claim to you."

God, why did his deep, rumbling voice make her insides clench? And not in a bad way. In a way that made her very aware of him and how close he was. It wouldn't take much to...

She forced herself to swallow. "I'm not looking to be

claimed, Dylan. I'm my own woman. I don't need a man to survive."

"But you need a man for other things."

"That's why I have Ford."

"You use him." He didn't even bother to form that as a question.

He was testing her. Testing her relationship with Ford. Seeing if it had cracks he could crawl through.

"Untrue." They had an easy, comfortable relationship that worked for their purposes.

"He's your go-to for sex."

She wasn't responding to that. "If you don't want to finish giving me a tour, I can explore on my own."

"I'm only trying to understand the dynamics between you."

Her eyebrows stitched together. "Why?"

"Because I want to do this..."

With his next step closer, she found herself pinned against one of the bedposts. Placing his hands on her shoulders, he took his time sliding them down her arms. All while keeping their gaze connected.

A little puff of breath escaped her parted lips and a bolt of lightning ripped through her.

But it was when he grabbed both wrists and raised her arms, pinning them to the post, she could hear nothing but her heart pounding in her ears. If he thought her nipples were hard earlier, they were now aching. "Dylan, what are you doing?"

When he dipped his head, his mouth hovered over hers.

He was about to kiss her.

She should stop him and leave. She shouldn't be kissing one man when she just fucked another.

"Tell me no, if you don't want this."

The problem was, she did want it.

She waffled back and forth between thinking kissing him would be wrong and letting herself allow it, simply to discover if that spark between them still existed or if she was only imagining it.

If it wasn't there, she could easily resist him and walk away. If it was...

She could be in trouble.

She owed no loyalty to Ford, the same way he owed no loyalty to her. They kept things simple and uncomplicated. They were also free to date or be with others.

But still...

Damn it. She needed to stop judging herself so harshly. Plenty of other people would be willing to do that for her. She shouldn't let the moral "rules" of others fill her head. She could make her own.

Her biggest concern was alienating Ford. He'd been good to her for years. Quietly supportive in the background. Only a phone call or text away if she needed anything. Including him.

"Erin..."

God, her name crossing his lips like that...

She closed her eyes when her name, in the same way he just said it, echoed through her mind.

She should be able to resist him.

She was finding that ability impossible.

One kiss. What would it hurt?

Opening her eyes, she saw his furrowed brow. A second later with a single nod, he released her wrists. "I'll leave you alone."

Before he had a chance to step back, she grabbed his face and pulled him to her, crashing their lips together. A puff of breath filled her mouth before he took control of the kiss, forcing her back into the bedpost again, intertwining their fingers and pulling her hands above her head once more.

His tongue drove into her mouth, completely claiming it. He stole her breath and made her knees wobble. She struggled to stay on her feet as her bones melted.

Holy smokes, he was a great kisser. So much better than she remembered.

Of course, back then, they were young and only finding their way. Typical teenagers figuring out their bodies and how they reacted to certain actions and situations. While fun and exciting, Dylan always kept his wits about him and stopped before they went too far, despite Erin begging him not to.

She wanted him to be her first because at the time, she thought he would also be her last. The universe had different ideas.

She quickly left the past behind when he wedged his knee between her thighs, spreading them. His thick thigh pressed against her throbbing pussy and the way he rocked it against her shoved her dress higher.

And higher.

Rudely reminding her she no longer wore any panties.

And the reason for that.

She needed to stop him before Ford's DNA ended up smeared all over his jeans. But his kiss was turning her brain to mush, and she figured a few more seconds of it wouldn't hurt.

Just a few more, then she'd stop him.

Only it didn't take long for him to collar her wrists with a single hand and work the other up under her dress.

Shit. Shit. Shit. The man was on a mission, and she needed to stop it.

She twisted her head and groaned, "Stop."

Too late.

"You're so wet."

Oh no. The floor needed to open up and swallow her whole.

But it was when he lifted two wet fingers to his mouth, her soul left her body. This time her "stop" was a loud screech instead of a groan.

He froze with his fingers barely an inch from his lips and his eyebrows slammed together. "What's wrong?"

"That..." She shook her head. "That isn't what you think. I mean, some might be but not all."

Her cheeks were on fire and her heart raced like a Thoroughbred when he glanced at his hand.

"Dylan..."

He stared at her. She knew the exact second he figured it out. It was the same time he released her wrists, dropped his knee, took a giant step back and growled, "You fucked him on my property?"

"Isn't that what this property is for?" she asked weakly.

His jaw shifted and he rubbed the pads of his two fingers together. "You let him come inside you?"

She blew out a breath and skirted around him. "I should go."

"Agreed."

The fire in her belly only moments ago was quickly doused. "I'm sorry, I should've stopped you."

His eyebrows almost hit his hairline. "You think?"

Her annoyance was quickly growing. He was just as responsible for the kiss as she. "Sharing a kiss is not the same as you fingering me, Dylan. We learned that over fifteen years ago, remember?"

His head jerked back. "Why the hell would you want to kiss a man after just fucking another?"

"I wanted to see if..." She sighed and shook her head. "Never mind. I never should've come today."

As she began to head toward the bedroom door that led back into the living room, he grabbed her arm and swung her around to face him. "Why did you?"

"Curiosity."

"About the resort or me?"

Both, if she was being completely honest. "The resort. You only happen to be one of the owners."

"Inconvenient fact for you, isn't it?"

The second she eyed his hand on her arm, he released her. "You've done a great job of creating your dream, Dylan. Now... I'm tired and heading home."

"I'd suggest taking a shower," she heard behind her as she opened the bedroom door and stepped out of the room.

She pinned her lips together so she wouldn't respond to that bullshit.

She escaped the farmhouse and managed to get back to her vehicle without any other delays, but on that walk, she realized that it hadn't been only anger coloring his words.

There was also pain.

Chapter Nine

Dylan glanced up from his laptop when Dayne's head appeared around the door frame to his office. The only difference between his and his twin's face was the fact that Dayne's included a grin and Dylan's held a scowl.

"Brother..." Dayne started as the rest of his body appeared in the doorway.

"Is there a problem with the finances?"

His brother blew on his knuckles and scrubbed them over his chest. "Of course not. You know I'm a financial wizard." He should be since he took six years to get his four-year degree in accounting.

Unlike Dylan, Dayne had decided in college that partying would be his major and accounting his minor. Needless to say, their parents had not been pleased with his screwing off, resulting in him having to fund those last two years entirely on his own.

"Then, why are you bugging me?"

The grin flattened and Dayne flopped into one of the chairs parked in front of the desk, hooking a denim-covered knee over the chair's arm. "I can't visit the person I shared a womb with?"

"Shared? More like crowded me."

"Luckily, it didn't take long for you to catch up to my superior size."

Dylan leaned back in his leather office chair. "Some parts of me actually surpassed your size."

The grin was back. "You've been hiding in your office the last couple of days."

"Not true. I took Rebel for a ride." Rebel was one of the dozen horses the ranch now owned. All twelve, plus two donkeys, were rescued from a kill auction down in Lancaster County where the perfectly good horses had been dumped for various reasons; most of which made his blood boil.

Dylan was determined to make the ranch a new beginning for more than only humans.

"*Mmm.* I saw one of the wranglers cooling him down. Looks like he went for a hard gallop."

"He was restless and needed to stretch his legs." They quickly figured out that Rebel was a retired racehorse and still loved to run. Dylan loved to give the Thoroughbred his head when he needed to clear his own. Only that hadn't been doing the trick the last few days.

Dayne cocked an eyebrow. "Are you sure it was Rebel who was restless and not you?"

"Why are you in here?"

"I come bearing good news."

Dylan could use some. "Then, let's hear it so I can get back to work."

"You could use a break."

Dylan lifted an eyebrow at his brother. "We only have three days until we're officially open and guests arrive."

"And we're on track. You know why?"

Dylan didn't bother to ask why because he would hear it whether he wanted to or not.

"Because you're anal about *everything*."

"Is that a bad thing?"

"Depends."

"Can you just tell me the good news?" *And then get out of my hair.*

"Ford accepted my job offer. Well, he countered on the salary... But it was minimal and he's worth it."

"According to you."

"You don't think he is? He built this damn resort in record time. Better yet, it's not done half-assed. He's an excellent contractor and a jack of all trades, brother. If he doesn't know how to build or fix something, he knows who will since the man has valuable connections."

"That he does," Dylan mumbled, thinking about Erin fucking Ford on this very property. His scowl returned.

"What's going on?"

Dylan pulled in a breath and on the exhale, lied. "Nothing."

"Bullshit. Remember? We were once one egg."

Dylan sighed. "When is he starting?"

"He already has. He also asked if I could hire a few of his employees to help with the maintenance. You know with a resort as large as this, something will always be breaking."

That was true. Stopped up plumbing, broken pipes, broken furniture, electrical shorts... the list was endless.

He knew hiring Ford as the ranch's facilities manager was the right decision and he should be happy the man took the job...

But he had mixed feelings about it.

For one reason and one reason only.

But he would not be discussing that reason with Dayne.

There *was* one person he would want to talk to about it, though. "What's he working on today?"

"One of the run-in sheds."

"Which pasture?"

Dayne's brow furrowed. "The far north pasture. Why?"

Dylan surged to his feet. "I want to welcome him aboard." He quickly skirted around his desk and past his brother.

"Why don't I believe you?" Dayne yelled as Dylan hurried out of his office and went outside to find the man.

———

EVERY TIME the utility vehicle hit a bump or hole, Dylan bounced violently in his seat, almost giving him whiplash. He made a mental note to make sure the roads were graded soon so they weren't so damn rough. They had paved the driveways and "lanes" around the lodge and event hall, as well as all the parking areas open to guest vehicles. However, the dirt roads beyond the farmhouse would be used by guests taking a long walk, going on a hike, or participating in one of the scheduled horseback or ATV rides.

Plus, come winter, smoothing them out would make plowing a lot easier. Once they made some of their investment back, he'd also like to put down stone to keep them from turning into mud come spring.

Of course, he had an entire list of improvements and additions for the future, as long as the ranch turned out to be a success. But for now, the resort was where he wanted it to be for the initial opening. Once they had guests, he planned on asking for feedback on what activities or amenities they'd like to see.

As he motored past the pasture on his right with the herd

of grazing horses, Rebel actually lifted his head and whinnied loudly. Dylan chalked it up to the fact the horse was appreciative that he hadn't been turned into dog food. At least that was what Dylan wanted to believe, when the truth was Rebel probably thought he had a carrot or apple in his pocket.

Another pasture on his left included a menagerie of farm animals they adopted from rescues or shelters. Along with the two donkeys bought from the kill pen, the rag tag group included four llamas, two fat Vietnamese pot belly pigs, six Nubian goats, and the five most senior Holstein cows from his father's former herd. They still produced milk but not at the capacity they used to, so if they had been sold off with the rest of the herd, they most likely would've been turned into hamburger or dog food.

Closer to the farmhouse, two dozen Rhode Island Red hens and one ornery rooster filled the chicken coop. Fresh eggs couldn't be beat. Neither could fresh goat milk, something Dani wanted so she could make cheese, and whatever else, for the guests.

Dylan made it clear to her before she adopted them from their previous owner, she'd be responsible for making sure those does were milked twice a day. However, she also promised to feed her guinea pig every day when she begged for one at six years old. That lasted about two days before Dylan had to take over Squeaker's care.

While they had plenty of barn cats to keep the rodents at bay, they were still missing dogs. He figured they'd be a part of the ranch soon enough since some of the full-time employees would be living onsite and he was damn sure a few would bring their pets. They were welcome as long as they didn't terrorize wildlife, the other animals, or guests.

Driving over the last hill, he finally reached the far north pastures. Inside the newest fenced area, he spotted Ford's dually pickup truck parked by the run-in shed. The three-sided shelter, built from wood and covered with a heavy-duty metal roof, was one of the last ones built since this pasture was one of the two farthest from the resort. Because of the distance, the rear of the shed also included an enclosed storage area to hold bales of hay.

The newly hired facilities manager had to be putting the finishing touches on the structure.

After driving through the open gate and parking next to Ford's dually, he heard classic rock blasting from the truck's open windows. However, he didn't see the vehicle's owner. Once he climbed from the UTV, Dylan couldn't miss the hammering over the loud music, so he headed in that direction.

He rounded the shed to the open side to see the half-naked man installing a bracket for a salt block. Dylan's feet stuttered to a halt, and he took him in, despite being irritated for being unable to stop from doing so.

Not only was Ford shirtless, his bare chest was slick with sweat from working in the heat of the day. A small patch of dark hair nestled between his defined pecs glistened in the unavoidable sliver of sun due to where he worked. Even his impressive six-pack abs were damp from perspiration.

Since Ford still had no idea he was there, Dylan muttered, "Hope you're wearing sunscreen," doing his damnedest to stop staring.

He failed.

Ford quickly straightened Jand, after containing his surprise, answered, "Always."

He pounded in the last nail before holstering the hammer in the leather tool belt hanging low off his hips. It had to be heavy since it pulled his jeans down enough to expose another belt. The Adonis belt. Those tempting grooves of muscle running south at an angle from his hips to another tool, one not used for construction but rather filling Erin with cum.

Dylan gritted his teeth at the memory of that unexpected discovery.

After pulling off his baseball cap, Ford swiped a forearm across his damp forehead, then whacked the sweat-ringed hat on this thigh before slapping it back on his head.

It was impossible for Dylan to pull his gaze free when his newest employee grabbed a plastic gallon jug off the ground where it had been sitting near a toolbox. Putting it to his lips, he chugged the water, obviously not caring that it spilled down his chin and chest. Dylan unglued his gaze from the man's Adam's apple bobbing with each swallow, only to watch the rivulets of water forge a path down his tan torso.

Unfortunately, Ford wasn't the only one thirsty in that run-in shed.

As soon as Ford had his fill, he yanked off his hat again and poured the rest of the water over his head. Once his hair was soaked, he shook his head like a wet dog, sending droplets flying, some of them even hitting Dylan. Dylan closed his eyes and licked away the drop that landed near the corner of his mouth.

Hearing, "Just finished up out here by installing the hay rack, grain feeders and, of course, this salt block holder," had Dylan's eyes flashing back open.

Jesus. He certainly didn't need to get a damn hard-on over a wet dog like Ford.

Dylan cleared his throat and diverted his gaze elsewhere, hoping his cock didn't betray him. The last thing he wanted was to be outed to the man standing before him. The one who fucked Erin "occasionally."

That reminder was enough to stop the blood from

rushing south. "My brother said you took the facilities manager position."

"I did. He made the offer hard to resist."

"Harder to resist than Erin?" *Damn it.*

Planting a hand on his hip, Ford dropped his head and stared at his boots.

Was he annoyed? If so, good. So was Dylan. "Have you spoken with her since the open house last weekend?"

Ford lifted his head and narrowed his dark eyes on him. "No. Should I have?"

Dylan shrugged. "I thought you two saw each other regularly."

"I said occasionally. We're not tied at the hip."

Do you want to be? At least that didn't slip out.

Ford watched Dylan carefully. "Is there a problem?"

Dylan struggled to keep his expression neutral. "No, I'm only surprised she's fine with a casual relationship since all she talked about in high school was how she wanted to get married and have kids."

"She got married, remember? Just not to you."

Dylan's tight jaw shifted. "But she's been a widow for a while now. I figured she'd be ready to settle down again."

"Did you ask her if that's what she wants?"

"I didn't get the chance before figuring out that you two fucked somewhere on the property during the open house."

"Did she tell you that?"

"She didn't have to. I discovered it on my own."

Ford's eyebrows shot up his sweat-beaded forehead. "How? You said that there'd be no cameras in the playrooms."

Dylan's head jerked back. "You fucked her in one of the playrooms? Nobody was supposed to be up there on Saturday."

"She asked to see them."

"How did she even know they existed?"

"I told her. I didn't know it was supposed to be a secret."

"For the locals, yes."

"She's not your average local."

"Apparently," Dylan muttered.

"So, you *do* have cameras in the rooms up there."

"You know there are. For safety. But that's not how..." *Shit.*

"Did something happen after I left her with you to finish the tour?"

"Would it bother you if it did?"

"I thought I made it clear that there aren't any strings between us. Erin is free to do what or whomever she pleases."

Ford now had both hands on his hips, once again pulling Dylan's attention there.

One thing Dylan discovered after learning to accept his sexuality, was that he liked his women soft and his men hard.

Unfortunately, Ford fit that bill. Fortunately, he doubted the man was bi.

He certainly wasn't asking but that didn't mean he couldn't fish for that info.

Chapter Ten

Dylan shook his head and thought, *screw it*. He might as well make his intentions toward Erin known. "I don't like the fact that when kissing a woman, I discover she had sex with someone else not even an hour prior."

Ford's spine snapped straight, and his shoulders pulled back slightly. "She told you that?"

"She didn't need to."

A realization filled Ford's face. Was he trying not to grin? "What I'm hearing is, you're angry because when you kissed her, she was full of my cum."

Dylan's chest tightened. "Wouldn't that piss you off?"

With lips pursed, Ford shook his head. "No. Once again, Erin is free to have sex with whomever she wants."

"And are you?"

"That's how it works. For some reason, you seem bothered by that concept. You don't like the thought of a woman you're pursuing being with another man." Ford's dark eyebrows pinned together. "Tell me... Are you jealous of her? Or of me?"

Dylan's eyebrows did the same. "What the hell are you talking about?"

"Are you jealous I fucked her? Or are you jealous she fucked me?"

"That doesn't make sense."

"Sure it does. I'm trying to figure out how you're looking at the situation and why it's bothering you."

He stated the obvious. "We used to date."

"When you were kids," Ford reminded him needlessly. "That was a long time ago and she moved on after you left. As I'm sure you did. Now that you're back, you want to rekindle what you had as kids and you think I'm standing in the way. She couldn't have been the only lover in your life."

"She was not." He had plenty of relationships in the years since leaving Fisher Falls. Actually, too many to count. Not all of them had been with women, either.

College had been eye-opening and changed his life. He also uncovered things about himself long buried deep because of growing up in Fisher Falls. He still kept most of it to himself but wasn't sure how long he'd be able to hang on to his secrets. Especially now that he owned an all-adult resort. One where someone's sexuality or personal preferences wouldn't be judged and where guests were encouraged to be uninhibited.

He was well aware it wouldn't be long before his true self was exposed.

Ford stared at him for far too long. When his expression changed, Dylan locked down his own. The man was too damn intuitive.

"All these months working with you on this property and I had no damn clue," Ford murmured.

It was safest to play dumb. "Clue about what?"

"About who you really are."

His pulse began to race. Could the man see right through him? "You still don't." Dylan assured him.

"You wear your mask well, boss."

"Don't call me that. I'm not the one who hired you."

"Are you pissed that your brother did?"

"No." He had no doubt Ford would be a great employee with his experience, knowledge and work ethic. The only problem he'd have with him was due to Erin.

"Are you sure? I only accepted the offer this morning and,"—Ford snapped his fingers—"here you are."

Dylan took a step closer. "I'm not here because he hired you."

"You're here to confront me about Erin, then. Clearly, you want her for yourself, and you think I'm a threat to that." Ford tilted his head to the side and studied Dylan. "Or maybe you're worried that I'm more of a threat to those secrets you're clinging to."

"I have no secrets," Dylan insisted.

"Sure. None of us do," Ford scoffed, shaking his head. "Well, I've got work to do. I don't want to get fired my first official day on the job."

Dylan ground his teeth at Ford's dismissal. He grabbed the other man's arm to stop him from picking up his toolbox. "I want to know why you think I have secrets."

Ford slowly turned back to face him, not bothering to pull free from Dylan's firm grip. "It finally hit me why you were eye-fucking me."

"I wasn't—"

Ford's mouth pulled up on one side. "Do you think I didn't notice? Or were you only checking me for sunburn?"

"Well, your health insurance hasn't kicked in yet." Dylan mentally groaned. The man was playing him. He needed to turn around and get the hell out of there before he stepped in more shit. Shit he might not be able to wipe off his boots.

"Do you want to finish your exam then, Dr. Dylan?" His hands went to his tool belt. "I can undress the rest of the way if you'd like a closer look." He unlatched his heavy tool belt and dropped it next to his portable toolbox.

Dylan's heart went from racing to pounding in an instant at the thought of seeing Ford totally naked. "Don't."

"Why? Will you be too tempted?"

Cocky fucker. "I have zero interest in you." Sometimes lies stuck like glue in his mouth. This one was no exception.

"Bullshit." Ford chuckled and shook his head. When he was done being amused, he sobered quickly and locked eyes with him. "Why don't you prove you don't?"

"How the hell am I supposed to prove that?"

"By doing this." Ford grabbed the arm holding him and jerked it hard, causing their bodies to collide.

Before Dylan could recover his breath and put space between them, Ford locked lips with him.

Dylan planted his hands on Ford's damp chest to push him away but as soon as his fingers met the man's hard flesh, the opposite happened. His grip tightened and, using his body, he pinned the slightly taller man against the run-in shed's wall.

What Dylan had been trying to avoid earlier was no longer avoidable. All the blood rushed from his brain into his cock. He couldn't hide his hard-on since it pressed against Ford's.

He closed his eyes and sank into Ford's heated, damp body, while deepening the kiss. Their tongues clashed, their lips wrestled, their breathing hitched.

Damn it. He wasn't proving Ford wrong; he was proving

him right. Especially when Dylan automatically ground his hips against him.

It had been a while since he'd been intimate with a man. He knew better than to look at one twice since returning to Fisher Falls. He had no idea that Ford swung that way. Or more like swung both ways like a broken screen door. The same as Dylan did.

While it was enlightening, it was also troublesome now that he knew. Dylan had checked out the man from afar plenty of times while Ford worked around the property but never thought to act on his attraction.

He figured since Ford had "occasional" sex with Erin, he was straight.

Shit. Maybe that was why they only hooked up sporadically. He could be hooking up with men on "occasion," too.

Did Erin know?

Dylan certainly hadn't shared his proclivities with her, either.

If she found out, how would she react? Would she not have a problem with it, or be disgusted?

The problem with this new discovery was, Ford now knew about Dylan's sexuality. Would he tell her? The man could easily make up a story about him, claiming Dylan hit on him and Ford rejected his advances. A story like that could end up being a cockblock when it came to rekindling his relationship with her.

Ford's hands at Dylan's belt had him twisting his head to free himself from the unexpected situation.

"Stop," he demanded between his panting. Once free, he turned away to hide his reaction because he was breathing so hard, he was becoming light-headed.

Or maybe that was from losing his head.

Or from the excitement of discovering the man he had

stared at for the last few months was attracted to him in the same way.

No matter what, he couldn't kiss Ford again. Not only was he Erin's "friend with benefits," but now also a ranch employee. Despite his denial, Dylan *was* one of Ford's bosses.

And having sex or even playing around with Ford could get messy in more than one way. Not resisting Ford could screw up their working relationship, his chance at Erin, maybe even the resort's reputation.

Did he just cause it to be tarnished?

He worked too hard and spent too much money to have the business fail before it even got off the ground.

He ground his teeth at his own weakness.

He needed to get the hell out of there. Now. Then they both needed to forget this ever happened.

Without another word or even a glance back, Dylan strode out of the run-in shed and directly to his UTV.

Luckily, Ford didn't try to stop him.

Because if he had, their cock-hardening kiss might've ended up being so much more.

WHAT THE HELL JUST HAPPENED?

Did he really make out with his new boss?

Thankfully he hadn't sold off his business yet. He would need to keep it after he got fired.

Because Ford just exposed Dylan's secret.

Or at least one of them.

But Dylan shouldn't worry about Ford exposing his sexuality since, for the most part, he kept his under wraps, too.

Fisher Falls was not the most accepting when it came to anyone not straight as an arrow. The men around here prided themselves on being "real men." *Grunt, grunt.* The area was full of farmers, hunters, fishermen and even some end-of-world preppers. The farther you traveled from the center of town, the more likely you'd run into someone who despised the government, as well as anyone who didn't act or look the same as them.

It was a risky move for the Lyons brothers to open this kind of resort here due to that fact alone. Would the ranch be gated and have security guards? Of course. But that could end up being a false sense of security for both the resort and the guests.

It was also risky for locals to identify as anything other than heterosexual.

Were people more accepting in this day and age? Some. But there were plenty of others who doubled down on their hatred of what they didn't understand.

It was why Ford never wanted to hook up with anyone from town other than Erin. Instead, he used hookup apps to find someone in the closest city. Of course, it was a pain in the ass to drive that far, especially in winter. Unfortunately, he had no choice, since it was the safest way to handle any wants and desires Erin couldn't fulfill.

Because of the loose structure of their relationship, she never asked if he was seeing anyone else and he didn't volunteer that information. That meant she had no idea he was bi. He had no reason—at least before today—to share that side of him. He also wasn't sure how she'd react if she ever found out.

One thing he always promised her: No matter who he was with—other than her—he would always wear a condom and get tested regularly. He also asked her to do the same if she was having sex with anyone other than him. Luckily, they trusted each other enough and didn't need verification to make sure they were sticking to their word.

Ford leaned back against the run-in shed's wall and ran a hand down his bare chest, remembering Dylan's hands on his heated skin. His palm drew a path down his abs until it hit the waistband of his jeans.

He was tempted.

But he shouldn't.

He was working.

Anyone could come along and catch him.

Did he care about any of that? Hell no. All he cared about right now was relieving the pressure and finishing what Dylan started by grinding his cock against Ford's.

Screw it.

After unfastening his leather belt and jeans, he shoved them down far enough to free his erection. He gave his balls a quick squeeze before shutting his eyes and pulling a long breath in through his nostrils.

This shouldn't take long, and he hoped to hear anyone approaching.

Circling the root of his cock, he squeezed that next, cutting off the blood flow for a few seconds. Then he began the age-old practice of horny boys and men everywhere... He began to stroke his length.

Keeping his eyes shut, he imagined Dylan on his knees in the finely ground stone with Ford's cock in his mouth.

He also pictured those intense hazel eyes rising to meet his, his mouth stretched around Ford's girth, his tongue collecting the tangy precum as it swirled around the crown.

Ford's hips and fingers twitched with every pump into his boss's imaginary mouth.

He was about to lose his load. Unfortunately, not in

Dylan's mouth or on his face or even deep within the man's ass.

Damn shame.

Clenching his teeth, Ford stroked faster.

"Fuck," he groaned when his cock pulsed and his cum shot out, landing on the dusty stone at his feet.

All spurred from a simple kiss.

One that might take a while to forget.

Maybe he needed to cruise his favorite app and take the hour-long trip to State College to help evict it from his memories.

Chapter Eleven

"Ford…" Erin started while pulling a pan of homemade meatloaf out of the oven.

"Yeah, darlin'?"

As soon as she placed the hot pan on a trivet in the center of the kitchen table, she turned to face him where he stood behind his seat. He was ready to plant his ass at the table and start chowing down since he'd worked hard all day at the resort finishing up small projects and was starving.

When she invited him over for one of his favorite meals, it took him less than thirty seconds to respond to her text with a "yes," while in his head he screamed, "Hell yes!"

Even though Danica had been working on the resort's menu all week and the employees got to be her guinea pigs, nothing beat a plate of Erin's glazed meatloaf, sour cream mashed potatoes, and braised cabbage.

Of course, with a cold beer to wash it all down.

He leaned over the table to set a bottle of Yuengling next to her plate, then tucked his thumb under her chin to tip her face up. He stared down into her deep brown eyes. "What's bothering you? I can see it in your face."

"I need to ask you..." She shook her head. "No, I need to tell you something. I know we don't owe each other anything other than friendship, but..."

"What?" he prodded.

"I..."

She was rarely this bothered over anything unless it was something out of her control. That realization made the tiny hairs on the back of his neck stand at attention. "What, Erin? Just spill whatever it is."

"The flame I thought was extinguished... It's rekindled."

He stared at her for a moment. *Flame? Rekindled?*

Dylan had mentioned kissing her, but had something else happened since then? "You slept with Dylan."

"No."

He shook his head. "Then what?"

"He kissed me."

Since she wasn't aware that Dylan already confessed to that, he decided to act like it was news to him. "Without your consent?"

"No! No. Nothing like that." She pulled away and rounded the table to take her seat before flipping a hand toward his place setting. "Let's start before it gets cold."

He settled in the chair across from her and took a big bite of the meatloaf. She never missed with her grandmother's recipe. She should share it with Danica. He was damn sure some of the resort's guests would love it as much as he did.

After swallowing, he said, "So, you want to fuck him."

She pulled in a breath, picked up her fork and stared at her meal.

"He wants to fuck you." Ford reworded it when she didn't respond and wouldn't meet his eyes across the table.

After scooping up some the mashed potatoes, she paused the fork in front of her mouth. "I would like to... explore the possibilities?"

"You don't sound sure."

"I would like to explore the possibilities," she repeated more firmly before shoving the fork into her mouth.

He nodded while chewing some of the savory cabbage. He chased it down with a mouthful of beer. "Since when do you need permission from me? Our relationship was never like that."

"I know, but not only is he an ex, he's your boss. I don't want to cause any issues for you or want it to be awkward for any of us."

The only issue between Dylan and Ford right now was their own kiss two days ago. Since then, the co-owner of Double D Ranch had avoided him like he was contagious. "Do you plan on being exclusive with him?"

A wrinkle appeared along her brow. "I don't know. I haven't thought that far ahead. It was only one kiss."

According to what Dylan revealed, she left out the part about him fingering her.

Since he wanted her to always feel free to share her feelings or her desires with him, maybe he could reassure her with a little confession of his own. "Let me tell you something, darlin'... Something I haven't told you because it wasn't any of your business, just like you kissing Dylan wasn't any of mine. We've kissed, too."

"Yes, we've kissed plenty of—"

"Dylan and I."

Her gaping mouth snapped shut and she carefully placed her fork on her plate. "What?"

"He's more than what he presents on the surface."

With wide eyes, she pressed fingers to her lips. "He's... bi? Holy shit."

"Very, and no one knows, apparently. Not even his family."

"Then, should you be telling me this?"

Good question. "Probably not. However, I know you won't share that info with anyone, and since I was an involved party..." He let that drift off. He gave her enough info that she could figure out the rest on her own.

"But that means... *You're* bi?"

"Very."

"You never told me."

He sat back and tipped the beer bottle to his lips. "No reason to share. Once I moved here, I didn't think it would be accepted in this area." He'd keep his travels to State College to himself for now. However, if she asked, he wouldn't lie.

Would he prefer to find someone closer, like Dylan Lyons? Maybe not "like" Dylan, but the man himself since he was hot as hell and sexy, too. Plus, from what was ground against him the other day, his boss seemed to not be lacking in the cock department.

From what he could tell, it wasn't a monster, but it also wasn't a button mushroom.

He looked across the table at the reason that particular option might never be available. He had no doubt who Dylan would pick, if given the choice.

"Well," Erin started, "this area still might be behind the times, but I think the resort and its guests will be turning this town on its ear. Let's hope it opens some minds along the way."

He could only hope, but... "Don't expect miracles."

Her lips thinned out. "I won't. And this is why I wanted to talk to you."

"To tell me that you're worried about what others might think if you're involved, even casually, with two different men?" He could certainly understand that concern.

"I'll admit, I'm a little worried about that."

"Wait until they find out you are doing two men at the same time."

"What are you talking about?" She frowned. "Do you mean at the *actual* same time and not in the same time period?"

He shrugged. "Why not?"

"Ford..."

He was surprised that suggestion shocked her. She had always been open-minded. But maybe a threesome was a step too far? Did he finally find her limit?

He sighed. "Look, do you still want me?"

"Of course."

"Do you want Dylan?"

"Yes. Wait... Do *you* want Dylan?" She shook her head and lifted a hand. "I mean for more than a random kiss."

One side of Ford's mouth pulled up.

"Ford!"

He laughed. "He *is* sexy as fuck, and I can see why you're tempted to rekindle that relationship."

"Yes, he is," she murmured. "But I just want to make sure I heard you right... You're talking about a threesome, right?"

"Sure. Why not? I understand there are a lot of reasons why someone might not want to get involved in a threesome, especially if they were looking for a serious relationship. Polyamory involves a lot of work. However, I'm only suggesting sex. Not a commitment." At least to start. If they went in with no expectations other than pleasure, then no one would get hurt.

Hopefully.

"This was so unexpected. So, how would we deal with this?"

Was she seriously considering it? Ford was game. If he could get Erin onboard, they only needed to convince one more person. "Have you seen his big bed?"

"Have you?"

"I helped carry it in and set it up." He's also fantasized about everything that could be done in that over-sized, custom-made bed.

"But you didn't test it out."

"I'm not sure Dylan would be interested in what I'm thinking." Erin's ex could be where the idea came to die.

"Was the kiss a dud, then?"

Not even close. "No, but he was pretty pissed afterward."

"From what?"

"From me figuring out his secret."

"When was this revelation?" she asked.

He answered, "A couple of days ago."

"And how has he been since then?"

"He's avoided me." Which was why he figured his idea would never come to fruition.

"Just like I avoided him since I wanted to talk to you first." She chewed on her bottom lip.

This woman was amazing and Ford never wanted to give her up, if he could help it. The thought of them being interested in the same man didn't bother her at all.

Erin had to be a unicorn, so he was relieved she didn't want to be exclusive with Dylan. At this point, at least. "You confessing to me about a simple kiss is making me feel guilty that I didn't tell you sooner."

"You didn't have to tell me at all," she assured him.

"Darlin', you didn't have to, either, but you did. I'm assuming out of respect for me."

"Would you have told me about the kiss you two shared if I hadn't brought it up tonight?"

"The truth is, probably not. I wouldn't have told you his secret if you hadn't. Anyway, I doubt it will ever happen again."

"Unless I tell him we're a package deal."

He stared at her. "What do you mean?" He knew exactly what she meant because he was the one to suggest a three-some, but he wanted to be absolutely sure.

As with any relationship, clear communication was key to keeping it healthy. That was especially true when it came to polyamory.

"Well, let's break it down. Despite him being pissed, he's attracted to you, right?"

"If that kiss"—*and his cock grinding against mine*—"was any indication, then yes."

"We know he's interested in me. I have no doubt you're interested in me, and now I know you're interested in him."

Her analysis was basic but true. "It doesn't have to be a threesome. We could each have a separate sexual relationship with each other."

She frowned. "Like a love triangle?"

"That *is* an option." But not Ford's preference. "Dylan might be more agreeable to that. At least to start."

"To start?"

"I'd prefer to have you and Dylan at the same time. Is that your preference, too?"

That wrinkle reappeared on her forehead. "Having two men at once?"

"Have you done it?"

"Have you?" she countered.

"I've had threesomes before," he revealed. "Only short-term, though. And only for sex and nothing deep."

Her lips twitched.

He chuckled. "Okay, a few things were deep, but not the actual relationship."

Her barely-there grin bloomed into a smile. "Who else but us could be sitting around the dinner table contemplating a threesome?"

"Are you into it? If we can convince Dylan, that is." Ford was trying not to get too excited about the possibility since a few hurdles needed to be overcome first.

"I'm worried about one of us being left out or dealing with jealousy."

Or even *feeling* left out, whether true or not. Those could all be hurdles. "It could happen. Threesomes can get messy. It's a risk, for sure."

"I don't want to screw up my relationship with you, either."

He reached across the table to grab her hand and give it a gentle squeeze. "You won't, darlin'. It's not me you have to worry about."

"He can be intense."

"I've noticed," he said dryly. "Maybe we can help loosen him up a little."

"This idea is growing on me. But poor Dylan, he has no idea what the two of us are cooking up for him."

When she tipped her beer bottle to her lips, he paused his eating to watch her throat undulate. His favorite necklace she wore around that delicate column was his hand.

"My prediction is he'll either love it or hate it. There won't be an in between."

"He was like that when we were kids. I was hoping he grew out of that black or white outlook."

"Even though I didn't know him back then, after working with and for him for the last few months, I can say he can still be like that. It's funny how Dayne is not like his twin in that respect."

"I bet if we suggested to have a threesome with Dayne, he'd be ripping off his clothes before we were even done talking."

"I don't understand how, even though they look alike, I have no attraction to Dayne."

"I was always the same. Dayne tried to pull pranks on me and pretend he was Dylan, but I always knew immediately."

"So, it's not just me," Ford murmured. And here he thought he had some special gift when it came to telling the identical twins apart.

"No, and I think it's proof that who you are on the inside is always reflected on the outside."

"That could be it. Now, we need to finish dinner so I can explore *you* on the inside."

Her eyes held a mischievous sparkle. "I only invited you over for dinner, Ford."

He winked at her. "But what's dinner without dessert, darlin'?"

Chapter Twelve

DYLAN FLIPPED through the live feeds of the cameras installed all over the resort's common areas. Since the property was three-hundred acres, they were needed, not only for security, but to make sure that everything was going as planned, especially during the hectic opening week.

Of course, since the guests' privacy was also important, none were installed in the cabins or the guest rooms in the lodge. Or in the farmhouse, of course.

From what he could see, everyone was having a good time. Guests were enjoying the pool and attached in-ground spa. A few sunbathers were taking advantage of the lounge chairs on the pool deck. Some of them were naked, others in bathing suits.

Signs posted around the pool reminded them that clothing was optional. The lodge lobby and dining hall were the only places where it was mandatory for guests to be dressed at all times.

He continued to scroll through the feed on his laptop and saw a small group heading out on a trail ride with one of their newly hired, but very experienced, wranglers. The wranglers were in charge of the herd's care, as well as guiding guests on short horseback riding excursions around the property and the longer rides through Moshannon State Forest, which butted up against the property.

He next checked the event reservation system to see if anyone was booking the playrooms above The Mane Event Hall. Since the resort was all-inclusive, they weren't charging extra for their use, but they had to be reserved in advance to avoid scheduling conflicts and to ensure the room was thoroughly cleaned after each session.

He was pleased to see that all eight themed playrooms were being used off and on throughout the day and night. He didn't pay attention to which guests booked them until a couple familiar names caught his eye as he scrolled.

The first one being Dayne.

His twin reserved room one last night, the medical examining room, where guests could play doctor, nurse, or just take advantage of the equipment. Dylan wondered who Dayne had been playing doctor with and where he found that person. Had he hooked up with a guest?

They hadn't made any rules about employees fraternizing with guests when off the clock. At least, not yet. They might need to. Not that Dayne was an actual employee, so the rules wouldn't pertain to him or Danica, anyway.

Ultimately, it was best to keep his nose out of Dayne's business in hope that he would stay out of Dylan's.

The next familiar name had his heart stopping and when it restarted, it began to pound.

Ford Harris.

Now Ford *was* a damn employee. He booked room six, the impact room, from...

Dylan's eyes sliced to the corner of his laptop screen.

Seriously? He was using the room *right now?* The fucking balls on that man. Not only was he in Erin's life, he had also kissed Dylan last week.

A kiss Dylan was having a hard time wiping from his memory. Every time he laid in his massive bed at night—unfortunately, alone—he relived the kiss he shared with Erin before it morphed into the one with Ford.

Every damn time, he ended up hard as a rock and having to jack off on his own.

Maybe he needed to be more like his twin. Find a willing guest, book one of the playrooms and forget both Erin and Ford existed.

It might work. At least for a little while.

However, right now, seeing his name put Ford front and center in Dylan's mind. He quickly went back to the camera footage to see who the facilities manager took upstairs for private playtime.

He rewound the recording from the hallway until he came across the exact moment Ford walked through the door to "Heaven."

He stabbed his finger so hard on the keyboard to pause it, he was surprised the key didn't shatter. He leaned in closer with narrowed eyes.

Was that...

Did he really...

The man not only had a huge set of balls, he was playing with fire when it came to his job.

He glanced to see for how long Ford had reserved the room, then at the time again. He slammed the lid closed on his laptop and shot to his feet. As he strode out of his office and patted his pockets to make sure he had his keys.

Just in case he needed them.

It took no more than two minutes to get to the rear of the

event hall, ten seconds to jog up the back stairway, and less than that to get through the door.

Immediately, he noticed room two was also occupied with the blinds drawn.

He beelined it down to room six, where another couple stood in front of the window watching whatever Ford and his partner were doing inside the "impact" playroom.

A male guest—Dylan drew a blank on his name—was pressed against the woman standing in front of him. He had one hand down her shorts and another up her shirt. Her mouth was open, and her head thrown back against his shoulder, but her eyes remained glued to whatever was happening inside that room. The man watched the action inside room six, too, while whispering into his companion's ear and playing with her.

Dylan ignored the twitch in his jeans and joined them at the window, leaving enough space between them so they didn't feel crowded. They acted like he wasn't there, and he did the same. What he couldn't ignore was what was going on the other side of the glass.

Jesus.

Erin, completely naked, was sprawled face down across the spanking bench. A rubber bit gag filled her mouth.

Her arms were bound with leather cuffs behind her, but the restraints, attached to an O-ring above her, lifted them toward the ceiling. Her ankles were also cuffed, and her legs were spread and raised, too.

She was completely vulnerable in that position. She had no use of her arms or legs to get free. The gag also prevented her from saying a safe word.

He sure as hell hoped they had another way of communicating that, in case their scene got too intense.

Ford stood at the end of the bench with only his cargo

pants pulled down far enough to rail her hard. With one hand, he kept jerking on the chain attached to clamps pinching her nipples.

Her ass was a bright cherry red with discernible welts. Most likely caused by the discarded riding crop nearby.

What the actual fuck?

He had no idea Erin was into impact play. But then, how would he know since they hadn't kept in touch once he graduated high school. Most people reconnecting didn't go straight for the, *"I love to be tied up and have my ass whipped. How about you?"* conversation.

Not that Dylan would share what he was into with anyone but a partner. It wasn't anyone else's business.

Once over his initial shock, Dylan realized neither Ford nor Erin were paying attention to their audience. They were lost in their own world, while Dylan's employee continued to fuck his ex-girlfriend.

With his pulse now rushing in his ears, he continued to watch them, unable to walk away. *Hell*, he couldn't even turn away. His cock, now as hard as steel, throbbed intensely with each heartbeat.

It hit him then, he had never seen Erin completely naked before. Of course, they fooled around as young kids— just normal teenage stuff—but he never let it get further than that since they were going to wait until she turned eighteen.

Even so, he was damn sure back then she did not look as she did now. She was much more mature and filled out. But it was her red ass that kept drawing his attention.

She allowed Ford to use a crop on her.

Was this the first time? Or did they play like this on a regular basis?

Did she like it? Seek it out? Or was Ford the one who

liked to spice things up and somehow convinced her to go along with it?

And leaving the blinds open? Dylan wasn't sure if he himself would be secure enough to do that. He valued his privacy and letting others watch him, whether by himself or with partners, went against his grain.

Erin didn't look worried, embarrassed, or even tense. Instead, her face was full of what Dylan could only describe as ecstasy. If he listened closely enough, he could also hear her moaning around the rubber bit every time Ford slammed his cock into her.

Dylan took a snapshot in his mind of the scene before him and tucked it away for later. Despite that, he wished like hell he was standing in Ford's place. But he wasn't, and Erin might not even want him there.

The woman next to him whimpered, then bucked against her man before releasing a long sigh. Most likely she just got off.

Dylan wished he could pull out his cock right then and there and do the same, but it was important to remember that he was one of the owners of this resort. Business came first. Pleasure second. He and his siblings needed to act professional while in the public eye, then they could do whatever they wanted behind the privacy of a closed door.

The male guest next to him asked, "You're the owner, right?"

"One of them," he muttered.

"I have to say, so far, we're really enjoying our stay. My wife and I have traveled all over the world and even stayed at every swingers resort we could find, but this place... I have a feeling it's a gem that, with time, will only shine brighter and brighter. I can't wait to tell our friends about it."

Dylan reluctantly pulled his attention from inside the

room to the couple next to him. "I'm glad you're enjoying your time with us, and we would love to welcome your friends here. We're also open to any suggestions, so make sure to fill out our online survey after you check out."

"We will," the man responded.

The woman pulled herself free from her husband's embrace. "Will we see you at dinner?"

When he could, he stopped at each table during one of the meals and made sure guests were enjoying themselves. If any issues were mentioned, he wanted to nip those in the bud immediately. Complaints were taken seriously since word of mouth would be the best advertising, especially since it was also free.

"Maybe," Dylan mumbled. "If not, enjoy the rest of your day."

The woman's lips curved up and she squeezed her partner's forearm. "We plan on it." With that, they turned and, with her husband's hand possessively planted on the small of her back, headed toward the exit.

Now he could concentrate on the other couple behind the closed door without any distractions. Dylan turned just in time to see Ford take a couple more hard thrusts before burying himself deep and staying there. Ford's hips and glutes flexed a few times as he came inside Erin.

To Dylan, it seemed like Ford took forever to pull out but maybe because he was being impatient. When Ford finally slipped from Erin, Dylan couldn't miss that the man was, once again, not wearing a condom. That twisted Dylan's gut.

Ford's slick erection bobbed freely as he leaned over, brushed his palms over her red ass and then placed a kiss on each cheek.

Then he straightened and turned...

They specifically didn't want one-way glass for the playrooms. Some people got off from people watching. Others loved to create a show for an audience.

Dylan and Ford's eyes met and held for far too long. Ford finally jerked into motion, approaching the window and giving Dylan an eyeful of his impressive girthy cock. His balls hung heavily over the elastic band of his boxer briefs. He also got a glimpse of powerful thighs lightly covered in dark hair.

Dylan wanted to see more. He wanted to see all of Ford. Unfortunately, the closer Ford got to the window, the less Dylan could see. When they only had the glass separating them, Dylan waited for Ford to say something.

He didn't. With his expression masked, his arm shot out and within seconds, the blinds were pulled shut, blocking Dylan's view of both the man and Erin, still tied up on the spanking bench.

Regretfully, Dylan would miss the aftercare Ford provided her. Most likely a bottle of water or one of the Gatorades kept stocked in the mini-fridge. Ointment for her welts. A massage to soothe her stiff muscles. Cleaning up her cum-filled cunt.

Maybe even him moving around to the front of the spanking bench and making her suck his cock clean.

If asked, Dylan would volunteer to do that for him. Or even lick Erin's pussy clean. He would do anything to taste the two people he wanted the most right now.

Would they shower together in the attached bathroom? Share cuddles and kisses? Would he praise her and tell her what a good girl she was?

Or would they have a conversation about Dylan standing outside the window like a jealous stalker.

His imagination was running wild.

But one thing he knew for sure: it should've been him in that room playing with Erin. Not Ford.

Chapter Thirteen

F ORD HAD no idea what was waiting for them on the other side of the door. He and Erin planned today's session on purpose. They also left the blinds open with the hope that Dylan would see them.

The other night, after dinner and sex, they laid in bed discussing how they could convince Dylan to join them. Since the three of them all wanted each other, it only made sense to do it as a throuple and not individual couples.

However, Dylan might not see it that way.

Of course, Erin once again expressed her concern. "My worry is that if our plan doesn't work and this ends up as a messy triangle, the easy relationship you and I have could be destroyed."

"Don't let it."

She rolled her eyes at his response. "Yes, because words are always stronger than emotions."

Ford now realized, after seeing the expression on Dylan's face when he closed the blinds, her apprehension the other night was certainly valid. This plan could either work or go horribly wrong. In the end, they decided it was a risk both were willing to take.

He took his time releasing Erin, making sure her extremities weren't numb, cleaning her up, then using ointment to soothe the raised, red stripes on her ass. He also watched her down his required bottle of water.

After helping her dress, he pulled her into an embrace, palmed her ass and squeezed. "Does it still burn?" he asked when she flinched.

"A little."

He squeezed again, more gently this time. "Good. That means every time you sit for the next few hours, you'll think of me and what I did to you."

A soft smile filled her face. "That I will."

"I think I'll cane you next time instead of using the crop. I might even do your back and thighs."

She pulled in a shuddered breath. Not from fear but excitement. "I think the crop was the right decision today, though. It left just enough of a mark on me for him to see it."

To not only see it, but Ford was sure Dylan would have a strong opinion on it. "Will you talk to him?"

"Yes, but not today." She glanced toward the door. "Do you think he's still out there?"

"Not sure. It depends on his reaction to what he saw. He had no idea you were into impact play, right?"

"I didn't tell him. Just like he didn't tell me he was bi."

When she chewed on her bottom lip, he pulled back and stared into her face. "What?"

"Should I feel bad about this whole plan?"

"No. He's a big boy. Me thinks him coming up with this adult resort idea means he's done a lot of naughty things with a lot of naughty people. He can handle what we did." He paused as he considered what could happen if Dylan decided he didn't want a threesome with them. "Even if the three of us don't end up playing together, would you stop being with me if he forced you to choose?"

She shook her head. "You've been my rock when you didn't need to be. In contrast, he ran off for bigger and better things, leaving me behind. At the time, that made me feel small and unworthy. I know better now, but even so, I'm not giving you up, Ford, not even for Dylan."

That was the answer he hoped to hear. "It's the same for me."

"What if he has no interest in what we want?"

"Then we would have to decide if separate relationships between us would work. Or if it would destroy our individual relationships like you mentioned the other night."

"I don't want him to get hurt by this whole idea."

"I don't want him to get hurt, either. Hell, I don't want *any* of us to get hurt. This is about pleasure, not pain."

Her lips tipped up. "Well..."

Ford chuckled. "You know what I mean. Welcomed pain can be very pleasurable, as you know."

"Just ask my ass cheeks," she teased and pulled out of his arms. "Okay, I think our time is up for this room. We can't continue to hog it."

Plus, the cleaning crew would need to come in and do their thing before the next guests used it.

The extensive cleaning crew was just one "department" at the resort giving locals much-needed jobs. Employment around the area was limited and nobody liked to drive an hour to State College if they could avoid it, especially in winter, unless the position paid extremely well. Not even professors wanted that kind of commute to Penn State University's main campus.

In the short amount of time between conception and

opening, the ranch was definitely helping out the local economy. A positive in Ford's view but, no surprise, not to everyone. Some of the more prudish residents of Fisher Falls were vocal about the resort being immoral once they found out the truth behind the all-adult "vacation" destination.

Ford unlocked the door and swung it open. "I can walk you to your car, if you—" He swallowed the rest of his offer the second he spotted his boss leaning against the wall nearby.

Waiting.

With his face unreadable and his arms crossed over his chest.

Erin went up on her toes, kissed his cheek and whispered, "I'll talk to you later." She stepped out into the hallway, gave her former high school sweetheart a nod and a calm, "Dylan."

"Erin," he ground out in response, but that was all. His eyes landed on Ford and stayed there.

When Ford began to follow Erin out, Dylan stopped him with, "Ford, you can wait. I need to have a word with you."

Was their plan working, or would it backfire, and he'd end up with a fist to the face?

"Sure," he murmured and noticed Erin gave him a quick, wide-eyed glance before heading outside. He turned his attention back to his boss. "What's up?"

Dylan's nostrils flared as he tipped his head toward the open doorway. "In there. Where no one will overhear us."

This definitely could go either way.

Ford turned and headed back into room six. The lingering smell of sex, as well as the ointment, filled his nostrils. It was almost enough to make him hard again.

While he expected Dylan to shut the door, what he didn't expect to hear was the turn of the lock. He turned to face Dylan. "So, what's up?"

"You really have to ask that?"

Ford shrugged. "You're already aware that Erin and I hook up, so it can't be that."

Dylan's jaw shifted. "I discovered something else today."

"That having the playrooms will help make your resort a success?" Ford didn't bother to hide his sarcasm.

Neither did Dylan. "Not if my employees use them instead of the guests."

"I waited until the last minute to book this one."

"I'll take it that you had Erin on standby, then."

"We were at her place when I pulled up the schedule online on a whim." Of course, that wasn't quite true. Booking the playroom was hardly an impulse, it was part of the plan. However, he did wait to make sure a guest didn't want the room first. "What did you discover?"

"You like beating a woman's ass."

Why did he make that sound like a bad thing when in reality, done right, it was the opposite?

Ford shrugged. "Man. Woman. Doesn't matter to me."

"Are you saying that Erin isn't special to you?"

"Erin's very special to me. As I am to her. I didn't *beat her,* as you put it, or force her onto that spanking bench. As you witnessed, she's into it." She was into a lot more than that, but he'd let Dylan find that out for himself. "And as you saw, she walked out of here satisfied."

Dylan took a step closer, edging in on Ford's personal space, but he didn't move away and instead, stood his ground.

"What about you?"

"What about me?" Ford repeated with confusion. "Are you asking me if I like impact play?"

"I'm asking if what you do to her gets you off," Dylan growled impatiently.

"You couldn't tell? I fucked her hard and filled her with my cum." Again. "Sounds like a satisfying experience to me."

Dylan's tight jaw flexed.

"You know, you don't have to be jealous about what Erin and I have. You could have the same."

The resort owner's dark blond eyebrows pinched together. "What do you mean?"

Time to plant the seed... "You could always join us."

Those eyebrows took a deep dive. "What do you mean, join you? Erin would never agree to that."

Huh. "It's been a long time since you two dated, boss, you have no idea what she would agree to."

Was the man grinding his teeth over him calling him that? The truth was, Dylan *was* Ford's boss, whether he liked the title or not. Maybe he just didn't like it coming from Ford since he did kind of put a cocky spin to it.

"And why would you think I want you?"

"I don't know... maybe that steel pipe in your pants?" Ford tipped his head toward the very noticeable erection straining against Dylan's zipper. "It's been almost a half hour since I closed those blinds, so I know it's not from seeing Erin trussed up, a gag in her mouth and getting fucked so hard she squirted all over my cock."

Dylan's shoulders pulled back and he spun away. It was clear that he was angry with himself for having that reaction. He might swing both ways but maybe he was struggling with it.

Or it could be the fact that he wanted Erin to himself.

There was one way to find out. "Have you kept your sexuality a secret from your family?"

Dylan turned back and went toe-to-toe with him. His hazel eyes were sharp and filled with tenacity. "My family doesn't need to know my preferences, just like I don't need to know theirs."

Ford had no idea what cologne the man wore, but he always smelled so damn good. Even after working in the barn or riding his favorite horse, Rebel. "I assume that means you'd prefer to keep what happens in this room between the two of us?"

"What do you think is going to happen?"

"You tell me. You're the boss. Do I need to fuck you to keep my job?" Of course, Ford was baiting him on purpose, but he needed that planted seed to take root. This was only the first step to convincing the man into a threesome.

"You're not going to fuck me, Ford." He leaned in even closer until they were almost nose-to-nose. "I'm going to fuck you."

Ford's heart did a tumble. What Dylan proposed wasn't on Ford's agenda today, so he needed to respectfully decline that invitation. With regrets, of course. "I'm not a bottom."

One side of Dylan's mouth pulled up. "Today you will be."

"Only if I wanted you to fuck me. Who says I do?"

Dylan tipped his head toward Ford's erection. "That steel pipe in your pants."

"Busted," he muttered. His ass would be, too, if he allowed Dylan to fuck him. It had been a long time since he had been on the receiving end, and he also wasn't prepared. "That just indicates I want to fuck *you.*" Dylan fucking him was *not* part of the plan he and Erin discussed.

"I'm not interested in anything you have to offer, Ford."

"Except my ass and my girl."

Dylan's chest expanded when he pulled in a deep breath through flared nostrils. "*Your* girl?"

"Well, between the two of us, I'm the only one fucking

her, so doesn't that make her mine?" He was not only pushing Dylan, Ford was also pushing his luck.

He really didn't need a fist to the face.

"But you'll share her with me?"

Ford shrugged. "I'm not greedy."

"What if I don't want to share her with you?"

"Then, I'd say you *are* greedy."

"I'm pretty fucking greedy," Dylan acknowledged. "When I see what I want, I go for it. Unfortunately, you're standing in my way."

"That problem could be easily solved."

"By you no longer being a cock block?"

"Like I said, you're invited to join us. You're as hard for me as you are for her. You might not want to admit it, but the proof is..." Ford's eyes flicked downward. "Obvious."

"You're saying, if I want Erin, you're a package deal? Does she know you're negotiating her sex life for her?"

"By your comment, I'll take it you're only interested in having sex with her and nothing more. Sounds like you're the one who doesn't see her as special."

"Bullshit. I didn't say that."

"You've been out of her life for a very long time, boss. Do you think you know the real Erin anymore? She's no longer a teenager and neither are you."

"I'm well aware of that fact."

"I'm sure you are after what you witnessed in this room."

Dylan ignored that. "I guess I have to go through you to get to her."

"Clean your ears out, I said you can *join* us. I realize that a threesome can be a little overwhelming—"

"Shut up."

Ford did not shut up, in fact, he continued. "At first, but I'm willing to walk you through it. Don't feel intimidated. It's simply two dicks, three mouths and assholes, six hands and one very juicy pussy."

"I told you to shut up."

Ford knew he was playing with fire and could be seriously burned, but if what he was doing worked out, it could be good for all three of them. One side of his mouth pulled up in a cocky grin and he said something he hadn't said since elementary school, "Make me."

When Dylan's intense hazel eyes focused on Ford's lips, he licked them.

Without warning, Dylan grasped both sides of Ford's face, jerked him closer and crashed their mouths together. When his tongue demanded entrance, Ford didn't deny it. He'd be a fool to do so because he *wanted* this man.

However, what he wanted and what he would get were two different things. The anger and frustration had to be due to Dylan repressing his bisexuality.

It wasn't a sexy kiss. It was combative. Even so, his boss made Ford's blood rush, his cock hard, his balls ache for relief and he refused to be submissive simply because Dylan wanted him to be.

No damn way.

Their tongues fought for control. Wrestled for power. Neither wanted to give in and both wanted to be the victor.

The second Dylan pushed Ford's tongue out of his mouth, Ford clamped down on Dylan's bottom lip with his teeth. He was careful at first but since this seemed to be a battle, he bit down. Hard.

Dylan fisted Ford's hair and yanked it to free himself. Once Ford released him, the resort owner pulled away, panting. He wiped the back of his hand over his bleeding bottom lip and growled, "Is that how you want to play it?"

"Do you want to fuck or make love?" Ford asked him.

"Fuck."

"Then, yes, that's how I want to *play* it."

"I like a challenge."

"Don't threaten me with a good time," Ford warned.

"What's your safe word?"

"I don't have one." He never needed one since he wasn't usually on the receiving end, whether during sex or a scene.

"Since nobody should enter these rooms without one, now you do. It's peanut butter."

"That's two words."

"So is 'get naked.'"

Chapter Fourteen

"I never agreed to this."

"Okay, then," Dylan responded. "Just know, if you're not interested, then I'm not interested in your threesome. I'll pursue Erin on my own."

Ford stared at him for far too long. Was he considering it? Truthfully, Dylan did have some interest in having sex with him and Erin at the same time. He hadn't done a threesome before, and he wasn't against it. He'd simply never sought out the opportunity.

Today, it was landing in his lap. However, he was well aware of possible issues doing one.

Jealousy, or someone feeling ignored.

He had to take into account that he would be the odd man out here. Ford already had an ongoing intimate relationship with Erin.

Dylan did not.

Did he want one with her badly enough to put himself in this type of situation?

Earlier, his attention couldn't be pulled away from what

"

Ford had been doing to Erin on the spanking bench. While watching, he fantasized about standing in Ford's place. Not long after, he also had flashes of Ford being the one tied up and getting the same treatment as given to Erin.

He couldn't tell what turned him on more.

The truth was, he wanted to fuck them both. Only, he never considered doing it at the same time and in the same place. A twist he hadn't seen coming.

But right now, Dylan really wanted to recreate that scene with Ford. He wasn't sure if the man would agree since he already stated he normally didn't bottom.

"If I did this with you, you'd consider our proposal?" Ford asked.

"Our?"

"Yes, *our*. Do you think I'd propose something like that without getting her consent first?"

Consent was a requirement on this ranch, whether it involved a guest, employee or even a visitor. But still, he found this proposal surprising. "She wants a threesome? With the two of us?"

"I told you she's changed. Just like you did. Only you had to leave to find your true self. She found hers here."

Dylan sneered. "I'm tired of people trying to make me feel guilty for leaving."

"That's not what I'm trying to do. You left for a reason and that reason belongs to you. You knew what you needed and shouldn't feel guilty about that." Ford tipped his head to the side. "Anyway, Erin discovered a lot about herself after you left. So, in a way, you leaving also helped her find her true self, too."

"Are you saying she's grateful that I left?"

"That's not what I'm saying. Look, I'm done talking about Erin without her being involved. If you have questions about or for her, you need to hear those answers directly from the source."

Dylan could respect that. "If we're done talking and you're not getting undressed, then there's no point in us being in this room." He didn't want to hold up the cleaning crew for no reason.

When Ford continued to stand there, Dylan shrugged and headed for the door. As he reached for the knob, the jingle of a metal belt buckle being released made him pause. He stayed facing the exit and listened carefully to see if Ford was just jerking him around.

However, the rustling behind him got his blood flowing south again. His ears picked up the thump of boots being removed. The slide of denim over long legs. The whisper of cotton over defined abs, broad shoulders and thick, corded arms.

He didn't have to use his eyes to see it, he could envision it in his mind.

"Are you leaving or staying?"

That deep, gravelly voice sent an unexpected shudder through him.

At first, when he discovered he was attracted to men, he thought it was a fluke. An anomaly. Something he'd outgrow. A lot of college kids liked to experiment, and he was no different.

The first time he kissed a guy, he was drunk.

The second time, he was stone-cold sober.

The first time he had sex with a man, he was nothing but a ball of nerves.

The second time, he wasn't much better.

Unfortunately, same for the third.

It took a while before he was somewhat comfortable with it. In the back of his mind, he kept worrying about the stigma.

Some days he still did.

With time and experience, he discovered what he liked and didn't. One being, he was attracted to specific people, not specific genders. To him, it didn't matter if that individual was a man or a woman. One of his past partners informed him that made him a pansexual and not bi.

Bottom line, Dylan didn't give a shit about labels.

He also had no desire to shout from the rooftops who he was at his very core. It was no one's business except his own. Not even the person he was having sex with. Because that was all it was... Usually a brief encounter that didn't include the sharing of personal details.

He never stuck around long enough for anyone to do a deep dive on him.

For him, Erin would be different. He hoped to rekindle the relationship they established so long ago that abruptly ended. However, if he wanted a shot at her, it seemed as if he had to go through Ford.

"I'm naked," he heard from behind him. "That's what you wanted, right?"

That was one of many things he wanted. "It's a start." Pulling in a bolstering breath, he turned...

And took in the man from the thick, dark hair on top of his head all the way south to his long, well-manicured toes. Clearly, the facilities manager took pride in his health and physique.

Dylan jerked when he heard, "Now what?"

Ford's question sounded huskier than normal, and his hard-on jutted straight out from his body. Seeing a pearl of precum clinging to the tip made Dylan's mouth water. However, he would not be servicing Ford today, despite the desire to do so.

His own erection, ready to get the party started, kicked impatiently in his jeans.

Ford cocked a dark eyebrow. "Are you only going to stand there and stare?"

"I'll do what I want since you're not making the rules."

One side of Ford's mouth hooked upward. "You know the saying about rules, don't you?"

"They won't be broken here. Not now. If you can't take simple instructions, then you might as well get dressed." He took a risk by saying that, but Dylan stood behind his words. If he allowed Ford to do whatever he wanted in this situation, they would end up butting heads and getting nowhere except frustrated. Or, an even bigger concern, Dylan might end up face down, ass up.

For that reason, he needed to take control and keep it. "Since you like to call me 'boss,' I plan on earning that title for something other than the fact that I sign your paycheck."

"I didn't expect to like being *bossed* around, but here we are." Ford planted a hand over his chest, then slid it down over his pebbled nipple and teased Dylan by twisting it.

"Good to know you're agreeable." When Ford continued south and reached for his own cock, Dylan barked out a sharp, "No. That's not yours to touch. In this room, at this moment, that belongs to me. You don't do anything unless I give you permission first. Do you understand?"

Ford's eyes turned even darker, and his Adam's apple bounced in his throat.

"Answer," Dylan ordered. "And make sure to address me properly when you do."

Ford's erection bobbed, but he curled his fingers into his palms, most likely to keep from fisting it. "I understand, *Boss*."

"Good." Dylan moved away from the door and pointed

toward the spanking bench. "Now, get on your stomach in the same position you had Erin."

When Ford hesitated, his eyes flicked from Dylan to the bench before landing back on Dylan, who breathed easier when the man finally headed over to the bench and climbed on. Not only did his muscular arms dangle over the sides, but he was also tall enough that his calves and feet jutted over the end. Dylan would solve that problem the same way Ford had with Erin.

Once Ford was settled in place, Dylan picked up the ankle cuffs from where they'd been left and secured Ford's legs, using the attached chain to raise them up. "Is your cock getting crushed?"

"Yes," came the muffled answer.

"Good." Dylan moved to the front of the bench where their gazes briefly held before he picked up the abandoned wrist cuffs. "Hands behind your back."

With a soft grunt, Ford placed his hands at the small of his back and Dylan quickly buckled the cuffs on him before hooking the attached chain to the O-ring above. Now he was trussed up in the exact same position as Erin was earlier. He was stuck there until Dylan released him.

Not in any rush, Dylan's gaze roamed over the man's stunning body. The only softness he could see was his sack. Other than that, Ford was all lean muscle and tanned, smooth skin. Black fur decorated his suspended legs. Even though it wasn't thick, Dylan couldn't resist running his hands over the wiry hairs. Not only did it tickle his palms, he could feel how tense Ford was.

But then, it took a lot of trust to be bound helpless in this position. Unable to escape unless he uttered two simple words. While Erin most likely trusted Ford completely,

Dylan was damn sure Ford didn't trust him in the same way. At least not yet. And possibly never.

After circling the bench and inspecting every inch he could see in that position, he stopped in front of Ford. "Now for your gag."

Instead of the same bit gag Ford used on Erin, Dylan instead loosened his belt, released the metal button and unzipped his jeans. He pushed his jeans and boxers down only as far as Ford had during his session with Erin, fisted his aching cock and stepped forward.

Dylan held the crown of his cock in front of Ford's mouth. "Open wide."

The bound man's jaw shifted, and he licked his lips but didn't do as ordered.

"You can use your words if you want this to end," Dylan reminded him.

The determined look in his employee's eyes assured Dylan that he would not be hearing the phrase "peanut butter." While he was damn sure, if given the chance, Dylan could break the man, that wasn't on the agenda.

Driving his hands into Ford's hair, Dylan used it to rip his head back, stretching his neck to the point of straining.

"Be a good boy and open up," Dylan ordered more softly this time.

A low groan escaped Ford when he heard the praise. His eyelids slid closed the same time his mouth opened.

With a whispered, "That's a good boy," Dylan shoved his cock inside.

He had to force himself to keep his own eyes open because, *damn*, it had been too long since he'd gotten head from anyone. In real life, anyway. He'd fantasized fucking this man's face every night since that kiss in the run-in shed. Only, it was now a reality.

Despite that, he had no plans on finishing in Ford's mouth. Though, he had a feeling Ford would prefer that over Dylan's next destination.

He thrust his hips slowly at first, letting Ford adjust to his length and girth. But the urge to go deeper and faster clawed at his insides.

He hadn't had sex with anyone since coming home to Fisher Falls. He'd been too busy working on building and opening the ranch and didn't want to be distracted. He figured he'd have plenty of opportunities to find a release once the resort opened and was booked full with horny guests. That was, if he couldn't win back Erin first.

Even so, he didn't expect to break his long dry spell with the man who helped construct the very structure they were in. The same man currently in a casual relationship with the woman Dylan had planned to pursue.

What a damn mess.

He still had a hard time wrapping his head around the couple wanting him to join them. Maybe not so much Ford, but Erin…

So surprising and unexpected.

When he glanced down to see Ford watching him intently, his hips stuttered and he lost his rhythm. He quickly recovered and continued.

He should really give the guy an alternate way to tap out since his mouth was full. Especially since his hands were bound, too.

Shit.

When he pulled out, a string of saliva bridged the gap between Dylan's cock and Ford's lips. Dylan gathered the spit, using it as lube to stroke his hard-on.

"Since you're in this position, unable to use your words or your hands, what method of tapping out do you prefer?"

Since Ford's attention was pulled to Dylan's hand sliding methodically from tip to root, he sounded distracted when he answered, "I already told you that I don't need one. However, a clear sign would be me biting you."

Dylan winced. "And if you had, you would've been punished for that." Once he picked himself up off the ground.

"I would've taken my chances."

That answer ensured Dylan would be keeping his cock out of Ford's mouth for the rest of the session.

Oh yeah. The man could be arrogant, even strapped down to the spanking bench and in a helpless position.

If Ford was a submissive, he would be labeled as a brat. But it was damn clear he took the dominant role in his encounters.

The same as Dylan.

Normally, that could be a problem, but not today. Today, Ford was at Dylan's mercy, and he put himself in that position willingly. He had every opportunity to walk out of that room before getting undressed, but he stayed because he was trying to win Dylan over.

That wouldn't be an easy win.

Dylan snagged the discarded nipple clamps off a nearby table next and showed them to Ford. "Lift up so I can put these on."

"Boss..."

The attached chain jingled as he bounced the metal clamps in his palm. "These should be the least of your worries. Especially if you normally don't bottom."

"It's been—"

"Save it. I don't care how long it's been."

With a mumbled curse, Ford arched his back, giving Dylan access to his chest. He attached one clamp to a tightly beaded nipple, draped the chain over the man's broad back, in case he wanted to tug on them like Ford had with Erin, then attached the other one.

Ford only grimaced for a second or two. When his expression changed to ecstasy, Dylan figured the endorphins were kicking in.

Dylan took in the flesh pinched between the rubber-coated crocodile-type clips and smiled. He flicked the exposed dark pink tip before combing his fingers through Ford's hair as a reward. "That wasn't so bad, was it?"

Ford grunted in answer.

"Whatever you do to Erin, you should be able to handle, as well, isn't that right?"

"Yes."

"Yes, what?"

"Yes, *Boss*."

Chapter Fifteen

"Good boy," Dylan whispered as he moved to the other end of the bench, petting Ford's back and ass as he went. "Seeing you like this makes my cock ache to be inside you. Is that what you want?"

Ford hesitated.

"Isn't that what you want?" Dylan repeated.

"Yes... Boss."

"If you're going to call me that in this room, I sure as hell hope that 'Boss' starts with a capital B instead of a lowercase one." In the BDSM world, a Dom's honorific, like Sir or Master, was always capitalized out of respect. A submissive's never was.

"It does."

"Good." He could be lying but Dylan had no way to prove it. "Seems we're finally on the same page."

He headed over to the cabinet that stored the smaller toys next. Inside hung a lot of assorted pleasure and torture devices.

One in particular caught his attention. He grabbed it off

the hook and tested the weight. Dylan thought it would be a perfect addition, even though nothing similar had been used on Erin.

But then, Erin didn't have a set of balls hanging between her legs.

Heading back to the spanking bench, he studied the item and murmured, "I remember buying this. Today seems to be a perfect time to try it out."

Ford had turned his head to watch Dylan and what he was doing, but once Dylan stood behind the man, he was out of sight unless Ford awkwardly craned his neck.

"Do you know what I'm holding?"

"No, Boss."

"You'll figure it out shortly."

Dylan's ears picked up on Ford's muffled groan of dismay. Only it turned into a moan of pleasure when Dylan stroked the velvety soft skin of Ford's sack, then kneaded his balls gently. When he stopped, Ford blew out a loud breath.

"If I remember correctly, on the product page this was called a 'humbler.' I wonder why?" He placed the clamp around the base of Ford's heavy balls, adjusted the fit and began to tighten the screws, causing Ford to jerk his suspended legs and make the chain clatter.

"You might want to stay as still as possible," Dylan suggested before hooking the testicle clamp to the same chain attached to the ankle cuffs. "If you don't, every time you move, you'll pull on your balls. That means you're in control. At least with this, anyway."

It was either going to be torture or give Ford extreme pleasure. Dylan was leaning toward the first one. Especially if Ford had to keep his legs extremely still to prevent the stretch.

"I had no idea you were such a sadist." Ford quickly added, "Boss."

"The two words are peanut butter, if you've forgotten."

Ford didn't have to participate in any of this. He had an easy out, if he wanted to take it.

It was apparent how stubborn the man was when he came back with, "I'm allergic."

"No, you're cocky."

"Unlike you, who's so damn humble?"

Dylan grabbed the testicle clamp and twisted it slightly. Just enough to cause discomfort. Ford tensed but barely moved, despite hissing out a, "Goddamn it!"

"Boss," Dylan added.

"Just... Just..."

"Just what?"

"Nothing," Ford muttered.

"That's what I thought. Can I continue?"

Even though Dylan stood at the opposite end of the bench, he caught Ford's nod.

"You know, peanut butter is great covered in chocolate," Dylan grabbed two small packets of lube and a condom from the room's basket. When he returned to stand between Ford's legs, he tore open one lube packet. "When's the last time you've been fucked?"

Ford blew out a loud breath and shook his head. "I don't know, Boss."

"I'll take that to mean years?"

"Yes, Boss."

"Damn, you're going to be tight, then." He took his time spreading Ford's muscular ass cheeks, drizzling some of the lube over his puckered hole, then spread the rest of the packet on his index and middle finger. "A little stretching couldn't hurt first."

Ford said nothing as Dylan stroked his lubed fingers around his tight ring.

"You need to relax. Being this tense isn't going to help," he murmured, dipping the tip of one finger in. He pulled it out, then pushed it in farther. He repeated that until his index finger was fully seated. Then he started all over again, this time adding his middle finger.

What sounded like a lion's chuff came from Ford as soon as Dylan sank both fingers deep inside him. He alternated pumping them in and out and scissoring them, waiting for the man to relax. If he couldn't handle two fingers, he certainly wouldn't be able to handle Dylan's cock. It was bigger than that.

And while Dylan might want to put him in his place, he didn't want to actually hurt the guy. Pleasurable pain was one thing. An injury was another.

Plus, despite his annoyance with Ford being involved with Erin, over the last few months of working together on the ranch resort, Ford had proved himself time and time again that he was a decent guy. Reliable. Loyal. Hard-working. Knowledgeable.

Not to mention, sexy as hell.

As facilities manager, Ford was one of their most important employees. He helped keep the ranch running smoothly. Because of that, he didn't want to torture the guy, only remind him who was in charge. At least, here at Double D.

Simply put, he also wanted to have sex with him ever since that kiss out in the far pasture.

Curling his fingers, Dylan easily located Ford's walnut-sized pleasure button. What Dylan called "the rocket launcher." He'd never been with any man able to resist losing control when his prostate was stimulated.

He couldn't avoid it himself. In fact, one partner played

with Dylan's prostate for so long, he cried mercy after he was drained dry. He was so exhausted afterward, he slept a solid eight hours after that.

He wouldn't do that to Ford. Not today, anyway, since he already came in Erin earlier. This time it was Dylan's turn to come.

He continued to play with Ford's P-spot until he was humping the bench and groaning. It was obvious he was trying to stop himself since every thrust moved his legs, which in turn, pulled on the "humbler."

That had to hurt.

"Do you want to come?" Dylan asked.

"Yes, Boss."

"From what I remember, Erin makes some damn good peanut butter pie."

"Will you let me come if I say it?"

"No." Dylan pulled his fingers out, wiped them off on a nearby hand towel and grabbed the condom next. He ripped open the gold foil package and rolled the lubed, latex disc down his throbbing cock.

He was so ready to put his dick where his fingers had been. Opening the second lube pack, he added even more to his covered cock and dripped more on Ford's hole. At least it wasn't pinched shut this time.

Even so, Dylan doubted he was stretched enough to not experience any discomfort.

Shifting forward, he pressed the tip of his erection against Ford's exposed anus. "Have you heard that peanut butter icing is great on chocolate cake?"

"I'm not saying it."

Did that declaration come from between clenched teeth?

"Don't tense," Dylan warned as he slowly and carefully

pressed forward, giving Ford plenty of time to accommodate his size.

Not only was the other man tight, his periodic clenching also wasn't helping. "Peanut butter's also good to spread between two pieces of bread along with your favorite jelly. Just like my cock is spreading your ass."

"You need to stop," came the plea. "Boss," was quickly added.

Dylan paused. "Say it, then."

"Not what you're doing. What you're saying."

"I'm giving you an out if you're uncomfortable."

"I don't want a damn out!" Ford's outburst caused his legs to jerk which, again, caused his balls to be yanked. His forehead hit the bench, and he began breathing in and out of his mouth loudly.

"You need to stay still."

"Shut up," Ford muttered.

"If you're not enjoying it—"

"Shut up and fuck me, goddamn it!"

Ford wasn't in the position to demand anything, but they'd already taken enough time in the playroom. Dylan needed to get back to work before someone came looking for him.

He certainly didn't want to be caught fucking Ford. Especially by Dayne or Danica. He'd never hear the end of it.

Grabbing Ford's ass cheeks, he dug his thumbs deep and spread them wider so he could watch his cock slide in and out of the man. It was a beautiful sight.

But seeing that, feeling the squeeze around his cock and hearing Ford grunt and groan wasn't helping him keep a smooth, steady rhythm. It only made Dylan want to fuck him hard and fast, and come deep inside him.

He struggled to prevent himself from doing that. For both their sakes.

However, the man was too damn tight, despite applying a generous amount of lube.

Dylan did not pause when Ford began to tremble. He did not stop when beads of sweat appeared on Ford's tanned skin. Instead, he leaned forward and licked up Ford's spine, collecting the salty drops on his tongue.

"Is that from the pain or pleasure?" Dylan murmured against the nape of Ford's neck. He was tempted to leave his mark there. Bite him hard enough to draw blood the same way Ford did with Dylan's lip.

"Frustration."

"Of?"

"Not fucking you... Boss."

———

His asshole felt like a ring of fire burning between his ass cheeks. Having Dylan's fingers inside him for a few seconds wasn't even close to being properly prepared. Especially since Ford didn't bottom. It had never been his thing and had been probably a decade since the last time. He should've had an "exit only" sign tattooed above his ass cheeks.

Too late.

His thighs now trembled. His toes curled to the point of cramping. Excess lube dripped down his taint and onto his sack.

He was torn. While he wanted his boss, he hadn't planned on being the one totally naked and face down on a spanking bench.

He certainly didn't expect the man to clamp a torture device on his damn balls.

Of course, that was a power move. Dylan wanted to remind Ford that he was the boss on the ranch. He was probably still bent about Ford using the playroom with Erin.

Ford would take one for the team today, because if things went his way, Dylan would join him and Erin. Once he did, if things between the three of them progressed, Ford would eventually get the chance to fuck Dylan, too.

Give and take, right?

If he had to give up something today so he could take what he wanted in the future, it would be worth it. Or at least, he hoped so.

Was it a risk? Of course. It could very well end up with Dylan walking out of the playroom afterward and never wanting to have sex with him again. Or would refuse to join him and Erin, their ultimate goal.

Or the ranch owner might simply try to sweep in and steal Erin away so he could keep her for himself, even though she already assured Ford that would never happen. She clearly stated that Dylan had to accept them both, or neither.

He trusted Erin. More than he did Dylan. But then, he'd known Erin for many years and had only known Dylan for less than one.

Since the kiss out in the pasture, he wondered why he was attracted to Dylan but not his identical twin. The only obvious differences between the two were their hair styles and, unlike Dylan, Dayne had no facial hair.

However, the biggest, and most important difference was their personality. Dayne lived life loud, boldly and sometimes didn't have a filter. Dylan was on the more reserved side. Quiet, thoughtful and highly intelligent. Though, sometimes moody.

Despite both being scorching hot, Ford found himself more attracted to Dylan's disposition. The two brothers were the perfect example of the saying, "Don't judge a book by their cover." Even a cover as nice as the Lyons twins.

Ford voluntarily got naked, not expecting any kind of intimacy or even kindness, but Dylan was surprising him. Maybe the testicle clamp and hanging his restrained limbs from the ceiling was a power move, but the fact the man was now brushing his lips back down his spine, after licking all the way to his neck, was more than unexpected.

That made Ford wonder if Dylan had to work at being dominant and it didn't come naturally. Unlike it did with Ford.

It was why he and Erin had such a great sexual relationship. Despite her being independent, and certainly not a doormat in any way, she loved to be submissive in the bedroom.

Letting Ford take control turned her on the same way being dominant did to him. But outside the bedroom, he would never tell Erin how to live her life, what to say or what to wear. She could switch easily from being a kick-ass woman in the streets to being submissive in the sheets.

He loved the fact that she didn't *need* Ford but wanted him. To him, that made all the difference. Plus, she'd never been the jealous or controlling type when it came to their easy relationship and Ford didn't want to do anything to ruin it.

Realistically, adding Dylan would change their dynamic. Whether it changed for the better or worse remained to be seen. It was a valid concern.

Despite the risk, if it worked out, it would be nice to have both Dylan and Erin in his life. He'd no longer have to drive over an hour away to meet up with some random dude when he wanted that particular itch scratched.

Add in the fact, when he met up with a stranger, he never

knew what he was walking into or who was behind the messages. It could be someone who hated the LGBTQ+ community and used a fake profile as a trap to hurt or kill him.

He always went into those situations cautiously.

Dylan's grunt as he straightened and rammed his cock home pulled Ford free of his distracting thoughts.

Plus, now at the angle he was in, Dylan was hitting that perfect spot. The one causing his cock to drip precum. It would be smeared all over the spanking bench by the time Dylan was done. Ford mentally apologized to the cleaning crew but he was damn sure that wouldn't be the worst thing they dealt with when working on the resort as custodians.

The way Dylan's cock dragged back and forth over his P-spot had his hips twitching uncontrollably all over again. He forced himself to stay still so the "humbler" wouldn't stretch his balls and he wouldn't see stars.

Ford was certain that if he wasn't currently tied up and on his stomach, he'd be on his knees. And not because he was giving someone head. That kind of device could be brutal if used improperly.

Without question, he never wanted it used on him again, even if done properly. To him, it felt more like punishment than pleasure. And that's why Dylan used it to put Ford "in his place."

Whatever. Ford would deal with it for the short time needed.

A hitch in Dylan's steady rhythm had him thinking the man was about to lose his shit. Ford wished he could say the same. While he was no longer gritting his teeth and could accommodate Dylan more easily, this still wasn't his preferred way of having sex. Especially since he was quite sure he wouldn't be getting off.

Chapter Sixteen

Ford closed his eyes and listened to the man's heavy panting, his soft grunts and occasional long, drawn-out, "Fucks."

If Dylan wanted Ford to come, he could easily do so by simply continuing to stimulate his prostate with his cock. However, it was becoming increasingly obvious that Dylan would rather edge him instead of giving him any kind of relief.

None of this was surprising since this whole scenario was more about putting Ford in a vulnerable position. Simply put, a power move.

Ford got it. If he really dug deep, he'd have to admit he did the same by fucking Erin earlier in the very same playroom with the blinds open. On purpose.

To force Dylan's hand. To make him react.

The whole reason Ford was currently face down with a cock up his ass.

Another groaned, "Fuck," along with jerky hip movements had Ford thinking Dylan was at his limit.

The knowledge that his boss was about to come made Ford wish he wasn't currently tied up. He was desperate to come, too. Only, Dylan wasn't having it, and Ford couldn't do it himself unless he humped the spanking bench. And if he did that, he and his balls would regret it.

Instead, he stayed as still as possible, packing away everything in his memory bank for a future use. The same as he did with that first kiss.

What played out in his head late at night were Erin and him joining Dylan in his huge custom-made bed. While all three were naked, of course.

Again, today was a step toward that goal. He only hoped the goal wasn't unattainable. If it was and all he got was a cock up his ass... lesson learned. The hard way.

Wait. What was happening?

The man hadn't even come yet and he was already pulling out? Was he into edging himself?

Ford cranked his head around in time to see Dylan scrambling to pull off the condom. Quickly pumping his cock in his fist twice, he shot his load.

Not into the condom, of course, but on Ford.

A few warm drips decorated one ass cheek, while the majority ended up in a thick puddle at the small of his back.

"That's one hell of a sight," Dylan panted. With his hard, but spent cock still in his hand, his head dropped forward while his chest rose and fell quickly as he recovered.

Ford was interested to see if his boss would leave him hanging or if he'd help give him some release. If the man needed suggestions on how to do that, Ford could come up with plenty of options. But after blowing out a loud breath, Dylan, with the empty condom dangling from between his fingers, went to toss it in the garbage.

The water ran in the small, attached bathroom and when

Dylan came back out, his jeans were pulled up and his belt fastened. He held no towel or anything to clean up Ford.

Again, no surprise since the ranch owner was trying to degrade Ford, not reward him.

He'd allow it. This time.

But in the future... If they hooked up again, the scene would look different.

Dylan stopped at the end of the bench and carefully removed the "humbler."

Oh, thank fuck.

He could handle being restrained. He could handle giving head. He could *somewhat* handle getting fucked. But that damn torture device was on another level.

If Dylan—or anyone—ever approached him again with one of those in their hand, someone would end up on their knees gasping for breath. It wouldn't be Ford.

Once Ford's family jewels were no longer stuck in the nutcracker, Dylan moved around the bench unbuckling the leather cuffs, freeing his arms and legs. Ford didn't realize how his limbs being suspended above him had cut off his circulation.

But then, he had been more worried about the circulation being cut-off from his testicles. Did he need those the same way he needed his hands and feet to do work? No, but *damn*, his balls were important.

He remained face down on the bench, only rubbing his arms, for two reasons. One, he still had a puddle of cum on his back and wondered if Dylan would get around to taking care of that for him and two, he figured his rubbery legs, now experiencing painful pins and needles, probably couldn't hold his weight yet.

If he tried to stand, he might collapse in a heap at Dylan's feet.

His boss would probably like that.

Ford held out his hand to get assistance with getting up. He wanted to remind Dylan how hard he still was. Of course, his extended hand was ignored without a second glance and Erin's ex headed toward the exit.

The man was simply going to leave?

Of course he was.

As Dylan reached the door, Ford yelled out a warning, "Erin's going to ask what happened between us after she left."

The ranch owner paused with his hand on the lock, not even bothering to spare Ford a second glance. "It's no one's business what went on between us."

That was bullshit. "Not even hers?"

With a shake of his head, Dylan flipped the lock and ordered, "Get cleaned up, then free up this room as soon as possible," before walking out and shutting the door.

Since his question wasn't actually answered, Ford decided he wouldn't lie to Erin. If she asked—and he knew she would—he would tell her the truth about what happened. He wouldn't be surprised if he had several texts from her already on his phone.

The quiet of the empty playroom surrounded him, only leaving him with his thoughts and his raging hard-on.

He could wait until it went down on its own, or...

He could solve the problem himself in a more enjoyable way.

After shaking out his arms to make sure they were usable, he lifted his torso carefully and once again twisted his neck so see the mess Dylan left behind.

He reached back and scooped up what he could in his palm. After bringing his hand in front of his face, he stared at Dylan's cum, then rolled over and sat up.

With his empty hand, he gently pulled his balls up to inspect for damage.

With relief, he saw the coloring wasn't too scary and it was quickly going back to normal. Now, to see if they still functioned as designed...

Keeping one hand cupped around his poor balls, he slid his other up and down his hard length, effectively spreading Dylan's cum all over his cock.

Then he used that cum as a lubricant to do a little self-help.

He closed his eyes and let his imagination take over with Dylan straddling Ford's hips and impaling himself on Ford's cock.

Over and over...

And over.

Releasing his sack, he collared the root of his erection using his thumb and forefinger and continued to pump his fist.

"That's it," he whispered, forgetting where he was, forgetting what just happened. Hoping that one day soon his fantasy would be a reality.

Ford squeezed his cock tight while pumping it with his fist, driving himself right to that delicious edge. The one he rode the whole time Dylan was fucking him.

But this time, he lost his balance and slipped over the side.

Oh yeah, his balls were working just fine.

He opened his eyes to see the cum trail on his stomach. He smeared his hand through it, mixing what was left of Dylan's cum with his own.

And smiled.

———

Erin found him in the barn with a curry comb in hand and a horse cross-tied in the breezeway.

When the gelding threw his head restlessly, Dylan stopped currying long enough to pat the dark bay's flank and murmur, "Easy, boy. We're almost through here."

When the horse side-stepped, Dylan did the same so he wouldn't get his toes crushed. "What's bothering you?"

Erin finished heading through the open barn doors and into the breezeway. "Is it me?"

Dylan's head whipped around, and he quickly masked the surprise on his face. "Not sure." With a jerk of his head, he indicated she should move closer. "Let's see."

"Will he bite?"

"Only if you taste good," Dylan teased softly, moving to the front of the horse and holding his halter to keep him still.

"What's his name?"

"Rebel."

"Does he act like one?"

"Too often," Dylan answered dryly.

She stroked Rebel's head, even though he kept throwing it like he was impatient. "What is he?"

"Thoroughbred. He must have sucked on the track since he ended up at the New Holland auction."

"Where you swooped in like a hero to rescue him?"

"I can only hope I saved him from ending up in a bag."

She brushed her fingers over his velvety-soft nose. "A bag?"

"Of dog food."

Erin grimaced. "Has he thanked you yet?"

"Sure. By bucking my ass off when he decided an evergreen looked like Sasquatch."

Erin rolled her lips under.

"You can laugh," Dylan invited.

She covered her mouth with her hand. "I shouldn't."

"I missed your laugh," Dylan murmured.

Erin dropped her hand, her amusement now gone.

But before she could address his comment, a chunky black cat came out of nowhere to weave around Erin's ankles, head butt her shins and meow loudly for attention. "Another rescue?"

Dylan shook his head. "Not that one. She was one of my father's barn cats."

Erin squatted down and scratched her under the chin. "What's her name?"

"Cat."

Erin glanced up with a frown. She knew it was a cat. "Yes, but what's the cat's name?"

"Cat."

It finally hit her... "The cat's name is Cat?"

"Every barn cat's name was Cat. Dad didn't consider them pets, they were employed as rodent catchers."

After running her hand down the feline's arched back one last time, she stood. "Makes sense."

"Sure, if you think so."

"You don't?"

Dylan shrugged.

"Then, give her a better name," she suggested.

"She answers to it."

"How many cats are here on the property?"

"Five and three of them are named Cat."

Erin giggled. "That's crazy. Is it like Thing 1, Thing 2 and Thing 3?"

"It's Cat, Cat and Cat. No numbers needed. Like any typical cat, they only pay attention when they feel like it."

"What's the name of the other two?"

"Whiskers and Ginger."

"Let me guess, Ginger is an orange tabby."

"Your guess would be correct, but you didn't come here to talk about horses or cats, Erin. Why are you here?"

The lighthearted conversation they were having was about to quickly come to a screeching halt.

Erin pulled in a breath before answering, "To apologize."

Dylan's brow wrinkled and his lips twisted. "For what?"

"For what happened yesterday."

His head twitched to the side. "Which part?"

She frowned. *Which part?* "What you saw upstairs in the playroom. Did something else happen that I missed?"

His expression once again closed up tight.

"You two didn't get into a fight after I left, did you?"

"No, nothing like that." His initial hesitation was a bit suspicious.

"It was a stupid idea."

"What was?"

"Thinking that if you saw us together, you'd be tempted to join us," she answered.

"In a playroom with the blinds open?"

"No... I..." She shook her head. "No, in private."

"What I did see, Erin, was once again, he didn't use a condom."

Why did that bother him so much? Unless he joined them, it didn't affect him at all. "Ford and I are long past that, Dylan. I told you that."

"Arc wc?"

What? "We haven't... We aren't..."

"Not yet, but you just said your goal was to tempt me. So, if I joined you two, shouldn't that be one of my concerns?"

"No."

His brow furrowed. "How would it not?"

"Simple. I don't have sex with anyone else but him." She

had free rein to do so, but she didn't. Anytime she was in the mood to have sex, she contacted Ford. He was always accommodating.

"He doesn't have sex with anyone else, either?"

"He gets tested regularly. But he always uses protection when he's with anyone else."

"Him being with others doesn't bother you at all?"

"No."

"That's not normal, Erin."

"Says who? Society? Our relationship is *our* relationship. We make it what we want. And right now, we don't want it to be exclusive."

"Would it be if you asked?"

"I didn't come here to discuss that, Dylan."

"Then, why are you here?"

"Again, to apologize for going about it the wrong way."

One eyebrow lifted. "Why do you think it was wrong? Maybe it wasn't and it convinced me."

His tone sounded a bit aggravated, which led her to believe he wasn't convinced. Was he being sarcastic? "Did it?"

Dylan scratched his forehead, then, without a word, unclipped the cross-ties and led Rebel by his halter to a nearby stall. He slapped the horse softly on the hind end with a soft, "Good boy," closed the stall door and turned.

"Well?" she prodded.

"I loved you, Erin."

Holy shit. She hoped to move forward and not rehash their past. "And I loved you. But we need to get past this, Dylan. It was seventeen years ago."

"Seventeen years wasted."

She sighed. Maybe coming to see him today was a mistake. "I'm sorry you see it that way."

"If I had stayed and asked you to marry me, would you have done it?"

Her chest tightened. "Yes."

"Then, do you realize our kids could be teenagers by now?"

Was this his way of getting back at seeing her and Ford together? Was this some sort of punishment?

She squeezed her eyes shut and pulled in a breath. "Dylan, that's not fair."

"You're right. Life isn't fair. You out of anyone should know that since you lost Hart."

"Please stop," she whispered. "My heart broke when you left. My heart broke when Kyle died. Please don't break it all over again."

She opened her eyes when Dylan's hand cupped her jaw, and he pressed his forehead to hers. "I'm sorry. I'm being a complete ass. We agreed to move on, and I'll admit that I'm having a hard time doing that. It was difficult to think of you with Hart. It's even harder for me to see you with Ford."

"Two years, Dylan. We had two years together in school. I've been seeing Ford for ten."

"But not seriously."

"Every relationship doesn't have to be serious," she reminded him.

"You were supposed to be mine."

"If you can't share me, then I never will be. Ford has been there for me during all the years you weren't. I will not kick him to the curb simply because that's what you want. And since you insist we head down this path again, I will remind you, you could've stayed," she said softly.

"No, I couldn't have. I needed to get out of this town. It felt like I was suffocating, and it would've held me back. I needed more."

"More," she murmured.

"Yes, an education, to see the world, to discover—"

"More than me."

"I knew I was different, so I needed to figure out who I was and not rely on who everyone expected me to be."

"You found yourself."

"It took a while."

"I found myself while living here," she countered. "You might've too if you had given it a chance."

"It wasn't a chance I wanted to take." When she thought he would explain that remark further, he instead asked, "Was Hart into what you're into?"

"No."

"When did you discover it?"

"After Ford and I became friends."

He pulled away and barked, "Friends?"

"Yes, friends. We were friends first. Then after Kyle's accident, Ford looked after me. He always made sure I was okay, that I was surviving."

"Very convenient," Dylan said dryly.

"It wasn't like that. Our relationship developed slowly."

"And now he beats your ass."

Erin pinned her lips together and shook her head. "You're simplifying something that isn't so simple. And he does more than that."

"Do you love him?"

Her head jerked back. "We're lovers."

"Do. You. Love. Him?" he prodded.

Chapter Seventeen

When Erin spun away from him, he had his answer.

He might not like that answer—especially since it made his gut churn—but he had it. "Does he know?"

She stopped in front of Checkers' stall and focused on the pinto Quarter Horse Dylan also rescued from the Lancaster kill pen. "I didn't say I loved him."

She glanced over her shoulder when he approached. "Erin, you didn't have to. If you two love each other, I don't want to be the third wheel in your relationship." Why the hell did that hurt to say?

"You wouldn't be."

It didn't go unnoticed how she didn't deny that they loved each other, either. "You can't know that. Do you really want to risk your relationship with him just so I can join you two for sex?" Changing the dynamic of any established relationship could lead to disaster.

"It wouldn't be a risk since we've discussed it."

But reality was much more complicated and eye-opening than simple conjecture. "Funny enough... So did we."

"We?"

"Ford and I."

Her brown eyes went wide. "When?"

"After you left the playroom."

"I have no idea what you two discussed."

"No?" His eyebrows raised. "He didn't tell you anything that happened in that room once you left?"

In contrast, her eyebrows pinched together. "No, I haven't seen or talked to him since then. Should he have?"

"I'd want to know if the person I loved was fucking someone else."

"Again, he's allowed to..." She blinked and, in an instant, her expression changed to disbelief. "He fucked you after I left?"

Dylan shook his head.

"Then, I'm confused."

"I think he was at first, too."

She stared at him with disbelief. "You fucked him?"

"Are you more surprised that I fucked him, or that he let me?"

"I mean, I know you two kissed. He told me that. But I didn't realize..."

"Didn't realize what?" he prodded.

"Well," she started. "Kissing men is..."

"Just like Ford, I like men and women equally."

"And he let you fuck him."

"I said that."

"He didn't fuck you?"

"No."

Her forehead scrunched.

"It had been a while for him, Erin. Not having sex with a man, apparently, but being the bottom."

"I guess that's my surprise since he tends to be dominant." From his experience, being a "bottom" could mean two different things. In the BDSM world, it usually meant being a submissive. In the non-kink world, it meant you were the one getting penetrated. However, Dylan didn't think any of those terms were set in stone.

Even so, he was surprised that none of what they did bothered her. "That's it?"

She shrugged. "Again, he can do what he wants. Or who. It's not his behavior that surprises me..."

"It's mine," Dylan finished for her.

"I had no idea."

"None?" *Bullshit.* "He told you we kissed but since he wasn't sporting a black eye or broken nose, that should've told you something." He tipped his head to the side. "I think you're covering for him."

He waited for her response and got nothing in return. It was obvious that she already knew he was bisexual because Ford spilled the beans. Dylan should be pissed about that. Crazy enough, he wasn't. "I wish you would've stayed to watch."

"Me, too. I'm sure it was..." She waved a hand around before finishing with, "Stimulating."

Stimulating was the perfect descriptor. At least for Dylan. "I tied him up the same way he had you tied up."

Her lips parted and a flush rose from the neckline of her sundress all the way into her cheeks.

"Did you... Did he..." She visibly swallowed.

Did the thought of what he did to Ford turn her on? He dropped his gaze to her nipples.

Sure did.

"You should've stayed," Dylan suggested. "You could've watched the man who dominates you be dominated."

"Did he volunteer for that?"

"If you're asking if I forced him, no. I also gave him an out. He didn't take it. What does that tell you?"

Her eyes flared with heat and her next words were breathy. "I would've liked to have seen that."

Interesting.

This Erin was *nothing* like he remembered. Of course, he didn't consider that a bad thing but would've preferred to be the one to have introduced her to this lifestyle, not Ford.

Unfortunately, that bell couldn't be unrung.

Now he wondered, if he had stayed in Fisher Falls and married Erin, would they have ended up as a typical vanilla couple simply going through the motions expected of them? All while hiding their true desires from each other, as well as others?

Most likely.

As much as he hated the fact that Erin married Hart when Dylan bolted after graduation, maybe it was for the best. Their sex life might've remained stunted and even slowly soured their relationship.

However, there was no point in what-ifs. They needed to move forward whether he joined the couple or not. Because it was becoming clear, if he wanted Erin, Ford was part of the package.

It also made him wonder about something else...

Ford had sex with Erin. Dylan had sex with Ford. Would Erin fuck Dylan without Ford around? Would this threesome be fluid? Or if he agreed, would they only have sex when it involved all of them at the same time?

He could test that theory. If Erin was willing.

He tucked a thumb under her chin, lifting her face to stare deep into her brown eyes, and lightly brushed his knuckles down her soft, heated cheeks. "Basically, you're saying I can't have you for myself and have to share you with Ford?"

He followed the path of her tongue when she licked her lips. "Yes."

"Every time?"

"I..." Her throat rolled when she swallowed. "I guess it depends. That would be something we'd need to discuss."

"A discussion like that indicates it wouldn't only be a one-time thing."

"Yes," she answered with a lot more confidence than he expected.

With the blood now rushing to his cock, his growing erection got jammed in an awkward position in his jeans. "We never had sex, Erin. Not once."

"Depends on what you consider sex," she countered.

Of course, they fooled around plenty as teenagers but that wasn't what he was talking about. "You know what I mean... We never fucked because we decided to wait."

As difficult as that had been. Especially since she'd been against the idea and was constantly tempting him to take it further. That was when he learned how strong his willpower could be.

He continued, "I would like to change that. Since you and Ford have an open relationship, he shouldn't mind, right?"

Her eyebrows pinched together. "What are you saying?"

"You have sex with Ford. I had sex with Ford. You and I haven't had sex together yet. Think of it like a job interview. Otherwise, how do you know I can satisfy you? Maybe I can't and you'll rethink asking me to join you."

She rolled her eyes. "Just be straight about what you want, Dylan. You don't need to make up crap to sleep with me."

He had no problem being direct, if that was what she preferred. "One, this has nothing to do with sleeping. Two, what I said was true. But if you want it straight..." He leaned in until they were practically nose-to-nose. "I want to fuck you. Not in the future. Today."

Her breathing hitched and goosebumps appeared out of nowhere to cover her tanned, normally smooth skin.

"Looks like you want that, too." He drove his fingers into the long dark hair near her ear.

"Without Ford?" whispered over his lips.

"Without Ford," he whispered back.

He closed the tiny gap between them to claim her mouth. With a groan, she clutched his T-shirt and welcomed the kiss. He took the opportunity to explore every inch of her mouth, reminding him of how good she tasted.

When they were dating, they kissed *a lot*. In the beginning they were inexperienced, so it was awkward, but they perfected it over time. Their first kiss the other week was also a bit awkward, and today?

Perfection all over again.

Almost as if they picked up where they left off seventeen years ago. The chemistry between them was as palpable now as it had been then.

He no longer *wanted* to take this further. He *needed* to. He needed to fuck her with an urgency he'd never felt before. Even as a horny teenager.

Barely pulling back enough to break their kiss, he murmured, "I take it that's a yes?"

"What do you think?"

His eyes flicked down to the pounding pulse in her neck. "I never want to assume."

"Is there somewhere close by where we can go?"

His house was only across the parking lot. Even so, that

seemed too far away. He wanted her *now*. Plus, if they headed over to his residence, they risked being spotted by nosy people. Not guests, but his siblings.

He really didn't want to hand them a reason to ride his ass.

Giving her a smile, he grabbed her hand and led her away from Checkers' stall and into the nearby tack room, the only place inside the barn with a locking door.

She walked to the center of the room and glanced around. "Here?"

"There's a lot of equipment in here." None of it really meant for sex but it could easily be used for that.

"For riding—"

"Yes." He surveyed the tack room and keyed in on a couple of interesting items.

Grabbing a nearby riding crop, he slapped the wider, flat leather end against his palm. The sting and any resulting welts could easily be controlled by the power put behind the strike. Next, he slapped it harder against his denim-covered thigh, the sharp sound of the impact, along with the action gave her a sneak peek of what was to come.

He circled her, brushing the end of the leather tongue across her collarbones and shoulders. He didn't miss her shiver and the way her dark eyes followed him.

After lightly tapping her ass with it, he set it within reach. Next, he pulled a well-broken-in stirrup leather from an English saddle stored on a wall rack. Stirrup leathers weren't much different from a leather belt. He could use it to beat her ass or tie her up.

With pursed lips, he spotted the four-prong hook suspended from the ceiling used to hang bridles when cleaning or oiling them. That discovery was a sign to use the crop to spank her and the stirrup leather to tie her up.

He looped one end of the leather strap and secured it to the bridle hook before crooking a finger at her to come closer. With a naughty smile and slightly parted lips, she didn't hesitate.

He pointed to the floor under the dangling stirrup leather. "Stand there."

He was pleased to see she didn't balk at taking orders. At least when it came to sex. He would never order a woman around, Erin or otherwise, in any other situation.

He circled her slowly again, this time slipping a spaghetti-thin dress strap off one slender shoulder before doing the same with the other.

This particular sundress had a zipper at the back, so with excruciating slowness, he pulled the tab down, making sure the back of his knuckles brushed against her warm skin as he went, following them with his lips.

When he was done, the light, colorful fabric easily slipped to the floor, landing in a whisper at her feet.

Since her breasts weren't large or heavy, she could get away without wearing a bra, so no surprise she wasn't wearing one. Her nipples, puckered tightly, made his mouth water.

They would have to wait.

Her thong gave him a great view of her ass. He visually inspected her firm cheeks to see if any of Ford's marks remained.

Barely. He could only detect a little bit of slight bruising where he left the largest welts. Dylan would change that when he also left his own.

Unless she had an issue with him doing so. "He turned your ass cherry red. Do you get off on being spanked like that?

"Yes. Do you?"

Did her voice have a little tremor? "I like to do the spanking." He trailed his fingers down her bare arms stopping at her wrists. He lifted them above her head. "Keep them there."

"I always do what I'm told."

He came around to face her and cocked an eyebrow. "You're always a good girl and never a brat?"

The corners of her mouth curled up and her eyes held mischief. "I'm only a brat when I want to be spanked harder."

"No need to be. If you want to be spanked harder, simply ask."

"I can't if my mouth is full."

He stared at her. "Very true. I'll keep that in mind."

Looping the other end of the stirrup leather around her wrists, he used it to secure her arms over her head.

"What if someone sees us?"

The only people he wanted to avoid seeing them was his sister or twin. He didn't give a rat's ass about the guests. They were all on the property for a reason. Most of them for something similar to what they were about to do. "You kept the blinds open in the playroom. Do you really care?"

She shrugged as much as her suspended arms allowed. "No."

"Do you hope someone sees us?"

"An audience would be," she finished on a sigh, "intoxicating."

"So unexpected," he murmured. He still couldn't believe this was the same Erin from their youth.

"It seems like we've both changed, Dylan."

That they have.

As he rose from slipping her panties down and removing them from around her feet along with her dress, he paused long enough to part her pussy with his fingers and tickle her clit with his tongue. Her whimper made his cock kick in his jeans.

Patience.

He paused again to suck one pebbled nipple into his mouth, then the other before going back and nipping them both playfully but hard enough to make her breathing uneven.

Since her ankles weren't bound and her sandals were planted firmly on the concrete floor, she leaned into him, silently encouraging him to do it again.

He didn't. They were limited on time, and he had other plans.

His gaze landed on a brush sticking out of a plastic tote used to hold grooming supplies like curry combs and hoof picks. That particular brush had stiff bristles used on a horse's body when it was really dirty, like when they were caked with mud.

He left her bound in the center of the room to grab it and test it over his palm.

Perfect.

He hoped Erin thought so, too.

He'd find out soon enough.

When he returned to her, he started to lightly sweep the brush over her skin. Anywhere the bristles touched left her skin pink with barely visible scrape marks.

It wasn't enough.

Normally if he was in charge, he wouldn't ask, but since they hadn't established a safe word yet—something he needed to do—he asked, "Too much?"

"No," she whispered.

He stopped brushing her skin and put his lips to her ear. "Before we go further, I need to ask what your safe word is."

She better have one. Especially after what he witnessed Ford doing to her.

"Pineapple."

That was a common one and easy enough to remember. "Pineapple, it is," he confirmed.

Personally, he preferred the "red light" system. He wished his partners did, too. It was nice to have more than only a word used to "stop." He liked the idea that green meant everything was A-okay or they wanted more, yellow was slow down or be careful, and red was to stop immediately. It was simple and effective.

He should've given that system to Ford instead of only a word. If the three of them actually became a regular thing, he would propose they switch over to that. Apparently, he hadn't been thinking straight at the time.

He silently chuckled in his head. Actually, seeing Ford naked and strapped down on a spanking bench certainly hadn't helped him think *straight*.

He took long strokes with the brush over her back, testing to see how much pressure he should use. He wanted it to feel good and turn her on, not make her flawless skin bleed. While some people were into blood play, he was definitely not.

He continued sweeping the brush over her back, her ass and the back of her thighs, then moved around to her front, brushing the front of her supple thighs and using the bristles to tease her pussy. He then ran it up her stomach and chest before concentrating on her nipples.

The path of pink left behind was picture perfect.

"You like that?" he whispered.

"*Yessss*," came out on a breath. Her eyes were closed, and she appeared relaxed, so he took that as a sign his pressure wasn't unbearable. If it became so, it only took a single word to stop him.

He once again sucked a now-red nipple into his mouth, soothing it by swirling his tongue around, as he continued to scrape the stiff bristles over the other.

He switched again.

And again.

But he needed to move on...

Chapter Eighteen

Forcing himself to pull away, Dylan set down the brush and picked up the crop next. He whipped his palm harder in front of Erin's face, making her eyes open at the sharp slap.

If his palm could take that strike, so could her ass.

But unlike the rest of her, he didn't want her ass pink, he wanted it as red as Ford had made it two days ago. He wanted his marks to cover any that remained from his facilities manager.

Was it like a dog marking a bush after another male peed on it? Sure. He also didn't care if anyone thought that.

He lightly tapped the wide leather end of the riding crop all over her body, only striking her slightly harder on her breasts and nipples.

"You know the word to say if it gets to be too much. Do you need a reminder?"

"No," she groaned. "I know what it is."

"Good..." He then frowned when he realized they

needed to get to know each other all over again. A lot changed in seventeen years. "Do you like praise?"

"I do," came out on a breath.

"Then... good girl." He bopped her playfully on her nose with the crop. "I don't want to do anything you're not comfortable with. Or do anything that turns you off. So, if I do, use pineapple."

"I will. Promise."

"Good girl," he whispered.

Did she shudder? *Well, then.* Yes, he was liking this version of Erin. A hell of a lot.

Maybe instead of being jealous, he really should thank Ford for helping her to discover her inner kink.

He'd consider it. But right now, he had more important things to do. One of them being turning her ass a gorgeous shade of red.

He smoothed his palm over one cheek, then the other, before picking his target and striking it. He made sure to hold back and not put all his strength behind it. He wanted her to enjoy it, not suffer or injure her. He'd also preferred her adrenaline to kick in before cropping her any harder.

Despite his impatience, he restrained himself until her ass cheeks were just on the cusp of red. Once they were, he warned, "I won't be holding back anymore. You know what to do if it becomes too much."

He couldn't see her face, but he could see her nod. So, with that, he let the crop fly. He left marks that began to rise into welts all over both cheeks, making her ass remind him of a peppermint stick.

Good enough to lick.

She did not use her word or cry out in pain, instead she seemed to fall into a blissful state.

The result was perfect.

"Holy shit, that's a beautiful sight," he whispered while rubbing his uncomfortably hard erection through his jeans. He wouldn't be surprised if his cock now had a permanent impression of his zipper.

He came around, tipped her chin up to check to see how far she had fallen into her subspace and whispered again, "So damn beautiful."

Oh yes, she enjoyed her ass getting spanked or whipped. Her relaxed state confirmed it.

He dragged a thumb over her full bottom lip and asked softly, "All good?"

She nodded.

With that, he took her mouth again. He wanted to nudge her out of her trance enough so she could answer an important question he should've asked before they started. Apparently, he had lost his head at the thought of finally fucking Erin and he needed to get his shit together before continuing.

It took a few seconds before she responded to the kiss but when she did, it quickly turned frenzied. They couldn't get enough of each other's mouths. He grabbed one of her breasts and squeezed it hard, rubbing his thumb back and forth over the pebbled tip.

With a groan, he reluctantly broke free. He tossed the crop aside so he could unfasten his belt and jeans. He paused with his hands on the waistband. "Are you on birth control?"

When she nodded, a lock of dark brown hair got caught on her eyelashes. He swept it away since she couldn't. As a Dominant, it was his job to take care of her when she couldn't take care of herself. That included looking out for her best interests. "Do you want me to use a condom?"

Her eyes turned as dark as night due to her pupils expanding. "Do you test regularly?"

"I do." Since he had no permanent or long-term partner,

to do so was not only for his safety, but anyone he played with.

"When was the last time?"

"Two months ago."

"That's a long time." She tucked her bottom lip between her teeth.

He locked gazes with her, so she'd know he stated nothing but the truth. "Erin, in that time, I haven't had sex with anyone except the same man you *occasionally* have sex with."

She sucked in a breath. "No one?"

"No. The truth is, I've been so busy with the resort, I haven't taken the time to find anyone. Ford was my first for almost a year."

"Seriously?"

"Seriously," he confirmed. "So, I'll ask again, do I need to wear a condom?" He wanted to fill her with his cum the same way Ford did. He wanted to see it coating her inner thighs.

He wanted it to remind her of who she fucked today. And if Ford happened to fuck her later, he would know, too. But it was solely her choice, and he would respect her decision either way.

"Then no."

"No, I don't need to wear one? Or no, I can't come inside you?"

"The first is no. The second is yes, please, Sir."

Sir.

He was not her Dom. Not yet anyway. But, *Jesus*, that answer along with her using that specific honorific set his libido on fire just like her ass and caused a roaring heat deep within his gut.

So damn ready to fuck her, he shoved his jeans and boxer

briefs down enough to pull out his throbbing cock. No surprise that the tip was shiny with smeared precum.

He pumped his cock as he slipped a finger between her folds to check to see how wet she was. He was pleased to find her soaked. "Good girl," he whispered again, now plunging two fingers in and out of her to spread her arousal.

Releasing a low, drawn-out moan, her hips rocked in time with his fingers. He added his thumb, pressing it against her clit. He circled and flicked it while continuing to finger fuck her and watch her face carefully.

Since she let him do everything he desired so far, Erin deserved a reward. "Spread your legs a little more," he murmured. "That's it. Good girl."

With flushed cheeks, another shudder ripped through her. Her eyelids drooped heavily, and her ragged breathing was peppered with little moans and whimpers.

"Beautiful," he whispered. "Look at you. Perfection."

"May I come, Sir?"

Her calling him *Sir* again almost made him lose his shit. Especially since he hadn't ordered her to call him by any title. "You may."

When she threw her head back, he was mesmerized with how her orgasm completely took over. Her soft wail, her closed eyes, her arching back, her slick pussy pulsating around his fingers...

All a thing of beauty. All of it making him desperate to fuck her. But since this was a reward, he made himself wait until the last ripple of her climax faded away.

When it did, she opened her eyes and gave him a soft, satisfied smile. "Thank you, Sir."

Jesus, he could get used to her using that title with him. Especially since he hadn't heard her use it with Ford the other day.

"My pleasure." With their gazes locked, he tucked his slick fingers into his mouth and sucked them clean. "So damn good that I'm tempted to make a meal of you. But not today, it'll give us something to look forward to."

He wrapped his arms around her, planted his hands on the hot skin of her ass and lifted her with ease. "Wrap your legs around my waist."

When she did, the intoxicating scent of her arousal filled his nostrils. After the little taste he had, it made his mouth water and tempted him to throw her legs over his shoulders so he could eat her until she came once more.

Instead, he dropped her weight and impaled her on his cock, planting himself so deep, it was impossible to go any farther. He had to pause and breathe through his urge to ram up into her relentlessly. He'd waited for this moment for such a long time, he never thought he'd get the chance.

But here they were. Finally.

Collecting himself, he gritted his teeth and called on his willpower so he wouldn't blow this whole thing.

It was time to get busy.

Using his tight hold on her ass, he lifted and lowered her over and over. With how deeply his fingertips were digging into her ass cheeks, it had to be uncomfortable. But unless he heard her say "pineapple," he was continuing.

Wrapping her fingers around the leather strap binding her, it alleviated some of her weight and helped her ride his cock. He swore her hips rolled so smoothly, her joints had to be made with ball-bearings.

Christ, it had been a long time since he fucked anyone without a condom. He could feel *everything*. Every tiny pulse. Every twitch. The way her pussy clamped tightly around him. The way her wet heat hugged him, and her juices rolled down his cock and coated his balls.

He needed to concentrate on something else or he worried he'd come too quickly. He didn't know if there would be a repeat of today, so he didn't want it to end too soon.

He also wanted to make sure she came again. Since he *did* want a repeat, he needed to prove he could satisfy her and not only himself.

For a distraction, he locked lips with her again. He needed to concentrate on the kiss and not her pussy milking his cock.

It was almost impossible.

He had no idea what Heaven was like, but this had to be damn close.

He missed this for the last seventeen years.

This.

Her.

His mind drifted to a "what if" that haunted him.

If he never left, she would've belonged to him and no one else. She would've been his alone. He had never wanted to share her and that was why it was difficult to think of her with Hart.

And now with Ford.

While he wanted to think he fucked up by leaving, the truth was, he hadn't. He would have suppressed his true inner self and that might've led to depression.

Even hating himself.

Possibly hating others.

Staying might have doomed the two of them, anyway. So, while leaving felt like a mistake, it was the right thing to do. Today proved it had been best for both of them.

But, *damn*, he could still grieve the loss of that time.

Once he was done doing that, he needed to get the hell over it and stop being an asshole about it. Stop obsessing on what could've been and look at what could be.

What happened the other day with Ford and what was happening today with Erin could be his future.

If he wanted it.

The offer was there. He only had to accept.

The unbearable pressure building inside him pulled him from his thoughts. He needed to dig deep to find that desperately needed control. The way she bucked against him, along with the sounds slipping from between her lips, he knew she had to be on the brink.

Or he hoped so, since he certainly was.

Luckily, he wasn't wrong.

She cried out and tensed, her body bowing against him. The second she came, he held her down so he was planted deep inside her when he chased her orgasm with his own.

His cock pulsed as intensely as her pussy when he filled her with his cum.

With eyes closed, he pressed his forehead to hers for a second as they both rode out the aftershocks and tried to rein in their out-of-control breathing.

When it was over, when they were both spent, he pulled back and they simply stared into each other's eyes.

He was sure his mirrored hers. And what filled hers was shock. Amazement. Maybe a tinge of regret. Not for doing this now, today, but for this only being their first time.

He decided right then and there, he would not let it be their last. And if Ford had to be involved...

Could he not only work with him but share Erin?

Could he get over his jealousy?

He might have to.

"You ready?" He wished they didn't have to part yet, but he also knew it was inevitable. Plus, he'd been unavailable for far too long already. He needed to check to make sure the resort was still standing and the guests happy.

When she nodded, he asked, "Are you okay?"

She nodded again.

"Barn cat got your tongue?"

Her grin matched his. "I'm still basking in that awesome orgasm. Thank you."

"My pleasure. Literally, it was my pleasure, too." He shifted. "Let me put you on your feet and untie you." He lifted her just enough to separate them before letting her slide down his body.

"My arms were starting to fall asleep."

He quickly removed the stirrup leather from her wrists. Before she could rub the circulation back into her hands, he massaged them for her. Aftercare was his job and so was giving her praise. "You did good."

"So did you."

He lifted his gaze. "I'm glad you were satisfied."

"We'll have to do this again."

"I agree. Better?"

"Yes, my blood is flowing again. Thank you."

He released her arms, and they dropped to her sides.

"You don't have to keep thanking me." He lifted his gaze again, but this time from securing his jeans and belt. "As I'm sure you know, it's my responsibility to make sure you're taken care of." When she went to retrieve her dress and thong, he stopped her. "Wait. Let me find something to reduce the welts first."

She glanced over her shoulder in an attempt to see the damage. "It's fine."

"It's not," he confirmed, even without seeing it. He lifted a wait-a-minute finger and went over to the barn's medicine cabinet. He dug around until he found a bottle of witch hazel. It had been purchased for the animals, but it would work to reduce the swelling on humans, too.

"Let me see," he murmured as he stepped behind her. *Damn*, that sight... If he hadn't only just filled her with his cum, he'd be rock solid again.

Pouring some of the witch hazel into his palm, he smoothed the liquid over her red, raised skin on both cheeks. "Give it a second to dry. That should help."

"Soaking in my tub will also help."

While he would love an invite to join her, he wasn't pushing his luck. Not today, anyway. All bets might be off in the future.

He plucked her thong from the floor and handed it over. While she pulled it on, he held her sundress. She took it from him next, pulled it over her head and let it drop into place.

Shame, that.

Even so, she was just as gorgeous in that dress as she was naked. She gave him her back and he zipped her up.

He grabbed a bottle of water from the small fridge in the tack room next. "Make sure to drink all of that."

She accepted it. "I will." She cracked the lid on the water and downed a healthy swallow.

"Definitely take that warm bath when you get home. Do you want aspirin? The first aid kit has some."

"No, I'll be fine."

He was tempted to say, "Good girl," again but they were no longer in a scene, and he didn't want to sound overbearing. Instead, he asked, "Can I check on you later?"

Her brown eyes went wide. "Like stopping over?"

He shook his head. "Just a simple text."

"Sure."

"I don't have your number."

With a tilt of her head, she shot him a knowing look.

Of course she saw through his request. He didn't have her number, and this was a good excuse to get it.

"Do you have your cell phone on you?"

He slipped it from his back pocket, unlocked the screen and pulled up his contacts.

When she held out her hand, he didn't hesitate to hand it over. She plugged in her digits. Then with a smile, she stepped toe-to-toe with him, pressing the phone to his chest. His hand automatically enveloped hers, but she didn't release it. Instead, she leaned in with her face tipped up.

It was only natural that they would share a parting kiss. Right?

After driving his hand through her hair, he cupped the back of her head as she went up on her toes and pressed their mouths together.

Even though the kiss was brief, it still made his blood hum. Especially when his palms picked up the heat of her spanked ass through the light fabric of her dress.

"I want to do this again," she murmured against his lips.

He also looked forward that.

Soon.

"Great minds..." He didn't bother to finish that common idiom, she knew the rest.

After releasing his cell phone, she dropped from her tiptoes, making him once again aware of their six-inch height difference. "I'm glad we're finally moving forward, Dylan, and no longer lingering in the past. Now, I have a tub calling my name." With a soft smile, she disappeared through the tack room door.

That was when he realized he was also smiling like a damn fool.

Because today ended up being a good day.

He hoped tomorrow was even better.

Chapter Nineteen

Ford stood over Dylan as he turned on the tub's faucet in his bathroom. "Did she say when she'd get here?"

His boss straightened from testing the water's temperature with his hand. "I told her seven-thirty." He wiped his damp hand along his denim-covered thigh, drawing Ford's gaze there.

For a second, it took him back to last week when Dylan had him strapped down to the spanking bench and was railing him hard. Surprisingly, that memory woke up his cock. While he didn't like to bottom, he wasn't mad about it.

He might even consider letting Dylan fuck him again.

But not tonight.

Tonight, they had other plans. They ran into each other two days ago in the event hall while he was fixing a light. Even though they hadn't been exactly avoiding each other, they also hadn't been actively searching each other out.

But it had been the perfect time, since no one else was around, to have a discussion about Dylan fucking Erin in the tack room and where they would go from there.

Ford had stopped in at her place after he caught a glimpse of her driving off the ranch the other day. If she hadn't been there looking for Ford, he had to assume she'd been looking for Dylan.

His guess had been correct.

She had shared with him everything that happened, including Dylan coming inside her. Instead of inciting jealousy, that confession made him instantly hard.

Unfortunately, she had already soaked in a warm tub and most of what Dylan left inside her had been washed away. However, the evidence of a crop striking her flesh was still visible.

He made her plant her hands on her kitchen counter and bend over so he could inspect those fresh marks. How much he got turned on over someone else whipping her ass and fucking her surprised him.

He chalked it up to that someone being Dylan.

It also made him wish he'd been there.

When asked, she admitted her ex had made her come twice during their time in the barn. Ford had been determined to match that number, if not beat it. By the time he left her that night, she was out cold from exhaustion. Though, thoroughly satisfied.

If she was okay with having sex with them both, nothing was stopping them from doing her at the same time. And while they were at it, doing each other, as well.

Ford asked, "Does she know I'll be here?"

"No. I wanted it to be a surprise." Dylan grabbed a container of bath salts from the bathroom counter and sprinkled some into the rising water.

"Are we really doing this?" His nostrils flared as he picked up a pleasant floral scent coming from the tub.

Dylan's eyebrows shot up. "Second thoughts? We

discussed this the other day in the hall." He went over to the light switches and dimmed the recessed lighting.

Dimmable bathroom lights had been a must when Ford helped build Dylan's addition. Now he saw why. It gave the large bathroom a more spa-like atmosphere.

Their plan was to pamper Erin. Make tonight an "experience" and all about her. "I know. It's not her I'm worried about. She's clearly shown she wants us both."

Dylan screwed the cap back on the bath salt container and put it away under the sink. "But you're concerned about the two of us."

"Of course. We're both dominant. That alone could cause issues."

"Only if we let it."

Right. Dylan was making it out to be simpler than it was. He needed to factor in human emotions, including jealousy and possessiveness.

"You said you've never been exclusive, so it shouldn't be an issue, correct?" Dylan asked.

"Yes, and you already know that. Not only did we tell you, but I certainly wasn't bent out of shape when you cropped her ass and came inside her the other day."

Hazel eyes met his. "It turned you on."

Ford wasn't ashamed to admit it. "Enough to fuck her right after you did. I only wished she had left you inside her when I did. I got there a little too late."

Dylan tipped his blond head and groaned out a, "Fuck."

One side of Ford's mouth pulled up at his boss's unexpected reaction. "Apparently, I'm not the only one?"

Dylan lifted his head. "We'll see what tonight brings."

"Hopefully lots of pleasure. For all three of us."

"I have no doubt we can team up to achieve that. But..."

Ford scrunched his brow. "But?"

"I'm sure you already understand why I struggle with my jealousy—"

"She was your first love," Ford finished for him, then added with a shrug, "Mine, too." When Dylan raised his eyebrows at that confession, he explained, "Just because we're not exclusive doesn't mean I can't care deeply about her."

"I figured as much. Now what?"

Ford shrugged. "Tonight, we make the best of the situation."

"Have you had a threesome before?"

"Yes. You?"

"No." Dylan frowned. "Has she?"

Good question. "Not with me, she hasn't." Usually, the guys he hooked up with were only into guys. Not that he had a deep and meaningful conversation with them about their sexuality. And he couldn't imagine asking around for a third in Fisher Falls since Ford and Erin pretended to only be "friends."

"Then that's our answer. She told me she hasn't had sex with anyone but you since Hart died."

Holy shit. He had assumed she had since she never told him otherwise. He also never asked, as it was her business and hers alone. Just like he didn't talk about any of his own sexual encounters. Or the fact it was only with men and that she was the only woman he was intimate with. "I... had no idea."

"Now you do. We have to assume this will be her first time, so we need to be careful."

"She might not like you treating her with kid gloves."

"I didn't say we should treat her like she's breakable. I said be careful. We'll give her whatever she wants and maybe even what she doesn't realize she wants." Dylan glanced at his cell phone. "She should be here shortly. We should finish getting ready and set the trap."

Ford's eyebrows pinched together. "Trap?"

Dylan grinned. "Follow my lead."

———

ERIN STOPPED at the entrance to Dylan's wing of the farmhouse. She pursed her lips as she read the hand-written sign taped to the door.

Door's unlocked. Follow the trail of rose petals to find me.

"What in the world?" she whispered, then softly snort-laughed at the last sentence. *Eat this note so my nosy siblings don't see it.*

She ripped the sign down and balled it within her fist. She was *not* eating it. She hadn't eaten paper since she about two years old.

But what was all this? Was Dylan trying to woo her? Steal her away from Ford?

While she liked a little romance, she already told him that she and Ford came as a package deal.

With a sigh, she opened the door, and the sound of soft rock filled her ears at the same time she saw a path of vibrant red petals scattered on the wood floor. Dropping the balled-up note on the small table next to the door, she called out, "Dylan?"

Of course he didn't answer. He expected her to follow his orders, not question them. Since she had worn sandals with shorts and a tank top, she kicked them off and placed them neatly by the front door.

She hoped he hadn't planned anything too fancy since she was casually dressed. The trail of rose petals leading to the closed bathroom door on the opposite side of the living area might say otherwise. It most likely wouldn't matter how she was dressed since she could pretty much guess she wouldn't be wearing clothes for too long.

She did what the note said and followed the petals to the bathroom. With her hand gripping the doorknob, she leaned closer and listened carefully.

Nothing but the music could be heard.

When she opened it, she poked her head in and whispered, "Dylan?"

No sign of him.

As soon as she walked in, her nose immediately picked up the light scent of lavender. The lights were dimmed low and candles flickered softly on the long quartz counter. A few larger pedestal candles on the floor circled the large stand-alone, jetted tub.

After shutting the door, she approached it and noticed more petals floating on top of the steaming water.

Oh yes, it seemed like he wanted her to join him in a romantic interlude. He went above and beyond to make it all so inviting.

She pinched her forearm to make sure she wasn't dreaming. No one had ever done anything like this for her before. Certainly not Kyle. Or Ford. Or even Dylan.

"Get in the tub," Dylan's order came from who knew where.

"Are you joining me?"

"In a minute. Do as I order, Erin."

Fine. If she had to.

She smiled. "Yes, Sir." Soaking in a warm lavender-scented tub surrounded by candles would certainly not be a hardship.

After quickly stripping off her clothes, she folded them neatly and placed them on the corner of the counter. When she went back to the tub, she drew a finger through the water to make sure it wasn't too hot or cold before climbing in with a sigh.

She loved taking baths. Besides having sex with Ford, she considered soaking in a warm bath as self-care. Especially when it was scented with bath salts, bath bombs or even bubble bath.

Slipping farther down into the silky water, until only her shoulders and head were exposed, she turned the jets on low and waited for Dylan to come through the door. He had to be hiding in his bedroom.

Why was he being so mysterious?

It wasn't like she didn't know he invited her over for sex. It had been quite obvious when his text simply asked, "Repeat?"

When she texted back her acceptance to his invitation, he gave her the time and place but no other details.

Even so, why was he hiding? Was he about to jump out in some crazy leather bodysuit with a whip in his hand?

She giggled softly at the thought of Dylan wearing a leather onesie.

After a few more minutes of waiting, she leaned her head back against the little waterproof pillow and closed her eyes. She might as well enjoy the wait. However, if he didn't make an appearance before the water turned cold, she was drying off, getting dressed and heading out.

She must've drifted off to sleep because when she finally opened her eyes, it wasn't only Dylan in the bathroom with her. Ford was there, too. Both stood by the tub, wearing only boxer briefs.

She blinked. Was she still asleep? Was this a dream?

It had to be. How lucky could a woman get? She had two hot, handsome men, with the impressive outlines of erections pushing through their cotton-blend underwear at her fingertips.

She had to assume their hard-ons were over her. Not each other.

Wait. "Is this real?"

Ford answered first. "I hope so."

"But... what is all this? Dylan never said you'd be here."

Dylan answered next. "I wanted it to be a surprise."

"Well, color me surprised," she said.

Dylan continued. "We came to an agreement and decided that there's no reason for us to be jealous of each other when the three of us can all have what we want."

"And what do we all want?" she asked.

"Each other."

"At once?" She wanted to make sure they *were* all in agreement.

"Of course." Ford looked pleased about the whole situation. As he should.

"On this ranch, you can have anything you desire, as long as it's legal and consensual, remember?" Dylan asked.

This was what she and Ford had wanted. Dylan to join them. She just never expected for him to agree. So, this was a new twist. One she wouldn't complain about.

"I never thought you'd agree," she murmured.

"You like us both. We both like you. We both like each other. It makes perfect sense," Dylan explained.

As long as it didn't cause issues between them. That was her only worry.

Or would it start off in a honeymoon stage and in the end, someone—if not all three—would get hurt or become bitter, ruining the relationships?

Did she want to risk losing Ford? Absolutely not.

Did she want to continue to explore a sexual relationship with Dylan? Yes.

So, this *could* end up being the perfect situation. Tonight could be the first step in seeing if it would all work.

"Did you two have sex together before I got here?"

The two men glanced at each other before they both answered, "No," at the same time.

She fought a smile. "Were you tempted?"

"We wanted to wait for you," Dylan said.

"Of course we were," Ford answered truthfully.

"So, no kissing or touching? Those hard-ons are caused from anticipation of what will come next now that I'm here?"

Ford winked at her playfully while Dylan stumbled over his answer. "I... We..."

Erin lifted a hand out of the water. "That sounds like a yes. I'm sorry I missed it."

"We could give you a replay," Ford suggested.

Below the water, her pussy clenched. "Yes, please," she practically breathed.

The men again looked at each other for a few seconds, communicating silently.

That was a good sign.

When they both took a step toward each other, Erin held her breath in anticipation.

Suddenly, their mouths were smashed together, Dylan's hand gripped the back of Ford's head while Ford gripped Dylan's waist as their lips moved, and their tongues tangled.

One of them groaned as they ground their cocks together and kissed each other with desperation.

Wow. She'd never seen anything quite so hot. She wanted to see more but also wanted in on it.

When they finally broke the kiss, both men were panting and staring into each other's eyes.

Now *that* might be even hotter than the kiss. Desire was apparent in their eyes as both sets lowered toward her in the tub.

Her nipples were so tight, they ached. Her pussy was getting wet, and it wasn't from the bath water. "Should I get out?"

"Not yet," Dylan's voice was thicker than normal.

"But you two are out there and I'm in here. Unfortunately, the tub isn't big enough for the three of us."

"Tonight, we want this to be all about you. We want to take care of you."

"I'm not here to have sex?" she asked Dylan.

Once the men stepped apart, he responded with, "Neither of us said that."

"Good, because after seeing that kiss, I'm ready."

"You're going to have to have some patience," Ford informed her, then followed with, "So are we."

Chapter Twenty

After shutting off the jets, Dylan took one hand and Ford the other, helping her out of the tub. As soon as she was on her feet, naked and dripping wet before them, Dylan went over to the enormous shower and turned it on. Unlike the tub, it *was* big enough for the three of them, with room to spare.

As soon as Ford stripped off his boxer briefs, his cock hung hard and heavy. Dipping his knees, he scooped her up in his arms and carried her over to where Dylan waited by the shower, also now completely naked.

The difference between the two wasn't the size of their cocks, it was the color of the nest of thick, wiry hair at the base. Ford's black; Dylan's a golden brown.

She drew a hand across Ford's warm, firm chest and whispered, "How did I get to be so lucky?"

"Just by being you," Ford whispered back, before pressing his lips to hers for a brief moment.

Those kinds of comments made her appreciate Ford even more. He always made her feel good about herself. Never once had he ever been critical or impatient.

Dylan tested the water temp before stepping inside the glass enclosure. Immediately, he was bombarded by the various shower heads and his drool-worthy physique became slick with water.

Erin wasn't sure where she should direct her gaze, since both men were more than worth staring at. The thought that tonight both of them would be all hers and hers alone caused a flutter in her belly from a combination of both nervousness and excitement.

Dylan ordered, "Bring her in."

Without hesitation, Ford carried her into the luxurious shower, letting her slide down his hard body and onto her feet before closing the shower door behind them.

The hot water pelted her from several directions as the men massaged shampoo into her hair and used a bath pouf to wash her from head to toe. All the while, taking their time to caress and kiss her all over, making sure not to miss even an inch.

Heaven. Pure Heaven.

They ignored each other and focused their attention solely on her, making her feel wanted, appreciated and basically... like a queen.

Would these two men eventually be her kings?

She didn't need to consider that right now. Tonight was simply for enjoying the attention being showered upon her.

Normally, she relished being on the receiving end of a hard spank, a good whipping, being bitten, strung up or tied down, and fucked relentlessly, but the way they pampered her without giving any orders... felt like being worshipped.

She could get used to that, too.

Could she envision this as part of her future? Absolutely.

She wasn't lying about being lucky. What woman

wouldn't want two men seeing to her sensual and sexual needs?

Standing behind her, Ford pinned his arm under her breasts so she could lean back into him. Settling her head against his broad shoulder, she closed her eyes, letting the fragrant steam and the two men take her away like one of those old Calgon commercials.

Suddenly, she was tightly sandwiched between them and when her eyelids lifted, she watched the two kiss each other deeply and passionately over her shoulder. As they did so, Ford's hard-on pressed against the small of her back while Dylan's pressed against her lower belly.

Reaching between the two men, she ended their kiss by cupping Dylan's cheek. She then turned his head so they could kiss instead, and when it was over, she twisted her head enough to share a kiss with Ford.

"Carry on," she encouraged.

Dylan's eyes met Ford's behind her. "Not in the shower."

In what seemed like an unspoken agreement, they both backed off. While Dylan turned off the multitude of shower heads, Ford stepped out and grabbed a thick, fluffy towel folded on the counter nearby.

He held it up and open in an invitation. "Come to me."

As soon as she did, he wrapped her up and began to vigorously dry her off. He even spent time toweling her hair dry as much as possible before grabbing another thick towel to use on himself.

After Dylan did the same, he grabbed a container of what looked like body butter from under the counter and scooped some out before passing it to Ford so he could do the same. As she stood naked in the center of the bathroom, they thoroughly massaged the silky, cocoa-scented moisturizer from her head to her toes.

And while they did that, she watched them work in the large mirror.

This can't be real life.

"You smell good enough to eat," Ford whispered against her ear.

"I hope I'm on the menu."

"Don't worry, you are," Dylan assured her. He then gave her a playful smack on her bare ass and pointed toward the closed bedroom door. "Go."

Of course, she went without delay. The pampering was spectacular, but she was ready to get down to the nitty gritty. Especially after eyeing up their equally spectacular bodies and more-than-ready cocks.

They were probably impatient to get to the real reason for tonight, too. But the question was, would they only fuck her, or would she finally get to see them fuck each other?

They would if she had a say in it. A simple kiss shared between them had lit her core on fire, seeing them fuck each other might make her combust.

Continuing the romantic theme, Dylan's bedroom was bathed in a soft reddish glow, giving them enough light to see each other clearly but not be harsh.

She considered his oversized bed, stripped down to only a dark, fitted sheet. "Do you want to protect the bed?"

With three of them, it would get messy.

"I always use a waterproof mattress pad," Dylan answered.

Smart.

He finished with, "And I promise you, it'll be needed tonight."

That promise made her thighs quiver.

She approached the bed, trailing a finger over the soft, silky sheet the same way she had with the tub. "Do you have tonight all planned out?" She paused and glanced over her bare shoulder.

"Only what happened in the bathroom." Dylan approached where she waited at the head of the bed. "We'll figure out the rest of the evening as we go."

"We'll follow our impulses," she murmured.

Ford also came closer. "And our desires."

Movement above her had her glancing up. *What the—*

"That wasn't there before." The large mirror above his bed hadn't been there when she toured his wing the day of the resort's open house.

"I decided to install it the other week."

She spotted very small hooks at each corner of the mirror. Not big enough to support any kind of sex equipment. "And the hooks?"

"So I can cover it with a piece of fabric if I get sick of staring at myself."

She wasn't sure anyone would get sick of staring at Dylan, especially while naked, and she was damn sure he slept that way.

"Or you want to hide it."

"That, too," he confirmed.

With her eyes to the mirror, she watched the men step into her space. However, their predatory gazes were not on their reflection. They were on her.

The hunger in their eyes told her that she would definitely be the "meal" tonight.

She dropped her gaze and turned. "Where do we start?"

Dylan pushed a lock of her still damp hair over her shoulder. "We're not going overboard with the equipment or toys tonight. I think it's best for us to concentrate on each other since it's the first time we'll all be together."

Ford wiggled his eyebrows. "And if everything goes

smoothly and we're all in agreement that this will work, we can play like we mean it next time."

A thrill shot through Erin. "I like the sound of that."

"We all do," Ford agreed. "Do you have a hair tie with you?"

Well, that was an unexpected request. "Sure, in my purse out in the car."

"Shit," he muttered before glancing at Dylan. "Do you have a rubber band?"

"In the kitchen. Not sure I want to run into Dani or Dayne like this." He pointed at his stiff cock.

Ford pursed his lips for a second. "Grab me a shoelace."

"What are you doing?" Erin's curiosity was now piqued.

Instead of answering her, he turned her and began French braiding her hair.

What? When did he learn how to do that?

"Grab something for me to tie off the bottom," he once again said to Dylan.

Dylan jerked into motion and headed for one of the cabinets or closets, or whatever the built-ins were considered, along the one wall.

The second Ford was done braiding her long, damp hair, he brushed his lips along the nape of her neck, drawing a shiver from her.

When Dylan returned, Ford held up the end of the braid. "Tie that off."

It clearly was not a request; it was an order. Erin expected Dylan to get bent about it, but surprisingly enough, he didn't. He simply did what he was told.

Interesting.

Would the power dynamics be fluid between the two men? If so, it might make becoming a threesome easier.

Ford released her braid. "We have one goal tonight," he started.

She turned in time to see the two men give each other a nod before Dylan finished with, "Make her come undone."

———

Ford leaned back against Dylan's heavy-duty headboard. One that wasn't only aesthetic, but meant to be used during bondage, or possibly even light, fun play.

This evening it was being used as support since he sat against it with his legs extended and open in a *V*. Erin, on her knees, had her wrists bound with silk rope at the small of her back.

That kept her off balance since she didn't have the use of her arms. So, he controlled her head with his own hands as she sucked his cock. The speed, the depth, all under his control.

Of course, since they'd done this many times over the years, he knew her limits but that didn't mean he wouldn't push them. He usually did.

One thing he appreciated about Erin was she never complained. She usually rolled with whatever he wanted because she trusted him. Completely.

He did the same.

He also trusted her to give a signal if he lost his head. Something that could very well happen with everything going on tonight.

With her mouth occupied by his cock and her hands tied behind her, the agreed upon signal would be waving the bandana she had clutched in one hand. So far, she hadn't given it. But then, right now he wasn't pushing her as hard as he could. Most likely due to being distracted by what Dylan was up to.

His partner—how he now thought of Dylan, at least in their non-work life—was also on his knees and behind Erin as he fucked her doggy style.

Ford's boss had his fingers dug into one hip and he alternated slapping her ass cheeks, making them a pretty pink. If Dylan kept striking her as hard as he was, they would soon be red.

But again, she could simply stop both of them with a simple shake of the bandana.

Ford whispered, "You're such a good girl," as he thrust up slightly at the same time pulling her head down. "That's it, suck my cock like you can't live without it."

Saliva had gathered at the corners of her stretched lips. Another beautiful sight like her flushed ass cheeks.

Unfortunately, hearing their flesh slap together along with the unmistakable wet sound created every time Dylan rammed his cock deep was going straight to his head—both of them. He had to draw on every ounce of willpower to avoid exploding down Erin's throat.

He *could* do that. Or he could do what he really desired. To come inside Erin after Dylan. The possibility of her pussy being filled with both of their loads was...

A heady thought.

He already came once earlier when they took turns eating her out. Because of that, he would have a bit more stamina now.

But... This whole situation was driving him to the brink. While he'd had threesomes before, for some reason, this one...

Was on a whole other level.

Most likely due to his established physical and emotional attachment to Erin added to his fiery attraction to Dylan.

He hoped, if this arrangement all worked out, he'd never have to drive to State College again to scratch his bisexual itch.

He had hit the wall when he watched Dylan's head between Erin's thighs earlier. He ended up kneeling above her head and jerking off until, with a deep grunt, he came all over face. After she licked away what landed on her lips, he scraped the rest over to her mouth to "assist."

So yes, he could come down her throat, but he had different destination earmarked for his next orgasm.

Once Erin came the first time from Dylan's mouth, Ford practically pushed the man out of the way so he could switch places and use his tongue to clean up her resulting arousal.

While he concentrated on her pussy, Ford kept his eyes on Dylan playing with her breasts with his hazel eyes dark and heated, and Erin's expression full of ecstasy.

Dylan would lightly smack her breasts and pinch her taut nipples, then he would twist and pull one without mercy while sucking and biting the other. Watching that made Ford's cock ache with need. Hearing her whimpers, sighs, moans and groans made him even harder. He desperately desired to either plant his cum in Erin's slick pussy or Dylan's tight ass.

He'd be okay with either choice. Or both. They had all night, if needed.

If everything went well, he hoped they'd have plenty of nights, days, or even early mornings in the future.

He'd been a little worried about how he and Dylan would work things out between them, but so far, they seemed to be in-tune with each other. However, that could possibly change if he tried to fuck his boss.

While both had agreed to be flexible, that didn't mean it would end up a reality. He and Dylan were both Dominants sharing a sub. An issue might come about when they tried to share each other.

Ford might have acquiesced in the playroom the other week, but he would not be doing that every damn time.

No way. If Dylan refused to switch, then it might be a dealbreaker.

And he refused to lose Erin. That meant Dylan would lose her.

So, it would be in the man's best interest to be open to switching. Otherwise, Dylan would have to find others to play with. It would not be Erin and him.

If Ford bailed on this threesome, so would she. She already assured him her loyalties lay with him. Dylan and Erin might have a past, but Ford and Erin were "current." They'd been seeing each other for a hell of a lot longer than Dylan and her had dated.

Truthfully, Dylan seemed like a reasonable man. It was one reason Ford agreed to get hired on full-time. While planning this evening, they had discussed the basics and neither balked at each other's suggestions or desires.

Both had no problem deciding they would skip doing anal with Erin this evening. They didn't want to overwhelm her with her first threesome.

He had done it a few times in the past with her, but he found it took a lot of prep to make it comfortable enough for her to enjoy it, anyway.

Their ultimate goal was for her to enjoy *everything* they did to her tonight.

Chapter Twenty-One

When Dylan's eyes locked with Ford's dark ones, his hips stuttered, and his rhythm was thrown off. Without the man even saying a word, it was obvious Ford wanted to fuck him tonight and he was damn sure Erin would love to be a spectator, or even take part.

Dylan agreed to be flexible.

Still... Like Ford, it had been a hell of a long time since he let a man have his ass.

When he was young and exploring his sexuality, he wanted to try it all. Since nothing was stopping him, he did. But while doing so, he had partners who would only top him.

In the beginning, one man drove him so out of his mind Dylan thought he'd enjoy bottoming with all men. That quickly turned out to not be true. Some were too impatient to properly prep him before shoving their cocks deep. Others just didn't care if he got off. It was all about them.

In the end, they hadn't been partners for long.

However, those experiences were valuable lessons on

what not to do when he topped. Or even what not to do when he had sex with women.

Normally, he would've spent more time doing foreplay with Ford that day in the playroom. But it *was* Ford, and jealousy had overcome Dylan, along with the urge to take his employee down a notch.

Add in the fact they didn't have a lot of time.

This evening, they could take as much time as needed, but he doubted Ford would be willing to be on the receiving end twice in a row.

Dylan considered his word to be solid and a reflection on him, so he couldn't back out on what he agreed to. But the worry that came along with that word threw him off his game.

He closed his eyes for a second, only long enough to break that hold with Ford. When he opened them, he focused on what Erin was doing. That quickly got him centered and back on track.

Watching her head bob up and down as she swallowed just about Ford's whole length… For a moment, he wished he was in her place. Without his wrists bound, of course. Dylan might not prefer to bottom but he sure got off on sucking another man's cock.

One reason being, he liked to be in control. He could do that by using his pace and the amount of suction. He could also edge the other man. One of his favorite kinks was when he'd take a man right to that sweet, sweet edge, then pull back or change course so his sex partner didn't come.

It frustrated some, while others loved it.

Erin wasn't edging Ford because she had no control in her current situation. Ford was guiding her head and mouth in the way he desired. Every once in a while, he might whisper a command or praise.

He liked to tell her she was a "good girl" *a lot* and, no surprise, she ate up that praise.

Ford would also push her limits slightly by holding her head down until her lips almost reached the base of his cock. He would keep her there until she fought for breath. Once she did, he would lift her head, give her praise, and let her continue on normally for a bit, giving her a break.

Despite him doing it over and over, she didn't once wave that bandana clutched in her hand. However, every time Ford did it, Dylan could see his partner fighting the urge to come.

Dylan didn't blame him because seeing that, hearing the wet suction of Erin's mouth, plus the visual of Ford's cock slick with her saliva... made him struggle not to come, too.

But first, he needed to give Erin her reward for being such a good girl. Then once she had her orgasm, he'd follow with his own.

His gaze rose from Erin to Ford. "Do you plan to come like that?"

With a tight expression, Ford shook his head. "Trying not to. I'd prefer to finish inside her."

Dylan asked, "After I do?"

Their eyes locked again, and Ford answered, "Yes."

Fuck, that was hot.

To be able to watch Ford fuck her while she was still full of Dylan's load...

Jesus, he needed to push that image from his brain right now. She also needed to hurry up and come. Like yesterday.

He pulled out and gave her ass one last stinging slap. "Flip her over."

Ford released her head, and when he slipped his cock free of her mouth, a long string of saliva remained binding them together until he swiped it free and used it to stroke his cock a couple of times.

Again, so damn hot.

Since Erin's hands were bound, the men rolled her over until she was on her back. Once she was, she planted the top of her head in the mattress, arched her neck and opened her mouth. Ford instantly obliged by feeding her his cock again, then patted her cheek and whispered, "Show me what a good girl you are and take it all."

Dylan dug his fingers into her supple thighs and spread her legs wide to expose her swollen and shiny folds. "Toss me the wedge that's next to the bed."

Ford reached over—somehow without dislodging his cock—grabbed the wedge cushion propped against the bed frame, and once he straightened, he handed it to Dylan.

"Ass up." He followed his demand with a sharp slap to her pussy. She made a sound around Ford's cock, but lifted her hips so he could position the wedge pillow under her ass.

Once she was in the perfect position, he dug his knees into the bed and powered up and into her, over and over. Her pussy soaked his cock while her mouth-soaked Ford's.

However, it didn't take long before Ford pulled out with a groan. Sitting back on his heels, he slowly stroked his erection. "Can't last letting her do that."

Dylan wasn't sure if Ford was explaining his action to him or himself. Either way, he could commiserate. If Erin didn't come soon, he'd be muttering the same damn thing.

He continued to plunge in and out of her but pinched her clit hard enough for her to jerk and cry out. Of course, she didn't use her safe word and instead encouraged him to do it again.

Of course, he did.

With his mouth to her ear, Ford kept whispering to her,

most likely to encourage her to come. He continued to tug on his cock but leaned over and sank his teeth into the soft flesh around her puckered nipple hard enough to leave an obvious pattern behind.

Digging her heels into Dylan's ass, she met each slam of his hips with her own. Now that her mouth was cock-free, she filled the space between them with mews and whimpers, moans and groans.

And the begging was the icing on the cake.

All of it music to his ears and proof she was enjoying her first threesome. Hopefully, it wouldn't be her last.

"Bite the other one," he encouraged Ford. "Harder this time."

"*Yessss*," Erin moaned. "Please."

Ford obliged by snagging the other nipple between his teeth and stretching it upward as far as it would go before releasing it and once again sinking his teeth in.

Erin bucked against both of them, yelling, "Can I come, Sirs?"

Ford sat back and gave Dylan a single nod. He returned it and used Ford's pet name for her to see if that would catapult her over the finish line. "Come, darlin'." Of course, he made that a demand, not a suggestion.

After hearing him call her *darlin'*, she froze for a second—as did Ford—then she exploded with both a wail and an orgasm. Both her pussy clamping down around his cock and the intense ripples were his undoing and he gave up the fight.

He. Was. Toast. "I'm going to fill you with my cum."

"Please, please, please," she whispered, writhing on the bed.

With one last thrust as deep as he could go, he spilled inside her.

He closed his eyes, and his hips twitched as she

continued to pulse around his cock, drawing out what could be every last drop.

He gave himself a few seconds to gather his sanity and once he got himself together enough to open his eyes... The look of hunger on Ford's face was almost enough to make Dylan instantly hard again.

Ford wasn't only pointing that at Erin, but at Dylan, too.

"My turn," Ford announced, climbing off the bed and coming around to the foot of it.

That was obvious. The angry color of his tightly fisted cock was proof the man was already skating on thin ice.

Before pulling out, he asked Ford, "How do you want her?"

"The real question is, how don't I want her?"

"Wait. Please," Erin panted. "I want to see you two together first."

"You can see us together later. I'm ready to fuck you now," Ford told her. "Don't you want me to fuck you?"

"Please, Sir!"

"Do you want me to add my cum to his? It's one way to have us both inside you at the same time."

"There are other ways," Dylan reminded Ford, other than sucking one cock while being fucked with another.

Double penetration was one. Of course, they wouldn't be able to try that tonight but if this threesome continued in the future, it would be on the table.

"Yes, Sir. I want any and all of that."

As agreeable as she was, Dylan had no idea if Erin ever had anal. If not, they would have to get her over that barrier first. It was a discussion that needed to be had before attempting it.

Ford took his place within seconds after Dylan pulled out. Dragging the head of his cock through her folds, he spread around the little bit of cum that slipped out. Then he lined himself up and, with his eyes on Dylan now at the head of the bed, Ford pushed himself deep.

Was Ford picturing himself fucking Dylan? Is that why he was focused on him?

His insides shook a little at the thought it might happen tonight, unless... he cut the night short. He recognized that would only delay the inevitable since he promised he'd be flexible.

He told himself again that he needed to keep his word.

Even so, he was torn. The thought of Ford fucking him both warmed and chilled him. Was he actually nervous about it? Yes, since it had been a long time since the last time he'd been fucked by a man.

Ford had shared with him that he regularly drove to State College for hookups. That meant he should be experienced enough to make sure Dylan didn't suffer through it.

Sex was about pleasure, not pain... Well... Abusive pain, anyway. Pleasurable pain was not the same. One was welcomed, the other not.

Erin loved her ass beaten. Or her breasts bitten. Or her nipples twisted.

It made the pleasure more intense and took her into her subspace, a state of bliss. A euphoria most likely due to a release of endorphins, resulting in an effect similar to taking opioid drugs.

A sexual high, truth be told.

Dylan had experienced that euphoria himself before he realized he preferred to dominate rather than be subjugated. He liked the power and control that being a Dom gave him.

Luckily, Erin was into pleasurable pain since he loved doling out a good whipping or spanking as much as Ford did.

Rising to his knees, he shuffled forward until his thighs

straddled Erin's head. Inserting a thumb between her lips, he pulled her mouth open despite the fact she would've opened it on her own if asked or ordered.

But that wasn't the point.

He shifted again and lowered himself until his balls brushed her lips. "Suck them."

When her mouth circled his sack, he wobbled a bit. Her mouth was hot and wet, and her tongue skilled as she teased and played with them.

He swallowed his groan and without much thought, his arm shot out and he grabbed Ford by the back of the neck, yanking him forward. Their mouths slammed together, and he plunged his tongue in the other man's mouth, giving him no mercy as he claimed it. Despite their tongues battling and their groans merging, Ford somehow managed to keep his rhythm steady while fucking Erin.

Dylan dug his fingertips deeper into Ford's corded neck to hold him there while using his other hand to snag Ford's nipple. Immediately, the other man grunted and deepened the kiss as Dylan went back and forth pinching and twisting his nipples until they were an angry red.

The perfect color.

It wasn't long before Ford twisted his head to end the kiss, but he didn't go far. His ragged panting pounded Dylan's mouth as he continued to pound Erin's pussy.

Dylan was impressed the man could concentrate on both. The steaming hot kiss was enough for Dylan to forget Erin had his balls in her mouth. It took her scraping her teeth along the delicate skin to bring him back to the situation at hand.

"I wish I had nipple clamps right now," he murmured against Ford's lips.

He had some in his personal toy cabinet, but he couldn't

be bothered to grab them now. He might break them out later if the two stayed for a second round.

Maybe even a third.

Once again, his insides fluttered from both anxiety and excitement, because he had no doubt what would happen in one of those rounds.

Before he could let that worry derail him, Erin released his balls. "I need to come again. Can I come, Sirs?"

Since Dylan recognized the sign of Ford's locked jaws, he answered for both of them. "Yes, darlin', come. Soak his cock." He also moved off of Erin so he wouldn't get an accidental headbutt in the nuts.

Nabbing one of Ford's nipples again, as well as one of Erin's, he twisted both as hard as he could. Once again, Erin bowed off the bed and slammed her pussy into Ford's cum-covered cock.

Ford and Dylan's eyes met once more. "She's... coming."

"Good," rumbled from Dylan as he watched not only Erin come, but a few seconds later and with another deep grunt, Ford did, too.

His pulse rushed at the thought of their cum mixing together in the woman they just shared...

Chapter Twenty-Two

Once Ford pulled out, they didn't let Erin move since they wanted their cum to remain inside her, but they did clean her up everywhere else. Afterward, he and Ford took turns in the bathroom. While in there, Dylan made sure all the candles were extinguished, and he pulled the drain stopper on the tub.

When he went back to the bedroom, both men massaged Erin's muscles, peppered her with light kisses, and Ford lazily combed his fingers through her hair after undoing the braid that had held it in place. Dylan had a feeling that this was part of Erin's normal aftercare.

The green-eyed monster tried to creep in, but he shoved it away. Jealousy didn't belong in any polyamorous relationship. It might not always be easy to overcome, but that would be necessary for the relationship to be successful.

While Ford tended to Erin, she sighed softly. "I don't want tonight to ever end."

"Then don't let it," easily slipped from Dylan's lips, surprising even himself.

She lifted her head, dislodging Ford's hands. "What do you mean?"

Dylan pulled in a breath and figured he might as well have them... "Stay." Before Erin could respond, Dylan added, "Both of you."

Ford's eyebrows shot up. "What about Dani and Dayne?"

"They're not invited."

Erin hid her face in his chest to smother her laugh. Of course, her body shaking gave it away, pulling a grin from him.

Ford didn't laugh or smile at Dylan's response. Instead, his eyebrows dropped low and pinched together. "You don't care if they spot us leaving tomorrow?"

Of course he cared, but he had to face the fact they wouldn't be able to keep this particular secret under wraps for long.

He rubbed a strand of Erin's hair between his thumb and forefinger. "They're eventually going to figure it out, anyway."

Erin asked, "They will?"

"Yes, since I can't imagine either you or Ford have a bed big enough for the three of us. Ford, are you worried about being seen leaving my place because you're an employee?"

"I assume if you're giving this threesome the green light, then they can't say much about it, whether I'm an employee or not."

That wasn't quite true when it came to his outspoken siblings. They could give a lot of unwelcomed opinions. But he wasn't the only owner of the resort. He shared that responsibility with his womb mate.

Ford's answer also reminded Dylan to bring up the traffic light system. Using it during their play would simplify the safe word issue. If Ford and Erin agreed to switch over, none of them would have to remember different safe words.

Especially in the heat of things.

Erin's question cut into his thoughts. "What do you mean we don't have big enough beds?"

"It's his way of saying he wants to do this again," Ford answered for Dylan. "And only his custom bed is big enough for the three of us. Plus,"—he glanced up—"That mirror sure is the shit."

Dylan agreed. It had been worth installing. "Not only do it again, but often. For that reason alone, it'll be hard to keep it a secret from my siblings. I mean, as long as you two want to continue."

"Let me think about it," she teased, nudging him.

Ford fought a grin. "I'll give it some serious thought."

"Funny." They could tease all they want, but Dylan had to admit, at least to himself, that he was relieved they wanted to continue. He needed to keep his jealousy in check, though. Especially after seeing Erin and Ford so comfortable with each other, whether wearing clothes or naked.

With a hand cupping her head, Dylan curled into Erin and his eyes drifted shut. But Ford's next question had them flashing open again. "Do you have a plug?"

Shit. Shit. Shit.

Of course he did, but when Dylan stocked them in his toy cabinet, he never expected them to be used on him. He reluctantly breathed out a, "Yes."

When Ford tucked a bent arm under his head, his lightly furred pecs flexed.

Dylan pulled his eyes from that cock-hardening display when Ford gruffly ordered, "Get that and your lube."

"I see where this is going," he grumbled.

Ford's eyebrows rose at the same time his eyes narrowed.

His firm expression also indicated that he was slipping into his Dom role. "Did you expect any different?"

His tone screamed *don't even think about talking back.* "No." Should he add "Sir" onto that? He wasn't sure he'd be comfortable with calling his employee that, even after hours.

Ford also hadn't demanded that yet. Maybe he wouldn't because when the tables were flipped, he might not want to use that same honorific for Dylan.

"Then be a good boy and get your plug. If you have more than one size, it'll be your choice, but be smart about it. Lube it up generously, as well as yourself. Once that's done, bend over and let us watch you put it in."

Dylan lost his breath, and a spark ignited in his gut. He had never, ever let anyone watch him put in a plug. Now Ford wanted him to do it in front of Erin?

Ford was right, though. Choosing the right plug would make what would happen later a bit easier.

He rolled off the bed, went to his toy cabinet and opened the double doors.

Erin whispered a, "Wow," behind him.

Ford murmured, "That's quite an extensive collection."

Inside the floor-to-ceiling built-in cabinet were loads of shelves, some of them full of themed storage containers. In addition, there were hooks to hang accessories, like rope, chains and floggers. It was also well stocked with a variety of oils, lubes and other bondage items. He tried to think of everything so he'd be ready for any situation.

When he'd sat down to make a list, he thought he'd be having sex with a variety of guests. Boy was he wrong! He never expected to end up in a poly relationship—if this was where it was headed—with his high school sweetheart and his facilities manager.

He dug around the small container holding anal plugs

and found one neither too small nor too big. He chose one large enough to help stretch him without a lot of discomfort.

However, it still wouldn't be enough to make penetration easy. Ford would have to go slow, and he wouldn't blame the man if he didn't. Not after what Dylan did to him up in Heaven's impact playroom.

After also snagging a container of his favorite lube, he returned to the bed, already sporting half of an erection.

Ford rose onto his elbows to get a clearer view, while Erin curled deeper into his side, only lifting her head high enough to turn her eyes Dylan's way.

His insides quivered at the little show he was about to give them.

"Hurry up and lube that plug, then turn around and get it done, because I need a nap." Ford added a warning, "And so will you."

Dylan popped open the tub of Boy Butter and spread a generous amount over the latex butt plug. Once done, he turned until his ass faced the bed. He slowly bent over, wondering if the heat in his face meant he was blushing. He sure hoped not. That would make what he was about to do so much worse.

After taking a couple of calming breaths, he pulled one cheek to the side.

"That's it, spread them wide. Don't be shy, boss."

He felt as far from a boss as he could get at the moment. Exposing his anus to his cx, as well as his employee, made his heart pound wildly.

He needed to get over any embarrassment or discomfort. If this threesome became a regular occurrence, they would end up seeing every inch of each other's bodies, anyway. They would also see each other in very vulnerable positions, like right now. Beyond that, they would watch each other lose control mid-climax or during certain scenes, and most people's "orgasm" face wasn't very attractive. Unless it was fake, of course.

Throughout his thirty-five years, he'd never been shy about his body. That made it even more aggravating that he was currently doubting himself.

Using his opposite forearm—the one with the plug-occupied hand—he pushed on his other cheek, trying to spread himself open wide enough. A soft growl of frustration slipped from him when he failed.

In the past, he had held the heavily lubed plug steady, squatted over it before sitting down and driving it home. For the most part, that made insertion easy. But Ford had ordered him to bend over. Dylan couldn't defy him. Not unless he wanted to be punished later for being disobedient.

He did not.

When trying to seat it again, the slippery plug almost escaped his fingers. They were close to watching it bounce on the floor and across the room. That would've been *hilarious*.

He frowned.

"Darlin', help him out," Ford ordered next.

"By holding him open or inserting it, Sir?"

"I'll let you choose."

Shit. Shit. Shit.

He didn't need to turn around or glance up in the mirror to know Erin had climbed off the bed and approached. He could feel her heat and pick up her scent. He also couldn't miss her breathing since she wasn't quite panting, but it was definitely accelerated.

After extracting the plug from his grip, Erin waited for Ford to direct her, even though she most likely knew what came next.

She was giving Ford the power.

"Your hands are now free, boss, so spread yourself wide. Don't be shy. Darlin', let him have another scoop of that butter first. He'll need it."

Digging his fingers into his own ass cheek, he again pulled one to the side as the container appeared within his vision. Taking a generous scoop, he worked it in his crack, over his hole—now pulsing along with his heartbeat—and even worked some inside.

"Work it in there good, boss." Ford's voice was thick. Dylan wouldn't be surprised if the man was hard again already.

Dylan was on his way there, too, himself.

"Darlin', make sure you drive it in there deep so there's no risk of it popping out."

Dylan held his breath as Erin dragged the lubed tip across his hole a few times before stopping at his entrance and pushing against it gently.

She'd put pressure on it, then let up. Over and over again. Working it a fraction deeper each time. At that pace, she'd be back there a lot longer than he preferred.

"Just do it, darlin'. He can take it. That plug isn't that big and I'm bigger than that. If he can't take that tiny toy, he's going to have a rough time taking me."

Jesus. Dylan didn't have a humiliation kink and that was what Ford was dishing out.

Ford followed up with, "And that's what you want to watch, right?"

A long, wispy breath escaped Erin's lips. "Yes, Sir. I want to watch you fuck him and make him come before you come inside him. And if I may, Sir? I would like to see a generous use of your mouth and hands, too."

"Both of us? Or do you want him restrained so he can't move?"

Oh shit. Please, Erin, don't agree with that. Not tonight.

"I'd prefer to see you two interacting with each other."

Thank fuck.

"And what will you be doing, darlin'?" Ford asked her next.

"Anything you order me to, Sir."

Ford's whispered praise of, "Good girl," even drew a shiver from Dylan.

She increased the pressure but still had to fight through him tensing.

"Relax, boss," Ford ordered.

Dylan closed his eyes and imagined himself shaking off his worry the same way a dog shook off water. He'd used plugs on himself plenty of times in the past, so he wasn't new to this. He needed to stop being an idiot.

Relax. The sooner you do, the sooner this display will be over.

He slowly pulled in a breath through his nose and just as slowly, released it out of his mouth, letting the tension go with it. Luckily, that technique loosened his muscles enough so Erin had no problem deeply seating the plug.

Dylan remained bent over until the uncomfortable stretch lessened to the point he could finally breathe again. He clenched his ass cheeks together, testing, then straightened. He felt so damn full.

He was surprised how quickly he adapted to the size. He hoped it would be the same with Ford's cock, a hell of a lot thicker and longer than the plug.

"That was quite a sight," Ford murmured as Erin once again joined him in Dylan's oversized bed. "I can't wait to exchange it for the real thing. Let's get some rest in the meantime."

Erin settled in the middle of the mattress and once again

curled around Ford. Dylan, moving gingerly, joined them, tucking Erin between them. It didn't take long for the three to drift off.

———

Ford's eyelids lifted enough to see no one had shut off the lights, so the room was still bathed in a reddish hue. Soft breathing came from the woman asleep with her thigh pinning his. Her fingertips were curled amongst his dark chest hairs and her cheek plastered to his pec.

Lifting his head, he saw Dylan spooning her tightly with his hazel eyes closed and his steady breathing a bit louder than Erin's.

Since Ford had fallen asleep on his back, he was sure he'd been snoring. Apparently not loud enough to keep the other two-thirds of the threesome awake.

After carefully extracting himself from Erin, he went to the attached bathroom, grabbed a drink directly from the sink's tap, splashed water on his face and stared at himself in the mirror for a few seconds.

Both his own sleepy brown eyes and his very awake erection stared back.

At least one part of his body recognized what time it was.

After fantasizing about it for weeks, he would finally get the chance to fuck his boss. Not only fuck him but dominate him. He wasn't sure which made him harder.

If Dylan went back on his word, Ford would never share Erin with him again. Their polyamorous relationship would be over before it ever took root.

It was great that both, or either of them, could have sex with Erin. It was also great if Dylan wanted to give him a hand job or blowjob. He certainly wouldn't refuse either. But if he couldn't top the man, Ford was done.

They had both agreed to be willing to bend. That meant Dylan could fuck Ford one time and Ford could fuck Dylan another. It didn't have to be exactly one for one. It only needed to be somewhat fair.

Ford also hoped that this poly relationship would be fluid and not need any strict rules. For example, if Erin decided to have a night where she only watched the two men have sex, then they should respect that decision.

Same with having sex individually, but they needed to discuss that in more detail. Would it bother Ford if Dylan had sex with Erin when he wasn't around? While he hadn't minded what happened between the two of them in the tack room that day, that didn't mean it would always be the case.

If Dylan or Ford, or even Erin, was feeling even just a little bit jealous or left out, they needed to be honest and explore why that was and quickly address the issue before it festered.

A relationship between two people was difficult enough, but three would be a whole other dynamic. Honesty, respect and loyalty would be the key to their success.

While Ford and Erin had an open relationship previously and didn't have to confess to each other if they went elsewhere for some fun, he knew Dylan would want to lock them down. He already hinted that he didn't want Ford fucking men in State College. He also stated flat-out he only wanted to share Erin with Ford and no one else.

Was Ford ready to be "tied down?" The only reason he never wanted an exclusive relationship with Erin was because Ford also had the urge to be with men. He was afraid if he chased that desire while being a couple, she'd feel he cheated on her and then their relationship would sour to the point it couldn't recover.

He didn't want to lose Erin but also didn't want to give up men. He had been completely honest about that with her right from the beginning, except he never shared that the "others" in his life were men. That was why they had stayed on the path they'd been traveling... at least until Dylan stepped into that path.

Would just any woman accept Ford's desire for men? No, but Erin wasn't just any woman. She was special. Proof was her being sandwiched between two men in the bedroom. She was open-minded and open-hearted.

Warmth pooled in his gut.

That right there was why he loved her. Something he never told her because they didn't have that kind of relationship. But now they might if these puzzle pieces fell into place.

Whether they would or not would be revealed when Ford went back in that room and if Dylan let him take control.

Again, if the man backed out, that puzzle would end up only consisting of a single piece and it wouldn't be him or Erin.

Ford hoped to avoid that disappointment.

Chapter Twenty-Three

When Ford reentered the bedroom, two sets of eyes turned his way. "If either of you need to go, I'd suggest going now."

"Me first!" Erin shouted with a giggle, then quickly rolled off the bed and disappeared into the bathroom.

Approaching the bed, Ford studied Dylan. He was looking a bit tense. "How's the plug feeling?"

Dylan sat up. "Fine."

Ford raked his gaze over his defined chest and arms. "When you go in the bathroom, take it out." He held out the large towel he found in the bathroom's linen closet. "You're going to need this."

Dylan's hazel eyes fell to it. "Maybe."

Ford tipped his head to the side and assured him, "Promise you will. Place it in the center of the bed." When his boss didn't move quickly enough, he followed with, "Get that done now," in a tone that didn't invite any argument.

That got Dylan moving faster. As he got out of bed and

put the towel in place, it was hard to miss the state of his cock. Despite his obvious nervousness, he was already semi-hard.

Ford could take that as a good sign, but didn't want to be too optimistic. Yet, anyway. He wouldn't be until he was buried deep inside the other man.

However, he was willing to make things easier on him. Unlike when Dylan fucked him. "Do you have a vibrating plug?"

One dark blond eyebrow popped up. "Yes."

"Get it. Erin will fuck you with it while you suck me. I want you so worked up you'll be begging for my cock." The resulting look Dylan delivered made Ford add, "I accept that unspoken challenge."

As Dylan went over to the cabinet holding his extensive toy collection, the bathroom door opened behind Ford.

A second later, Erin was at his side, bouncing on her toes. "What are we doing?"

Her excitement was palpable, and he struggled to hide his own. "*I'm* doing him."

"I figured that. What's he digging for?"

"Do you think I can't hear you?" Dylan grumbled with a shake of his head and still facing the cabinet.

She pressed a hand over her mouth to smother a giggle. "What are you searching for?"

"A vibrating plug," Ford answered before Dylan could.

"*Ooooh*," she breathed. "But—"

He cut her off before she asked too many questions. "You'll see." Once Dylan turned and handed it to Erin, Ford ordered, "Go do what you need to do."

After an exchange of glances, Dylan obeyed and headed to the bathroom. He'd prefer that Dylan say, "Thank you, Sir," but it was better not to push his luck tonight. He grabbed the tub of Boy Butter and handed it to Erin. "Lube that up good."

"For you?"

He shook his head. "No, for you to use on him."

"But—"

"Darlin', " he warned with a growl.

Her smile was blinding, and she gave him a sharp salute. "Yes, Sir!"

He hooked her around the waist, yanked her into him and planted a fat kiss on her lips. "You're the best," he whispered against her mouth.

"I can't wait to watch the two of you," she whispered back, reaching up and cupping his cheek. Her eyes were heated and she practically vibrated with eagerness.

It was infectious. "I hope he doesn't chicken out."

"He won't."

Ford nodded and, with his eyes on the bathroom door, reluctantly released her. "He's taking longer than expected in there."

"He could be giving himself a pep talk. Or struggling to take out the plug. Should I go in and help him?"

"No. Let him take whatever time he needs."

With her bottom lip pulled between her teeth, she nodded.

While they waited, Erin generously lubed the anal vibrator and Ford positioned himself at the top of the mattress. With his thighs spread, he sat on his heels and adjusted the towel so it properly protected the bed.

Ford held his breath when the bathroom door opened. Would Dylan be willing or would he back out?

"You good?" Ford asked him. The man's eyes flicked from the thin, black, beaded anal plug in Erin's hand to him.

With his expression locked down, Dylan responded, "Yes."

Ford took him at his word and pointed to the center of the bed. "On your knees, facing me."

Taking a deep breath, Dylan's chest rose and fell. He also did as he was told.

Ford patted his bare thighs. "Come closer and give me your mouth."

When their knees touched, their gazes locked for a second.

"Give me your mouth," Ford demanded again.

"Take it," Dylan challenged.

Ford raised his eyebrows. "You want to be a brat? If so, I can treat you like one."

As a Dom himself, Dylan knew exactly how brats were dealt with. Did the man *want* to be punished? That would be a twist Ford hadn't expected.

However, he wouldn't let Dylan push him. Not this time. The time for rough play would come later. Dylan needed to be comfortable with Ford topping him first.

His hand snaked out to grab Dylan by the back of the neck, yanking him closer until their mouths slammed together. He demanded entrance and his tongue explored every corner. Ford claimed Dylan's mouth and would soon be claiming his ass as well.

In the back of his mind, it dawned on him that Dylan wasn't resisting. In fact, Ford only received a low groan in response.

His boss was suddenly being submissive? To test that, Ford pushed the kiss deeper, thinking Dylan would want to battle with their tongues.

He didn't.

The fine hairs on the back of Ford's neck prickled. Was

this a trick? Dylan went from a Dom to a brat to being submissive within minutes?

This had to be a trap.

When Ford twisted his head enough to end the kiss, they were both rock hard and breathless.

Dylan gripped Ford's beard with his other hand planted on Ford's pumping chest. He searched his boss's face but only saw the heavy eyelids, the heat behind his hazel eyes and slightly parted lips.

Nothing jumped out at him as suspicious.

Ford needed to stop being paranoid by thinking Dylan was setting him up in some way. His reactions, or lack thereof, could stem from an internal struggle.

Ford leaned back and, while keeping a tight grip on Dylan's neck, pushed his head down. "Now, give me your mouth again. This time on my cock."

Dylan's face hovered over Ford's pulsing erection. "Do you want to hold it," he swallowed hard and the added, "Sir?" seemed a bit forced.

That must have been painful for him to say. Using the honorific wasn't one of Ford's requirements so it actually surprised him when Dylan did. *Without* being instructed.

Of course, that had him once again thinking this was a trap. He expected Dylan to fight him at every turn.

The two of them would need to have a discussion about this turn of events. Preferably without Erin present and when both were not naked and hard.

For now, the night needed to progress. If it was up to Ford, he'd go right to having Dylan climb on his lap and ride him like a pole dancer. But he would be a nice Dom and do what he said earlier by getting his boss worked up so he was more relaxed, even begging for it and unable to hold out any longer.

Like Dylan, Ford was overthinking what was about to happen. Even so, he realized calling Dylan "boss" wouldn't work in this situation. He needed to find a pet name for him for those times he was the bottom and not an equal. He'd save it for when Ford was bottoming. He'd simply make the title a capital 'B' in that situation and still use the lowercase 'b' during the workday.

That would keep things interesting.

Since he was the Dom in this situation, Ford still needed a missing piece of important information. "What's your safe word?"

When Dylan's eyes lifted to his, he met Ford's gaze straight on, just like a brat would. "I use the traffic light system. I planned on suggesting we all use it so we don't have to worry about remembering different safe words. Especially in the heat of the moment."

That was smart. "I'm good with that. Erin?"

Perched on her knees behind Dylan, she nodded. "Sure, but how does it work?"

"It's simple. If we're checking in and we ask for a color, you use 'green' to mean you're good or to keep going, 'yellow' for caution or slow down, and 'red' to stop immediately," Ford explained. "During play, green can also be used to tell us to take it up a notch and yellow would tell us to drop it down a notch, even if we don't ask."

"Easy enough. But what if I'm gagged?" she asked.

He glanced down at Dylan, now fisting the root of Ford's cock but he hadn't put it in his mouth yet.

Damn shame, that.

However, what they were discussing was important. Especially since Dylan's mouth would be full in a minute or two.

Dylan explained, "If your hands are free, then one tap for

green, two for yellow, and three for red. If someone is bound and gagged, we can continue using the bandana method like we did earlier."

He glanced across Dylan to Erin. "Are you good with that?"

"Yes."

"Then, it's set." One side of his mouth pulled up. "Time to gag you, *boss*." *Damn*, he still needed a better pet name for the man. Maybe he'd just go with it and see what came out naturally. He pushed down on Dylan's head. "Take it."

He wasn't expecting a slow smile to cross Dylan's face before he swallowed Ford's cock so deeply that the crown bumped the back of this throat.

Holy shit.

Dylan stayed there for a few seconds before he slowly lifted his head while dragging his tongue along the underside of Ford's length.

Ford wanted to drop his head back, close his eyes and just ram into Dylan's mouth over and over until he came down the man's throat.

He pulled his shit together because he was not getting robbed of his chance to fuck Dylan tonight. He could come down the resort owner's throat during a lunch break. In fact, he might put that on his work schedule.

As guarded as Dylan had been so far, he was the complete opposite while sucking Ford's cock. In fact, he was so enthusiastic about it, Ford's suspicions ramped up once more.

No matter what, the man was skilled. It could be he just enjoyed giving blowjobs and got off on giving them, too. Some people did. Erin loved to suck his cock, and she got extremely soaked while doing so. If Dylan was the same, then he should be thankful Ford insisted on putting a towel down to protect his fitted sheet. Erin, too, since she'd most likely be the one stuck in the middle of the bed later when they fell asleep.

His attention was pulled from Dylan's bobbing head when Erin asked, "Now?"

"Yes."

Dylan paused mid-bob as Erin turned on the toy's vibration and began to insert it. She was being slow and cautious, even though this beaded plug was long and narrow, unlike the one Dylan removed in the bathroom.

Ford stroked Dylan's hair and watched Erin fucking him with it for a few heartbeats. While he couldn't see exactly what Erin was doing back there—even in the mirror above them—he *could* see her reaction.

Obviously, she was enjoying this, evident by the gleam in her eyes. She also played with Dylan's heavily hanging sack.

A moan and a sudden twitch proved she was hitting the right spot. She was now an expert when it came to locating the prostate. She loved watching Ford's cock leak uncontrollably whenever she stimulated his.

Between sucking Ford's cock and Erin playing with him, Dylan begging Ford to fuck him might actually become a reality.

He pushed Dylan's head back into motion. "All the way down." When Dylan responded immediately by doing what he was told, Ford whispered, "That's a good boy."

Dylan's groan in response to the praise vibrated around Ford's length. He wasn't expecting that reaction. Instead of stiffening up, Dylan relaxed even more and got back to sucking Ford's cock with even more vigor.

Ford really needed to relax and enjoy it instead of overthinking this whole thing. But before he could do that, Dylan began to tremble a few moments before everything on him went tight. A sign that Ford should check in.

Using handfuls of the man's dark blond hair, Ford jerked Dylan's mouth free. "Color?"

Dylan's eyes were dark, his lips shiny and his voice gruff when he answered, "Yellow. Unless you want me to come, Sir."

"I don't. Not yet." He met Erin's inquisitive gaze over Dylan's bare back. "Darlin', I'm ready to switch with you. He's going to eat you like the good boy he is while I fuck him. If he's not doing it the way you'd like, I want you to instruct him. If he doesn't follow those instructions, he'll be punished."

Her, "Okay," came out breathy.

She probably had some residual cum still inside her from their two loads earlier, but Ford didn't care. If he found that a turn-on, Dylan might, too. If not, the man would need to get over it since Ford wanted to keep Erin involved and not feeling left out at all.

Erin tipped her chin down. "Leave it in?"

"For now."

Erin pumped the vibrator in and out a few more times, before driving it deep one final time, getting off the bed and coming around to the headboard. Ford glanced down at Dylan, whose eyes were now turned toward Erin.

Ford tapped him under the chin to get his attention. "You're going to eat her pussy until she comes. Understood?"

"Yes... Sir."

Ford's whispered, "Good boy," drew a tremor from Dylan.

He thumbed off a bead of precum clinging to the crown of his cock and dabbed it onto the tip of Dylan's nose before extracting himself from where he'd been positioned.

He waited for Erin to settle in his place, then leaned over and, while kissing her thoroughly and drawing his tongue through her mouth, he pinched her nipple hard. When she gasped, he gave her another quick kiss and went to the bottom of the bed.

He took in the sight of Dylan bent over with his knees spread and only the ring of the beaded anal plug visible. A string of cum connected the tip of his erection to the towel underneath.

Seeing that made Ford's mouth water since he also got off on giving head.

The mattress listed slightly when he climbed on and shuffled closer. He noticed Dylan's head wasn't buried in Erin's pussy yet.

Was he starting to panic? Was he worried that Ford would be rough?

"You're not doing what you were told," he warned the other man. "Spread your pussy, darlin', and show him where your clit is."

"I know where it is," Dylan muttered.

"I wasn't sure since you look a bit confused."

"I'm not—" Dylan shook his head, grabbed Erin's hips and yanked her closer. Then his head dropped, and he blocked Ford's view of her pretty pink pussy.

"Don't forget to instruct him if he needs it. Make sure he doesn't let up until you come."

"I will," Erin assured him.

"And when you come, I want to hear it. The louder you are, the more I'll trust he knows what he's doing."

Dylan had no response to that because he was too busy with his mouth on her clit.

Chapter Twenty-Four

Erin's facial expressions proved that Dylan's skill at giving head could be applied to both men and women equally.

"When he's a good boy, tell him," Ford added but wasn't sure if Erin was paying attention at this point. She already appeared lost in what Dylan was doing.

Ford hooked a finger in the ring of the vibrating anal bead/plug combo and pulled it almost all the way out. After letting it buzz for a few seconds at the rim, he drove it home again.

He managed to do that two more times before getting overly impatient to be inside the man.

When Dylan and Ford met to devise tonight's game plan, they had a lengthy discussion on whether to use condoms or not. In the end, they decided against it with the caveat they would have to stick to the threesome in the future and not wander elsewhere. Despite the requirement of not straying outside their triad, they would continue to get tested on a regular basis.

Ford already trusted Erin completely and he had to trust

that Dylan wouldn't be hooking up with the resort guests. Or anyone else for that matter.

They had to be "all in" on the threesome, or all out. This couldn't be a one foot in, one foot out relationship, especially if the only protection between them would be Erin's birth control. As it was, those pills would only guard the three of them against one thing: pregnancy. Ford didn't think any of them were ready for that, threesome or not.

He shook that thought free because he needed to concentrate on making this a good experience for Dylan. This way he wouldn't be against bottoming in the future. Because if he was, then this would be their one and only night together.

Ford was sticking to his guns on that point.

He continued using the toy until Dylan was not only groaning and moaning against Erin's pussy but bucking against Ford's hand.

He had wanted Dylan to beg for it before he replaced the toy with his own cock, but the man's mouth was occupied, and he didn't want to interrupt Erin's current state of bliss.

Ford would use his own judgement that the man was ready.

Slipping the toy free, he climbed off the bed, put it aside and grabbed the tub of lube from the nightstand.

He watched the two on the bed for a few seconds while applying the lube to his own cock by stroking up and down the length to spread it around. When done, he took the tub and got back into position on the bed.

As he studied Dylan's very fine ass, he was tempted to leave marks on it the same way he liked to do with Erin.

Patience. If tonight works out, you'll have plenty of opportunities for that in the future.

That gave him more motivation to make sure everything

went smoothly tonight. What happened next might make or break this threesome.

Dig deep for that patience.

Using a copious amount of Boy Butter, he made sure Dylan was well prepped inside and out. Then, holding his breath, he lined himself up.

It was finally happening. Keep your shit together.

When Dylan's ass cheeks clenched in anticipation, Ford whispered, "Relax."

Without lifting his head from Erin's pussy, Ford saw the man's rib cage expand. Ford waited for him to release that deep breath, along with some of that tension, and pressed onward.

"Relax, boss," he murmured. The man was so damn tight, Ford was having a difficult time entering.

He decided small movements would make it easier for both of them. It helped him work his way inside slowly, but steadily. He stopped about halfway, giving them both a break. Especially after the thought of not only fucking his boss and Erin's ex, but fucking another Dom, almost finished him right then and there.

With Dylan clamped so tightly around him, Ford needed to distract him. He ordered Erin, "Pinch your own nipples." He swatted Dylan's ass. "Keep eating but watch her."

Holy shit, did it turn him on every time he bossed Dylan around, especially since the man was a Dom himself. Ford did not expect that heady power trip.

For a few seconds, he watched Erin twisting her own nipples in the mirror above, then asked, "Is he paying attention?"

Erin glanced down to check. "Yes, Sir."

She had no reason to use that honorific right now, but he let it go. "Is he still eating your pussy?"

"Yes, Sir."

"Do you think he'd look better with a few stripes decorating his ass?"

When Erin's eyes flicked up to his, she hesitated a second. "No, Sir, not tonight. But I'd love to see that in the future."

She wasn't the only one. "Do you think he'd enjoy it?"

"Yes, Sir, I do, since you're so good at it."

"Thank you, darlin'. Now, I'm about to bury myself to the root. If he stops eating you, I want you to flick his ear hard with your fingernail until he begins again. He always needs to put you first over himself. That also means he must make you come before either of us do." He again swatted Dylan's ass. Of course, softer than he normally would. "Do you understand your assignment, boss?"

A muffled, "Yes," came from between Erin's thighs.

"Yes?"

"Sir," was added, again reluctantly.

Ford turned his attention back to his pleasurable task and pulled Dylan's ass cheeks farther apart. "My cock in your ass is such a breathtaking sight. I wish you could see it, boss." He glanced up at the mirror on the ceiling, then asked Erin, "Can you see it clearly?"

"No, Sir."

Damn, that was a shame. While he had hoped Dylan could watch himself getting fucked, Ford didn't want to switch positions.

Next time they'd put that mirror to good use.

He slapped Dylan's flank at the same time he jutted his hips forward, driving himself to the hilt. He paused again, but not for Dylan's benefit this time.

Ford silently counted to ten, took a few deep breaths,

grabbed the man's hips to hold him in place and began to pump.

At first, he kept his thrusts short. Slowly, he lengthened them until he was driving all the way in and pulling almost all the way back out.

Dylan arched his back and tipped his ass upward. The moan against Erin's pussy was most likely due to Ford dragging his cock over the man's prostate every time he pushed deep and again when he slid out.

If it had just been the two of them, Ford would've closed his eyes and gotten lost in what was happening, but he couldn't. He was in charge right now. He was also responsible for making sure Erin was getting what she needed from the man face-planted between her legs.

"Darlin', are you good?"

Her eyelids barely lifted when she moaned, "Oh yes. So good, Sir."

She kept tugging on her own nipples since he didn't order her to stop. He was enjoying the show too much.

"Warn me when you're about to come."

"Yes, Sir," she moaned.

"Are you close?"

"Yes, Sir."

"Whatever you need to get you there, tell him."

She nodded.

"I want to hear it, darlin'."

She dropped her gaze back to Dylan. "Fuck me with your fingers and suck my clit hard... *Yes*... like that..."

"Is that what you want?" Ford asked.

"*Yes*... Oh, yes... Sir..."

"Are you about to come?"

"*Yessss*," hissed from her.

"Eyes on me when you do. I want to see how hard he

makes you come." They locked eyes over the man they currently shared. "Let go of your nipples, shove his face deep and ride it. Mess up that beard."

She drove her fingers as best as she could into Dylan's short, dark blonde hair and lifted her hips at the same time shoving his face down. With a loud cry, she bucked against him as she came.

After a few more hip twitches, she flopped back to the mattress with a satisfied sigh.

One side of his mouth pulled up due to the dramatic display. "Are you done?"

A huge smile spread across her very pleased face. "Yes, Sir."

"Dylan, you can stop now." He still needed to come up with a better pet name, one that wasn't degrading. "Darlin', use your mouth to clean up his."

When he tapped Dylan's hip, the other man rose up enough so the two could share a very thorough kiss. Ford knew exactly what they tasted, since he had eaten Erin's pussy too many times to count. He reveled in the scent and tang of her arousal and could never get enough. He assumed Dylan would soon feel the same way.

"He was yours for a minute there, darlin'," Ford announced. "Now he's mine."

He snatched the resort owner by the hair and roughly yanked until Dylan rose up on his knees. Ford followed to keep them connected and clamped an arm across his chest to pin his boss against him.

Putting his mouth to Dylan's ear, he growled softly, "Are you ready for me to come inside you?" *He* sure was.

Dylan murmured, "Yes, Sir."

"Are you sure you don't want to come first?"

"If that's what you please, Sir."

"Such a good boy wanting to please me." Ford's whisper drew goosebumps from Dylan.

Ford continued thrusting up and into him, and when he pinched Dylan's nipples as hard as he could, he swore his cock was squeezed just as tightly. To test the theory, he did it again.

"So damn tight," Ford groaned against his neck, before sinking his teeth into the corded muscle.

Small amounts of fluid spurted from Dylan every time Ford hit his prostate. Too bad it was going to waste.

However, it didn't have to. He had an idea. A kinky one, of course.

"Darlin', suck his balls again," Ford ordered Erin.

After spinning around, she dropped to her back and tucked her head between Dylan's spread thighs, encircling his balls with her mouth and sucking hard.

Damn, he would love it if she did the same to him while he fucked Dylan.

Another time, he told himself. He'd put that on his long list of things for the threesome to do.

"Good girl." Ford was pleased she was totally into this experience so far. Even though this was a new dynamic for her, she hadn't hesitated or been intimidated at all. She had jumped right in enthusiastically. "Stroke his cock, too."

Not even being remotely gentle, Erin squeezed Dylan's cock from root to tip like trying to get the last little bit of toothpaste from the tube, milking more prostatic fluid from him.

That enthusiasm would be Dylan's downfall.

By keeping his thrusts short, he focused on the man's P-spot while Erin continued to tug on his cock, causing a moaning Dylan to jerk against him.

"That's it," Ford murmured against damp and heated

skin. "I want you to put stripes on her, but this time, not from a riding crop."

"Yes... Sir," Dylan forced out while Ford tweaked both of his nipples as hard as he could.

Ford recognized all the signs and obviously, so did Erin when she arched her back. The man was about to blow. "Keep it up, darlin', and get ready."

Ford paused his thrusting the second Dylan's body bowed, his head slammed back against Ford's shoulder, and his hips jerked in time with Erin's pumping fist.

Dylan's groaned, "Fuck," sounded like it came from deep within his soul. He jerked and twitched as his cum shot out and landed on Erin's breasts.

"Beautiful. Keep going, darlin'. Don't leave a drop."

It didn't take long for Dylan to cry out, "Red," around his panting.

"For me or her?" Ford asked.

"Her. Please, Sir."

Ford knew what it was like when his cock became super sensitive after an intense orgasm. "Stop what you're doing, darlin', but don't move." He reached around and swiped a finger through the man's cum on Erin's chest before lifting it to Dylan's lips. "Take it."

"Sir—"

"I didn't ask," Ford reminded him in his Dom voice. "Take it, Dylan."

After what Ford could only assume was an internal struggle, Dylan took his finger into his mouth and circled it with his tongue.

Ford slipped it free and repeated the action, but with three fingers next. He shoved the cum-coated digits into Dylan's mouth again and didn't remove them as he went back to thrusting up and into his boss.

Erin's was still reclined with her head tipped back to watch them. Seeing her smeared breasts, knowing he just made his boss eat his own cum, and having his cock deep up his tight ass was his limit.

Guaranteed he would pay for his actions next time but, *damn*, it was worth it.

He continued to pump through his own climax until it was over, then he planted himself to the root.

Once he could think straight again, he and Erin exchanged smiles, and he slipped free from Dylan. But before the man could move away, Ford pointed to the smeared cum remaining on Erin's breasts and ordered, "Now, use your mouth and clean up your mess."

Chapter Twenty-Five

With one hand holding open the refrigerator door and the other shifting foil-covered aluminum pans and plastic storage containers around, Erin leaned in closer, looking for something to quiet her growling stomach.

Erin walked into Dylan's wing earlier not knowing what the plan was or how much time she'd spend with him. It turned out they planned to surprise her.

Boy, was what happened a surprise. A happy one.

She really didn't think the men would work it out and the threesome would ever happen. Especially since they were both Doms.

Two Doms sharing one sub. She shook her head and sighed.

Between cat naps and sex, they shared with her their discussion and agreement about being flexible, which, in their case, meant both of them being a switch. It surprised her that Ford would agree.

When he took control during that second round, he was clearly in his element. She also noticed something interesting.

Beside the fact that Dylan had a freckle on his left inner thigh, she noticed he had totally blissed out while Ford fucked him.

In the beginning, Ford ordering him around made her ex tense up and a little defiant, but it didn't take long for him to embrace bottoming for Ford. Again, completely unexpected. Though, it was true she didn't know Dylan at thirty-five as well as she knew him as a teenager. Not even close, but she hoped to if the threesome proceeded.

Obviously, people changed emotionally, physically and sexually as they aged and gained more experience under their belt. Erin was proof of that.

It took Ford showing her the light when it came to the Dom/sub relationship. At first, she'd been shocked when he even hinted at it, then assumed he was kidding around. After that, those hints became suggestions. He also began to slip in some BDSM whenever they had sex, which she now recognized had been vanilla.

He slowly nudged her into the lifestyle by taking the time to show her what it was and explain the dynamics, what a turn-on it could be and how satisfying. As long as she was open to it, of course.

It turned out, she was.

While he started out slow as to not overwhelm her, she began to get impatient and encouraged him to take it further each time. Now, after years of playing together, they knew each other's likes and dislikes very well.

Despite the fact she had nothing or no one to compare him to, she considered Ford a great Dom and trusted him one hundred percent. He took care of her during light, fun sex, or a heavy scene, as well as afterward.

While he could be very dominating and controlling, as

soon as the scene was over, he was the exact opposite. He let her be independent.

She could only assume, now with the potential of two Doms in her life, her independence might be reduced. Especially if they turned this into a permanent polyamorous relationship. An exclusive threesome where they were dedicated to each other and none of them had sex outside the group unless all three agreed upon it first. A democracy of sorts.

They could bring in a resort guest one night for a foursome. Or maybe they'd enjoy a night of voyeurism, where two of them watched the third have sex with someone else.

The three of them discussed some of the endless opportunities being tied to an all-adult ranch resort that existed specifically to give a safe and supportive space for guests to lose their inhibitions and follow their desires.

Footsteps behind her, paired with a surprised, "Erin?" had her straightening and slamming the fridge door shut. She smothered her gasp and quickly pretended like she belonged in the farmhouse's kitchen, even though she didn't and was now busted.

"Dani!"

"What—"

"Do I want to eat?" Erin finished before Dylan's sister could ask the rest of her question. "Sorry, Dylan said it was okay. I was checking to see what was in the fridge." *Because we're starving for reasons I don't want to have to explain. Please don't make me since it involves your older brother.*

She grimaced and her eyes sliced to the door separating Dylan's wing and the shared kitchen.

Dylan, come make an excuse... please.

Next time she was packing a cooler full of snacks.

She tugged at the hem of Ford's T-shirt, the only piece of clothing she was wearing. Erin wondered how much of her pale butt Dani saw while she was bent over and staring inside the fridge. At least her cheeks weren't bright red from being spanked. Both hard and often.

Dani blinked a few times, then, as if someone pushed her *Start* button, she jerked into action and came closer.

Erin, self-consciously tugging at the T-shirt again, stepped aside to give her room. She also did it so Dylan's sister wouldn't get a good whiff. She was sure she smelled like sex, especially after having it with two men. Without condoms, or a shower yet.

She again shot a nervous glance at the closed door to Dylan's wing. *Please, please, please, if one of you come through that door, let it be Dylan.*

"I brought home a pan of chicken piccata along with some sides, leftover from tonight's dinner at the lodge. I got a hankering for it, so I came down to break it out and heat it up." She raised a single eyebrow. "Want some?"

She could see the burning curiosity in Dani's eyes and the fact she struggled not to ask why Erin was standing in their family's kitchen only wearing a T-shirt. One that didn't even belong to her or her brother.

Shit.

"Umm..." Truthfully, she wanted to go hide in Dylan's wing and not break bread with his sister. But if she hightailed it out of there, like a roach when someone flicked on a light switch, it might make it look even more suspicious. She needed to act like this was all normal. Unfortunately, she had no acting skills and would have to wing it. "Sure. If you don't mind. That sounds good. I'm ravenous."

"From?" If Dani was attempting to hide her amusement, she wasn't trying too hard.

"The workout I just had." *Shit. Don't panic.*

Danica's head tipped to the side. "Did Dylan install a gym in his wing when I wasn't paying attention?"

"Something like that," Erin murmured.

Dylan's sister was sharp. She'd have no problems putting two and two together.

When the door opened behind Erin, her heart skipped a beat, then began to race.

Despite being afraid to look, she couldn't resist watching Ford blow through it. He went from fifty miles an hour to a dead stop the second he spotted Danica pulling out the pan of leftovers from the fridge.

"Danica," he greeted carefully.

Dani's eyes went wide, and her mouth dropped open before she quickly plunked the tray of chicken piccata onto the counter. Probably so she wouldn't drop it in surprise.

With Ford only wearing a pair of Dylan's sweatpants—hanging deliciously off his hips—Danica's eyes instantly zeroed in on his lightly-haired, broad chest. Then they took a slow stroll south to take in the rest. Erin could imagine she was appreciating his sexy Adonis belt and defined six-pack abs. Add in that delicious dark, narrow path of hair leading from his navel to the trimmed patch around his cock.

Gray sweatpants, which tended to draw the female gaze on a normal day, combined with Ford's obvious lack of containment underneath them, made it impossible to conceal the outline of his nicely sized cock.

Apparently, neither Erin or Danica were immune from staring at it.

When Ford cleared his throat, Erin glanced over at Dylan's sister and their gazes met. Erin could see Dani fighting the urge to smile. Or drool. Or possibly both.

"What are you doing here, Ford?" Dani sounded over-the-top sweet. "Since you're dressed like that, I have to assume you were working out as well? Is my bonehead brother teaching fitness classes now?" She raised her hand with the palm out. "Let me guess, you're about to respond with, 'Something like that.' Where do I sign up for that kind of something?"

Ford, also attempting to look as if he belonged in the Lyons' family kitchen and that his presence was normal, deflected with, "What's in the pan?"

Erin helped him by unpinning her lips to answer, "Chicken piccata."

Seconds later, Dylan stepped through the door Ford had left open, took them all in, pulled in a breath and shook his head.

"Brother," Dani greeted, now wearing an over-exaggerated grin.

Erin was surprised she didn't wiggle her eyebrows and give him a, "*Bow chicka wow wow,*" along with it.

Dylan's tight mouth turned downward. "Sis."

"She's about to heat up some leftovers," Erin announced like this gathering in the kitchen was an everyday occurrence.

"Great," Dylan responded dryly. "Is there enough for everyone?"

Dani grabbed a spatula from a drawer and jabbed it toward the door to Dylan's wing. "Depends how many more of your students are about to come through that door."

Dylan's brow scrunched low. "Students?"

"Yes, of your"—she made air quotes—"fitness classes."

He blinked and glanced at Erin. She bugged her eyes out at him in a silent message.

"Yeah, *uh*... That's it," he grumbled. Dylan jerked his chin toward the aluminum covered pan. "Are you going to heat that up? Or just gawk at us?"

"I can multitask," Dani assured him and turned on the oven.

"Good, because I'm starving," Ford said.

"A good workout will do that to you." Dani rolled her lips under as she tented the foil over the pan.

"Wouldn't a microwave be faster?" Ford asked.

"Sure, if you want rubber chicken." Dani turned, leaned back against the counter and crossed her arms over her chest. "So..."

Dylan dropped his head and groaned.

"What kind of workout involves two men losing their shirts and one of them landing on Erin? Are you even wearing panties under that T-shirt?"

Of course not. She obviously wasn't wearing a bra, either. She hadn't thought about getting caught red-handed while searching for sustenance.

She and Ford shared a glance. Of course, he looked amused and didn't seem as freaked out over the situation as Erin and Dylan, despite the fact they all knew it wouldn't remain a secret if they stayed overnight.

Dylan must not have been mentally prepared to explain the situation sooner than expected. Now he had no choice.

"How long will that take to heat up, sis?"

"Longer than it will take you to go put on a shirt," Dani quipped.

With a single nod to his sister, Dylan announced, "I think I'll go put on a shirt," and headed back toward his wing.

"Good idea," echoed Ford and followed Dylan.

But, *lord*, did both men's asses look spectacular in the sweatpants. Though, Dylan's fit better, of course, and, unfortunately, covered the cut muscles at his hips and half of his own happy trail.

Dani called out, "Ford, if you want to remain shirtless, I

won't care. I'll only puke if I have to sit across from my half-naked brother while I'm trying to eat."

Ford hesitated in the doorway like he was considering it, but then he did a vanishing act through the opening when a hand grabbed his arm and jerked.

Apparently, *someone* decided that wasn't an acceptable plan. Only, now Erin was left alone with his sister. "Maybe I should go put on some—"

"Panties? Probably a good idea because you never know when our brother might come out here with the munchies. Not the brother running late-night, half-naked exercise classes. The other one."

Erin glanced toward Dayne's portion of the house before swinging her gaze back to Dani. With a nod and her holding the T-shirt's hem down as she went, she also went to get dressed.

———

DYLAN HELD the door open for Erin as they headed back into the kitchen. This time dressed. When she slammed on the brakes, Dylan bumped into her. That caused Ford to curse under his breath as he almost collided with Dylan.

He stared at the dining table that was now set and behind one of those place settings sat his twin.

He silently groaned. He knew they wouldn't be able to keep this a secret from his siblings if Ford and Erin made this a regular thing, but he had not been prepared to explain it right after their first actual threesome and, worse, at two in the morning.

A sigh slipped from between his lips.

"I set the table." Dayne announced his achievement with a grin, like he was five.

Dylan bit back, *"Do you want a cookie?"*

His brother waved a hand around the table. "Come. Have a seat."

"The piccata needs ten more minutes to be thoroughly heated," Danica added.

"I don't mind eating it cold," Dylan muttered as Erin was the first to head over to join his siblings. "Did we wake you, Dayne?"

"No, when I walked into the house, I could smell the food being warmed up."

Dylan raised an eyebrow at him. "You were out?"

"Why are you surprised? I mean, if anyone should be surprised in this scenario, it should be me, brother." Dayne jerked his chin at Ford and the lines at the corners of his eyes deepened. "Ford."

"Dayne," Ford returned the greeting.

"This an odd time to sit down for a family meal, isn't it?" Dani asked, still amused at the situation.

"We're only missing Mom," Dayne pointed out. "Maybe we should call her."

"Why the hell would you wake up Mom?" burst from Dylan as he approached the large wooden farm table.

"Maybe she'd be interested to see what her offspring were up to. Though, she'd probably be pleased we were sharing a family meal together."

"So, do you think she wouldn't care that you don't roll in until two a.m.?"

Dayne pursed his lips and scrubbed a hand over his jawline. "I don't think that's what would catch her attention." His gaze bounced from Ford to Erin and back to Dylan.

"It would be our sister's delicious chicken piccata?"

With a smirk, Dayne answered, "Sure."

"She's already tried it," Dani volunteered. "And she does

think it's super fucking awesome. As is everything else I make."

"You direct the kitchen staff," Dylan reminded her.

Dani shrugged. "Still my kitchen, my cooks and my choice of ingredients. Just think of me like a conductor of an orchestra. I might not be the one playing the individual instruments, but I guide the musicians."

Dylan rolled his eyes.

"So, Ford... I'm assuming you won't be late for work tomorrow morning since you're already here?" Dayne, apparently already bored with the direction of the conversation, brought it right back to where Dylan preferred it didn't go. Though, realistically, it would be impossible to avoid. He swore his twin didn't even have a sliver of decorum.

"I'll need to go home to change," their facilities manager answered, pulling out a chair and settling in across from Dayne.

"You didn't bring a change of clothing?"

"No."

"So, all of this," Dayne waved his hand between Ford, Erin and Dylan, "was simply an impulse?"

Chapter Twenty-Six

OF COURSE it hadn't been an impulse. The only impulse decision was him asking them to stay the night. Dylan certainly wasn't telling Dayne about the plan he and Ford came up with. It was none of his brother's business, just like it wasn't any of Dylan's business who Dayne had hooked up with tonight. As long as there weren't any guest complaints, it didn't matter.

The resort was meant to be judgement free. Dylan also wanted the guests to be as open about their sexual desires, or their kinks and fetishes, as they were comfortable. He didn't care what they did with their partners or other guests as long as everyone consented.

The goal was to have everyone feel safe with their individual choices. That should also apply to him and his siblings.

"We were simply going over some... things," Dylan explained to his brother.

Of course, Dayne immediately looked at Erin, now sitting

next to Dylan. "Did you get hired on here at the ranch without me knowing?"

When her mouth opened to answer, Dylan grabbed her knee under the table and squeezed to stop her from answering. "She *is* a customer service rep."

Dayne's eyebrows shot up. "Okay? So, you three had a late-night meeting about our customer service?"

"It wasn't late night," Dylan mumbled. Was he only digging the hole deeper by making excuses?

"They must've had their meeting, then decided to work out afterward," Dani explained.

"I still don't understand why you'd have a business meeting in your residence instead of in our offices and not invite others. You know, like the other people who have a stake in it. Instead, you do it with your ex-high school sweetheart and our current facilities manager?"

Both of his siblings stared at him, waiting for his explanation.

One they knew wasn't coming and if it did, wouldn't be truthful.

Dayne stared at Erin across the table. "Or did you hire Erin as our newest employee?"

Her mouth gaped as she turned to Dylan for the answer. They hadn't really had an opportunity to discuss her job. They hadn't really had a chance to discuss her life in general.

Dylan still didn't know how Hart died, leaving her a widow. Ford never talked about it and it wasn't like they'd been sitting down, sharing a beer and having heart-to-hearts.

Obviously, he knew Ford and her had a connection. Dylan had been also trying to reestablish a connection with her. Up to now, he hadn't been in a rush to know everything. He'd been simply fighting for the opportunity to discover it. He figured once that occurred by establishing the threesome, all those blank gaps would eventually be filled in, along with the chance to dig even deeper.

However, that wouldn't be happening in the early hours of the morning sitting around a table with his family sharing reheated chicken piccata.

"She was only giving suggestions on what we could implement in the future. Having good customer service will help our guest retention rate. To make this resort a success, we need to strive for a high return rate and also for word-of-mouth recommendations." That actually sounded pretty damn good, if he said so himself.

"What you say is true but also complete bullshit." Dayne locked gazes with him. "You don't need to lie to us unless you're embarrassed. Are you?"

Dylan's eyes flicked from his twin to Erin, then to Ford. He couldn't speak for himself and not have it affect the other two. Would Ford have a problem letting the world know he was bisexual? Would Erin have an issue with the locals knowing she had sex with two men at the same time?

It wasn't Dylan's decision whether to publicly out them. Nor was it theirs to do the same to him.

But the two people sitting at the table with him wouldn't be judgmental, otherwise they wouldn't have joined him building and running the resort. However, they *could* be complete pains in the ass, as some siblings could.

Dayne loved to break balls, especially Dylan's. Danica wasn't some shy, wilting flower, either. She had plenty of opinions she had no problem sharing. Loudly.

"I'm not embarrassed. It's just nobody's—"

Dayne cut him off. "The burning question is, are you het or bi?"

Dylan's heart thumped heavily in his chest. "Why do you care?"

"Because you've always had that stick up your ass and now I'm wondering if you've replaced it with something else."

"At least my head isn't up my ass like yours is."

Dayne chuckled and sat back in his chair like the cat who ate the canary.

"Why do you care?" Dylan asked again.

Dayne's head twisted toward Ford. "How about you?"

Dylan informed their employee, "You don't have to answer."

Ford sat back in his chair and stared at Dylan for a few seconds before his eyes turned back to Dayne. "I'm bi. Always have been bi and I'm not embarrassed to admit it. But that doesn't mean others are as open as I am. As part owner of this resort, you should be aware that not everyone wears their sexuality on their sleeve. I don't around town, and you know why. We also don't share what Erin and I are to each other. Everyone simply thinks we're close friends. And do you know why? Because it's none of anyone's damn business."

"I'm family."

"So? We all have our secrets. Even from family."

Dayne cocked an eyebrow. "But why does he feel the need to hide it from us?"

"Why don't you ask yourself that," Ford suggested.

Dayne shrugged. "I'd be the last person to judge him. Tease, yes. Judge, no."

"Maybe he doesn't want anyone riding his ass about what he does."

"Or who he does," Dani added in a murmur.

"So, you're riding his ass?" Dayne wore an asshole grin when he turned to Dylan. "I didn't take you for a bottom, brother."

"He's not," Ford responded quickly, cutting off Dylan's answer.

"I didn't take you for one, either."

Ford's chin rose and he looked squarely in Dayne's eyes. "I'm not."

"*Ah.* Got it. You're sharing Erin but not each other."

"Why are you so determined to know our dynamics?" Erin's irritation at Dayne was beginning to show.

"He only wants that info so he can needle me," Dylan answered for his brother.

Dayne tipped his head to the side and shot him another grin. "I try to find any excuse."

"We know," Danica said next.

"You aren't any better," Dylan told his sister.

"We're siblings. It's what siblings do."

Erin clapped her hands together and exclaimed, "Boy, am I starving!"

Danica laughed softly and Dayne's grin widened.

"Anyway, I can't wait to hear what customer service suggestions you came up with, Erin." Dayne turned back to Dylan. "Should Dani and I expect a summary email or a face-to-face meeting?"

When the timer on the oven beeped, it took everything Dylan had not to jump out of his skin. Dani got up and headed over to check on the leftovers, saying, "Maybe we should just hire her for real. Our PR company does the marketing but doesn't deal with that aspect."

"I think that's a great idea, sis," Dayne said.

"I have a job," Erin murmured.

"We'll pay you better," Dayne told her.

We will?

"You don't know what my salary is."

"Dani's right," Dylan's twin said. "We could use someone who's knowledgeable in that department."

"I have a job," Erin repeated, her eyes now burning a hole into the side of Dylan's face.

"Do you like it?" Dayne asked.

"It's..." She grimaced. "It's dealing with the public, so honestly, it's exhausting some days."

"Worldwide?"

Erin nodded. "Yes."

"Here you would only be dealing with our current or potential guests. You'd be smoothing things over if there are issues. Handling... Well, if you've been in customer service for a while, you know what you'd be handling. I don't have to tell you."

She asked Dayne, "Will the customer always be right even when they are very, very wrong?"

"Absolutely not."

"Will I have to sit there and take abuse from a disgruntled guest?"

"No. We'll ask you to smooth things over as best as possible but the second someone comes at you being abusive, language or otherwise, you'll have every right to shut them down or pass them on to me or Dylan."

She sat up straighter. "Hold on. Is this a serious job offer?"

"Sure."

Funny how Dayne hadn't cleared this with Dylan first. But then he hadn't cared about Dylan's opinion when he hired Ford, especially when he knew the contractor had been seeing Erin.

"What are the benefits?"

Was she seriously thinking about working for the resort?

Did what Dylan thought was a joke become a serious offer? Did he even have a say in this?

"Can we discuss this tomorrow, instead?" Dylan asked his twin.

"The three main players of this ranch are all here right now," Dayne reminded him. "Do you have a problem hiring her?"

What the hell. Dayne was purposely putting him on the spot and Dylan would look like an asshole if he said yes.

It wasn't that he didn't think she'd be capable—despite having no firsthand knowledge of her skills in that respect—it was the fact he'd be having an intimate relationship with two of his own employees. Though, their employee handbook didn't prohibit any kind of relationship.

But then, their employee handbook was pretty damn thin. Basically, the "rules" were: show up for work on time, do the work you were assigned and treat each other, as well as guests, with respect.

Besides a customer service specialist, which would most likely be Erin's title if they went forward on this, they really should hire someone to be a human resources specialist, too, since their employee roster was growing. He and Dayne had been handling the HR stuff on their own and neither were experts. In fact, they'd been winging it. And when it came to benefits, payroll and the rest, it could be overwhelming. He didn't want anything slipping through the cracks that might cause issues with the government. Or cause lawsuits.

Owning a business and having employees was not easy.

Neither was having two nosey siblings who were smartasses.

Dylan tracked Dani as she returned to the table wearing oven mitts and carrying the large aluminum pan. His stomach growled in response.

"You didn't answer," pulled Dylan's attention back to his brother.

"I don't have a problem with it as long as she wants the job." That at least gave her an out if she was feeling pressured.

"Erin?" Dayne inquired.

"Depends on the benefits. I've been with my organization for years now. I was one of the first remote customer service reps they hired."

"Honestly, hiring her to manage guest services would be better." Dani removed the tray's cover and took a seat. "She could handle that whole portion. Manage the reception employees, manage customer complaints and inquiries..."

Sometimes he actually liked his siblings. They might bust his balls, but in the end, they always looked out for each other. However, while hiring a guest services manager would be smart, would it be good to hire someone he was sleeping with? It could get awkward. His eyes swung to Ford.

He grimaced. It was bad enough he was having sex with one employee, but two? "I think the three of us should have a sit-down tomorrow. This way we can discuss this new position and all it would entail in detail when I'm not so wiped."

One side of Dayne's mouth hiked up. "Good idea."

Dylan turned to Erin. "This way the managing partners can discuss salary and benefits, too, and come to you with a solid offer. Will that work?"

Erin lifted and dropped a shoulder. "Sure."

"Okay, now that's settled, let's eat," Dani said, beginning to serve the leftovers.

Dayne handed his plate to their sister to fill. "Can we get back to discussing why Ford and Erin are here in the middle of the night?"

"No," Dylan answered.

"So, Erin..." Dayne started.

Dylan shot a glare his way.

Dayne laughed and lifted a hand. "This has nothing to do with your threesome, brother, I swear." He turned back to Erin. "How come you had a crazy knack for telling us apart so easily?" He shoveled a piece of chicken into his mouth and chewed.

While he and Dayne might look the same on the outside, Erin could always see their differences. In some ways, they thought and acted the same, but in others, they were completely unalike.

Dayne had always been wilder. Somewhat of a loose cannon. While Dylan had always been the calmer, more responsible twin. Admittedly, he had always been more reserved, too. Still was, despite his kinky desires. Just because he had certain sexual proclivities didn't mean he had to be loud about it. Unlike his twin.

Back in high school, his brother had tried several times to trick her into thinking that Dayne was him and failed every time.

"Just luck, I guess," she answered, accepting a plate from Dani.

"Bullshit," Dayne said around a mouthful of parmesan green beans.

"Fine. If you really want to know... That time you kissed me? I felt nothing. No butterflies and certainly no spark."

Dayne jabbed his fork toward Dylan. "And you felt that with him?"

"Absolutely." Erin shot his twin a smile, then forked some garlic mashed potatoes into her mouth. "*Mmm*. This is delicious, Dani."

"It certainly is." Their sister rolled her lips under.

Dylan dropped his head and chuckled at his sister's double entendre at the same time Ford burst out laughing.

He couldn't agree more. Any day Dayne was put in his place was a good day.

Chapter Twenty-Seven

Erin glanced at the text message one more time to make sure she was headed in the right direction.

About an hour ago, Ford sent her an invitation to eat lunch with him since he was out working on the ranch. She not only accepted that offer, when she spotted Dylan a little earlier in the lodge, she asked him to come along. He and Dayne had a virtual meeting with their PR company but said if they were finished in time, he'd catch up with them.

Since Ford never packed his lunch, she carried a small cooler Dani was kind enough to fill to make sure they had what they needed for an impromptu "picnic."

One perk of being a Double D Ranch employee was the opportunity to eat for free in an employee break room off the lodge's kitchen. Most employees took them up on that offer since Dani's menu inarguably included the best food in the area. So no surprise, after his initial text asking her to join him, he followed up with: *Bring food from the kitchen.*

After the Lyons made her an offer she couldn't pass up, she officially began working at the ranch about two weeks ago as their new Guest Services Manager. Not only were the benefits decent, but the salary was a little better than what she'd been making, even after almost ten years at her former company.

It wasn't *buy-a-mansion-and-a-yacht* kind of money, but enough to pay her bills and live comfortably.

Before making the offer, the Lyons siblings also wrote up a detailed job description. Her new position managed the reception and reservation staff, ensuring rooms and cabins weren't overbooked and that the check-in and check-out process kept running smoothly. Her responsibilities also included responding to and solving guests' requests or complaints, as well as fielding all suggestions to improve current services or add future services. She was tasked with answering any questions that past, current or even future guests had. If she couldn't, she tracked down the information or passed it on to the appropriate staff member. All in hopes for repeat business or to draw new guests.

Basically, she was a liaison between the guests and upper management. That being Dayne, Dylan and Danica. They also had weekly meetings with her to go over problems, suggestions and strategies for improvement.

She loved the position more than she thought she would. Her previous job had kept her stuck in her tiny home office for over eight hours a day. She only interacted with customers on the phone and never in person.

Being contained in those four walls day in and day out was sometimes claustrophobic. While at the resort, she could stroll around, interact with the guests one on one and have actual conversations about potentially improving their stay, whether right away or in the future.

The guests also appreciated being heard by management,

which made them want to return or recommend the resort to their friends. They considered that a win-win.

Bookings were already picking up and they were almost at full capacity this week for the first time since the grand opening. She was pleased she had a small hand in that. One thing she heard over and over was, their guests really liked the fact, besides having management that listened, they were also hands-on. Like Erin, they were regularly walking around and checking in with guests to make sure all their needs were being met.

That particular praise made her smile since Dylan was definitely hands-on.

Since that first night when Dylan and Ford surprised her, they now got together on a regular basis. Beside using one of the playrooms twice—with the blinds drawn for privacy at Dylan's request—they also spent plenty of nights in Dylan's portion of the farmhouse.

It helped that his bedroom was well stocked for whatever mood they were in. If they didn't have a desired item, he added it to his collection.

The nights they played together were the same nights they stayed over. For Erin, waking up sandwiched between two very sexy and handsome men was the ultimate fantasy turned reality.

How crazy was it that one of those men was Dylan? She never imagined she'd be with him again after he ran away from Fisher Falls.

Maybe it was best that he did. Their lives would look so different if he hadn't. She had no doubt she would be stuck in a traditional marriage—whether with Dylan or not—and raising children right now. She might have ended up as a housewife dependent on her husband, where her choices were limited.

She'd been headed that way after she married Kyle. At the time she thought that was what she wanted and if Dylan hadn't left, she would've pursued that kind of life with him after she graduated.

But after Kyle died, Ford opened up her world, making her realize she might have ended up unhappy. Even eventually divorced, since it turned out that traditional relationships were not for her. It was why she embraced the easy connection she had with Ford for so many years.

She pulled fresh air deep into her lungs as she strolled in the warm sunshine.

She was lucky Ford helped her find her true self, whether that had been his goal or not.

The ranch might help others find theirs.

Now that things with the three of them were slowly falling into place, she had no regrets allowing Dylan back into her life.

He had changed. So had Erin. And Ford, well... She swore Ford knew who he was since birth.

Even better, allowing herself to live the life she actually wanted—and not one pressured into by society—made her more confident. She truly believed she could do anything, be anything, and she no longer cared what others thought. She also no longer felt the need to explain herself to anyone outside of her small circle. And that circle now included Dylan and his siblings.

However, she was also realistic when it came to anyone outside of the ranch. If this threesome continued on their current path, they would only get closer and eventually, they'd have to deal with judgement from some—if not most—of the residents of Fisher Falls.

While she didn't expect anyone else to understand it, she only needed them to not be assholes about it.

Speaking of assholes…

She paused and squeezed her butt cheeks together. Today was the first day Dylan insisted she work with a small butt plug in. He had bought her a beautiful stainless-steel plug with a bright blue jewel on the end, but before she could use it, he was starting her out with something smaller.

She knew where this was leading, and she wasn't against it. She'd had anal sex with Ford in the past but at the time, it hadn't been the best experience due to being an impulse and not planned in advance.

Now that the three of them were enjoying each other's company on a regular basis, Ford wanted to change that. Dylan took over the prep part with enthusiasm, of course.

Erin continued on her trek toward the new bunkhouse. Dylan had hired a few of Ford's old construction crew to work on the ranch since, when it came to animals—both two- and four-legged—something always needed to be replaced or repaired.

But in this case, extra hands were needed to build a bunkhouse to house both permanent and seasonal employees. Basically, if there was bunk space available, any employee needing a roof over their head—assuming they didn't mind living in communal housing—could grab a spot. The employee housing was also being expanded by building six cabins behind the new bunkhouse for staff in upper positions. Managers like Ford.

Of course, Ford opted out of taking one of the cabins since, like her, he owned his own home on the edge of town. Would it save him a monthly mortgage payment if he sold it and claimed one of the nicely sized cabins? Of course. But he wasn't at the point of wanting to sell yet and said he'd consider it in the future.

Erin had also been offered a cabin and turned it down—

for now—for the same reason as Ford. Too much was still up in the air. She was only newly employed by the ranch and their threesome was almost as new. If it went bad—the job or the relationship—she would need somewhere to go.

She adjusted her grip on the cooler and turned the corner of the almost completed building.

Hammering and drilling could be heard from inside the structure. Plus, all kinds of equipment and supplies were in stacks and piles around the exterior. She spotted a long ladder extended up to the pitched roof of the building.

Dylan designed it so the sleeping quarters were on the top floor and the main floor would consist of the shared bathrooms, kitchen and living space. When finished, the bunkhouse and the cabins wouldn't be anything like the ones she'd stayed in during summers at Girl Scout camp.

She shuddered. The ranch employees would have flushing toilets instead of latrines, of course, as well as actual clean showers instead of gross stalls the girls shared with spiders and other creepy crawlies.

She also couldn't forget the bats.

She shuddered again when her nostrils burned, remembering the pungent smell of lye sprinkled over a hill of human waste. It was still her least favorite memory.

Or so she thought.

She looked around for Ford but couldn't find him. He stated he'd be working outside today since the weather was perfect, so she began to circle the exterior until she heard him call her name.

When she glanced upward, she spotted him perched on the slanted roof with a nail gun in hand.

No.

Her sight narrowed and suddenly blurred.

No.

Her pulse thumped in her ears and her lungs seized, making it impossible to draw a full breath.

No.

"Ford," she forced out but not loud enough for him to hear.

No.

"Ford..." she tried again but failed.

Digging her fingernails into her palms, she tried to focus.

He was going to fall.

He needed to get down from there.

No!

"Ford!" He must have finally heard her since his blurry figure jerked into motion. He rose from where he'd been squatting and pointed a huge smile in her direction. "Hey, darlin'! I'll be—"

"Ford!" That scream came from deep within her soul.

With a furrowed brow, he made his way to the roof's edge and glanced down at her. "What's wrong?"

"Please, please, please." Her whispered chant came out broken. "Come... down."

He needed to get off the roof *now*.

"I'm fixing—" His dark eyes went wide for a second before he quickly put down the nail gun, moved to the ladder and began to descend. "I'm coming down."

"I can't. I can't. I can't." With that, she fell to her knees and pressed the heels of her palms into her eye sockets to block out both the current vision and the past memory. She didn't want to look until his two feet were planted firmly on the ground.

"You can't what?" came a deep voice behind her. *Dylan.*

She tried to block out the sound of Ford's boots making their way down the metal ladder, but it was impossible. She could hear them over her own pounding heartbeat.

Strong arms engulfed her, and Ford's soothing whisper filled her ear. "It's okay, darlin'. I'm safe and right here. Nothing bad happened. It's okay. I'm fine."

"Jesus," came from Dylan.

With her face buried in Ford's hot, damp neck, she curled her fingers into his chest and clung to him.

He was alive and in one piece. He was talking and walking. He was fine.

He was fine.

"Breathe," Ford encouraged as he rubbed her back. "Breathe."

She pulled air in through her nostrils and blew it out of her mouth.

She did it again, making sure her exhale was twice as long as her inhale, a method used in meditation. Breathing exercises had helped her for years after losing Kyle tragically.

After one more deep breath, she managed to open her eyes. The haze had cleared, and she was no longer looking down a long, dark tunnel.

Ford went nose-to-nose with her, his eyes full of concern and his expression serious. He gripped her chin with his fingers. "See? I'm okay. Nothing happened to me." He helped her to her feet but still kept her locked in his embrace. "I'm here. I'm not going anywhere."

Dylan now had one hand planted on her back and the other swept strands of hair away from her face. "You okay?"

She nodded despite still being chilled to the bone. "I can't lose you, Ford."

His voice caught when he assured her, "You won't."

She knocked the side of her fist gently against his chest. "You can't make that promise when you do things like that."

"Darlin', it's my job. I go on roofs all the time."

"You didn't tell me that." She also never asked—on

purpose—hoping his employees had been doing the more dangerous work. But it was hard to block out him climbing ladders and working two stories up when she actually witnessed it.

"This was exactly why I didn't. I didn't want you to worry."

"Of course I would worry. I love you and don't want to lose you." She didn't think she'd survive having another loved one ripped away from her so soon.

His fingers, now gripping her biceps, flexed. It took him a few more seconds before he responded, "I love you, too."

Since the bulky tool belt hanging around Ford's hips pressed against her painfully, she leaned back until he freed her. It also gave her the opportunity to search his face after that confession. "You do?"

His answer included a soft smile. "Of course. I have for years."

"You never said anything." Just like working on roofs.

"Because we didn't have that kind of relationship. We agreed to keep it open and easy." He stroked her cheek with his knuckle. "You never told me, either."

"Because..." She shook her head. "I didn't for the same reason as you. I didn't want you to think I was pressuring you into an exclusive relationship."

He tipped his head to the side. "You have never pressured me for anything, darlin'. Not once. You are the most flexible person I've ever met. It's why our unconventional relationship still works after all these years."

Despite knowing Dylan stood listening closely behind her, this conversation was important. Especially when they just revealed that they loved each other.

It wasn't a surprise, but more of a relief.

"I loved what we had." Would they lose it?

"And now?" Ford's concerned expression returned.

No, they could only make it better. "I'm loving what we're building here. All three of us."

He pressed his lips to her forehead, murmuring, "I do, too. I never thought I'd want to be in any kind of committed relationship, but I see it headed in that direction."

She tipped her face up to him. "Does that bother you?"

Ford shook his head and glanced over her shoulder.

She knew at exactly who. She turned. "I'm sorry, Dylan. I don't want you to feel left out."

"I don't. What we had is old, but this is also new. There will be some growing pains. Truthfully, I wasn't looking for a committed relationship, either. But, I agree, it's working toward that."

He was right. What she had in the past with Dylan was old, but what they were building was new. They needed to keep looking forward.

"Do you mind?" she asked tentatively.

"I wouldn't keep inviting you two over if I did." Dylan's answer rang true.

Ford gave him a nod. "And we wouldn't keep coming over if we did, either."

When she stepped into Dylan's arms, he squeezed her tight and put his lips against her temple. "When you're ready, and only when you're ready, I want to hear about your reaction to Ford being on the roof. I can guess but I never want to assume."

After all these years, she thought she had that grief under control, but seeing Ford working on the roof brought it roaring back to the surface.

"It's up to you if and when you want to have that conversation, darlin'. If you don't and I have your permission, I can tell Dylan another time."

She nodded. Ford had been on site when the accident occurred, so he knew more details than her. He had shielded her from the worst of it. He'd also dealt with heavy guilt since it happened while Kyle was on a job for Ford's construction company.

Of course, Erin never held it against him. An accident was just that. Ford had always followed safety protocols and required his employees to do the same, especially since it had been his business, insurance and reputation on the line.

But sometimes, no matter how careful someone was, things happened...

"Please. I don't need to relive it." Pulling in a bolstering breath, she picked up the small cooler from the ground where she'd dropped it. She didn't want the day to be ruined due to her unexpected meltdown. "Dani took the time to pack us a delicious lunch. I don't want it, or this beautiful weather, to go to waste. We won't be able to do this come winter and it'll be here before we know it."

"Why don't we go and sit by the lake to share it, then," Dylan suggested, taking the cooler from her fingers.

Ford agreed. "That's a good idea."

That short walk and getting away from the bunkhouse might help blow out the rest of the clinging bad memories of her husband falling off a roof and breaking his neck.

While it had been quick and she was assured he didn't suffer, everyone he left behind sure did.

Dylan offered Erin his empty hand and when she took it, he intertwined their fingers. Ford stepped up to her other side, took that hand and gave it a gentle squeeze.

Then she walked hand in hand with her two men over to the beautiful lake to share their delicious lunch and soak in some of the warm sunshine. They spent their lunch talking about the future and ignoring the past.

Chapter Twenty-Eight

Ford was normally a heavy sleeper, but to think he wouldn't wake up with what was happening next to him was laughable.

Or maybe they did it on purpose.

Either way, the bed rocking, along with Erin's moans, groans and gasps, as well as Dylan's grunts as he pounded his cock into her, was enough to wake the dead.

He glanced over at the clock to see it was still a couple of hours away from sunrise. Since all three of them had the day off, they had a private trail ride scheduled for later that morning.

Only, someone decided to go for a ride earlier than planned.

After sliding up the heavy-duty headboard into a seated position, Ford shoved the covers off his lap, circled his erection with a tight grip and milked his cock from root to tip.

Erin, flat on her back, was being fucked missionary style. With her legs wrapped around Dylan's hips, she met him thrust for thrust. Her nails raking down his back left behind scratches deep enough to see in the faint light. At the same time, Dylan had his lips latched around her nipple, pulling it deep.

Erin threw her head back and gasped when Dylan's jaw shifted. Ford easily figured out what he was doing since Ford had done it plenty of times himself. His teeth were scissoring the tip of her nipple. Erin loved it when it was done with the right amount of pressure. Based on the ecstasy filling her face, Dylan must have figured out what that perfect amount was.

Ford should join in, but he was actually enjoying the show. What was happening in the early hours of the morning wasn't atypical. They had sex with each other individually, as well as when all three were involved, and it could happen any time of the day or night. If one of their triad was in the mood, they could always find at least one other, if not both, eager to play.

The openness and variety within their budding relationship made Ford pleased with the arrangement.

Sometimes one watched as two of them fucked. Like right now. And sometimes two of them watched the third masturbating.

For a couple of nights, they went as far as finding a resort guest willing to join them. They only let one man fuck Erin—wearing a condom, of course—before they decided that neither could tolerate it. Ford and Dylan quickly discovered they had a limit to sharing her, even though she didn't seem to have any issue when it came to sharing her men.

On another night, they invited a male guest to play with them in their favorite playroom, the impact room. Dylan and Ford took turns turning that man's ass so red that the next morning during breakfast service, he still couldn't sit down.

That was a fun night. Ford had used a tawse on the man and didn't have to hold back as much as he normally did when he used it on Erin. When Ford got around to finally fucking the guest, the man's ass was on fire. Amazingly enough, he still begged for more.

Unfortunately, at the time, Ford had been at his own breaking point. Especially since in the same room, Erin was bound to the St. Andrew's cross, facing away from them. Dylan was using a braided loop cable slapper on her, a new toy—and soon to be in his top ten favorites—that packed a punch. The leather was braided in a loop around a metal cable and, with the right touch, left such delicious marks on the person receiving the strikes.

At the time, watching Dylan work her and hearing her ecstatic reaction to each blow almost made him lose it. Add in the fact, once she was quivering and dripping down her own thighs, Dylan removed the plug from her ass and replaced it with his cock.

This all resulted in a memory Ford wouldn't soon forget.

He doubted the resort guest would forget it, either.

His grip tightened on his erection as he continued to tug. Cupping his balls with his free hand, he squeezed them to the edge of pain.

He lost himself in the sounds coming from the other two thirds of their triad. The sharp slap of skin-to-skin contact, Dylan's deep grunts and Erin's answering gasps and whimpers. While doing so, Ford also fantasized about fucking Dylan at the same time their lover fucked Erin.

They've done it a few times but neither Dylan or Ford lasted long when they did. They both agreed that next time the men would take turns eating Erin out first until she came at least twice so she wouldn't have to get herself off as her men laid collapsed on the bed next to her, trying to gather their wits.

Ford now jerked his cock so quickly the motion became a

blur. He debated whether to just blow in his own hand or all over Dylan's ass.

Erin's face was another possibility.

Or he could dive right in after Dylan was done and add his load to the mix.

The options were endless.

When his head fell back and cracked against the headboard, the action next to him jerked to a stop. With a wince, Ford opened his eyes to see both heads turned in his direction and one side of Dylan's mouth pulled up. "We wake you?"

Ford answered, "I sleep like the dead but apparently I'm more of a zombie type of dead than an actual corpse."

Amusement tinged Dylan's invitation, "You could join in."

"I could, but right now I'm enjoying the show. Continue."

Dylan tipped his head toward Ford's lap. "You're ruining my concentration."

Ford cocked an eyebrow. "Like you ruined my sleep?"

"I love watching Erin's face in the throes of ecstasy, but I also enjoy watching you masturbate."

Ford could have said the exact same thing. "And this is a problem?"

"Yes. Do me a solid by slipping in behind Erin. This way I can watch you jerk off and see her beautiful face at the same time."

His first instinct was always to push back on any of Dylan's suggestions or demands since they still bumped heads more often than not. The push and pull they had made sex between them extra spicy. Sort of like makeup sex after a fight, when that hot emotional energy was turned into physical energy.

It was no surprise that Dylan did certain things—like

fucking Erin right next to a sleeping Ford—to get a reaction from him. They still tried to "one up" each other on occasion. They considered the competition healthy as long as it didn't cause jealousy. Erin always ended up the winner, of course.

But this time, Dylan's idea was a good one, so he slipped behind Erin by putting his back to the headboard and spreading his thighs wide enough so Erin had room to recline between his legs and use his thigh as a pillow. But that also meant he needed to be extra careful with his stroking so he didn't accidentally punch her in the face in his enthusiasm.

Grabbing Erin's hips, Dylan jerked her back to where he wanted her and slammed his cock deep again.

Their eyes met over the woman they shared as Dylan thrusted hard enough to make Erin jerk against Ford. With one hand wrapped around his throbbing cock, Ford continued to stroke, squeeze and pull while with the other, he snagged one of her nipples and twisted it hard.

Erin hissed out an encouraging, "*Yessss...*"

He tipped his eyes down from Dylan to her. "Yes, what?"

"Yes, please, more, Sir."

"I'm not your Sir right now, he is. You need *his* permission." He still needed to get used to saying that. So did Erin. For years, he was her only Dom, now they had to get used to Dylan also stepping into that role.

Her eyes shifted to Dylan, who had his bottom lip caught between his teeth as he drove into her, not even skipping a beat during that interaction.

"Have you been a good girl?" Dylan demanded through clenched teeth.

The praise made her quiver against Ford. "I've been a perfectly good girl, Sir."

"Do you think I should let him reward you for being so *perfectly* good?" Dylan asked next.

"Yes, Sir. *Please.*"

Dylan's gaze lifted to meet Ford's again. "You have my permission to twist as hard as you can. Let's see if you can get her to say a certain color."

While Ford loved a challenge and tended to push Erin to the point where she teetered on saying "red," he didn't like taking it far enough where she actually had to use it. He always restrained himself.

But then, unlike Dylan, he'd had years to learn her limits while her ex was starting from scratch.

He and Dylan both agreed, if they ever wanted to do a scene with someone who could take it rougher than Erin, or even do things she didn't want to do, they'd have no problem finding a guest on the ranch more than willing to step into her place. As always, she'd have the opportunity to be in attendance, either simply observing or by joining them in play.

But they'd never involve anyone else without her approval first. The same way she wouldn't do the same. It all boiled down to respect and being open with each other about their wants and needs.

Some days he was perfectly fine with having a quickie or missionary-style sex with Erin, like Dylan was doing now. On others, he wanted to take things far enough she'd drop into her subspace. Of course, that took more time and effort than a quick fuck.

Dylan was also learning to enjoy the bliss that came with being a submissive. As was Ford. He had to admit, doing so had enhanced his sex life so far. He had no doubt that Dylan felt the same way, even though he hadn't stated it out loud yet.

He would, when he was comfortable with that acknowledgement.

Patience was also key when dealing with any kind of relationship, poly or otherwise, but it was especially important when more than two people were involved. A typical couple's relationship was difficult enough. Adding others required more work to keep it successful. However, a few weeks ago over dinner, they did agree that the work they were putting in had been worth it.

The moment anyone in their throuple decided it wasn't, they promised to openly discuss it.

"Kiss me," Dylan demanded, the fire in his eyes roaring bright.

At first, Ford thought he was talking to Erin. It turned out he was wrong.

When he leaned in, Dylan rose up and their mouths fused together. The more their tongues battled, the faster Ford stroked his own cock, and the quicker Dylan pumped in and out of Erin.

She reached up and cupped Ford's cheek with one hand and Dylan's with the other. Her ragged whisper reached his ears. "So beautiful. I love watching the two of you together."

It turned out they both enjoyed putting on a show for her, too. Either she watched them while she played with herself, or she eventually joined in once her pussy was soaked and her inner thighs slick.

Ford was sure it was that way right now as their shared kiss became more intense and Dylan continued to plunge his cock into her.

With a jerk, Dylan broke his mouth free, drove his hands and knees into the mattress, met Ford's eyes head on and slammed into Erin one more time, making her cry out and her body arch to meet him.

Ford had to stop stroking to avoid coming while watching that. When Dylan finally landed back in the real world, he announced between harsh pants, "I left you a gift. What you do with it is up to you."

"So generous," he teased. But in truth, it was no secret that Ford enjoyed fucking Erin after Dylan filled her with his cum. If they were both going to fuck her, he always chose to go second. Dylan never fought him over it since he wasn't into it as much as Ford.

What could spark one person's fire could effectively douse another's.

Ford asked, "Did she come?"

Dylan only nodded since he was still trying to rein in his breathing.

Erin's blissed-out expression made him ask, "How many times?"

Her heavy eyelids lifted, and she turned brown eyes up to him. "Since he woke me up? Three."

Shit. How did he miss all of that? "That means I have to give you four."

"It doesn't have to be a competition. One more will be fine," she assured him.

"For you," he countered. "He'll never let me live it down if I can't at least match him."

Personally, he'd be fine with jerking off and decorating Erin's face with his cum, but he also didn't want to pass up the "gift" Dylan left for him.

Choices. Choices.

Obviously, Dylan already knew what Ford would choose when he rolled away from Erin. "Let's switch. I know how much you like to churn that butter." He added a grin.

Churning butter was a juvenile way they described Ford fucking Erin after Dylan. Besides seeing Erin's ass thoroughly spanked, seeing Dylan's cum clinging to his cock while he fucked her was a huge turn-on for him.

He had no idea why it was but, luckily, neither Dylan nor Erin judged him for it.

Hearing Dylan use that phrase, though, proved his boss had loosened up a bit after first coming home to Fisher Falls. Dayne mentioned it loudly and often that his twin had finally pulled the stick out of his ass.

Ford could vouch it was true that his boss was a whole different man behind closed doors but not when he was dealing with the public or most of the guests. Dylan still tended to act reserved and professional. To look at him during work hours, one would think the man had no kinks or fetishes, or that he like to dominate in bed.

Ford preferred the closed-door version, and he was damn sure so did Erin.

Once both men changed places, Dylan reached over Erin, grabbed her legs and pulled them toward him until he could reach her ankles. He then held her legs up in the air, keeping her spread wide.

Ford drew a finger through her pussy lips, collecting some of Dylan's cum before smearing it over the crown of his cock.

"Keep her spread open. I want a little appetizer." He dropped to his belly and shoved his face in her hot, slick pussy.

He wasn't eating her out to clean her up, but to bring her to that next orgasm. He was working on borrowed time, so he needed to be quick about at least tying Dylan when it came to Erin's orgasms.

Since Erin always benefitted from their friendly competition, it kept her from getting annoyed at them for constantly butting heads.

Between Dylan's help and his own cunnilingus skills, it didn't take long for Erin to climax, thankfully. As soon as she did, and even before the ripples faded away, he dragged himself up and over her, plunging his cock to the hilt.

"Keep your legs up and spread, darlin'," Dylan ordered her. "I need my hands for other things." He adopted Ford's pet name for Erin, but he only used it when he was in control.

Those *other things* consisted of him winding a section of her hair tightly around his fist and pulling tightly on her scalp. Beside a sharp release of breath, she had no other reaction.

They recently discovered how much she liked her hair pulled. Almost as much as getting spanked.

While keeping the tension on her hair, Dylan drove his hand between her legs and pinched her clit, making her cry out and squeeze Ford's cock. That was not helping him get to his goal of giving her two or three more orgasms. If anything, it was sabotaging him.

When Ford glanced at Dylan, he saw it clearly in his face. He was trying to get him to blow sooner than he wanted. Luckily, it backfired. When Dylan pinched her clit again, her ass jumped off the bed, driving Ford so deep, he hit the end of her.

That brought about orgasm number two. One more and he'd at least be even.

Gritting his teeth, he kept sliding his cock in and out of her pussy, hoping she'd get there sooner than later. Because if not, he'd have to admit defeat. He'd been straddling that sweet edge for too long and was about to lose his footing.

It was at that point he made a fatal mistake. He looked down at his cock plunging in and out of Erin and saw Dylan's creamy cum coating it.

Fuck.

He was done.

He drove up and into her one last time and remained planted deep as he made his own deposit into the woman he loved.

Dropping his head and closing his eyes, he rode out the last of his orgasm. When he finally fell from the clouds and back to Earth, he already knew Dylan would be grinning like an asshole.

He lifted his gaze.

Yep. He was right.

He sighed and slipped to Erin's side to finish recovering.

A deep chuckle spilled from Dylan as he extracted himself from Erin and away from the head of the bed. He whacked Ford's arm. "It was a good effort."

"Five orgasms was more than enough for me. Thank you, boys." An obvious attempt at keeping the peace.

She went to climb off the bed, but Ford stopped her. "I got it this time."

When Ford was in the Dom role one night, he'd made Dylan crawl on his hands and knees to and from the bathroom to get the washcloths needed for cleanup. That was another memory he wouldn't soon forget.

His only regret was that he didn't record it so he could watch it whenever Dylan was being extra bossy during the workday.

He hoped to get him to do it again soon. Only, Dylan didn't have a humiliation kink. Like Erin, he basked in praise —as did most living, breathing humans—so Ford had showered him with compliments when he returned.

Since that wasn't happening this morning, Ford headed to the attached bathroom, cleaned himself up, grabbed what he needed for his lovers and quickly returned so he could grab a few more hours of shut eye.

After handing one damp cloth to Dylan to clean himself up, Ford told him, "I'll take care of her."

"My job," Dylan murmured as he used the washcloth on himself.

"Technically, yes. But I got it this time since you helped get her to two more orgasms."

"She would've had zero from you if it wasn't for me."

While Dylan's response was a bit cocky, Ford couldn't deny it was also true. "You're telling no lies. And I gave you the credit, *boss*."

Erin bugged her eyes out at them. "Again, this isn't a damn competition. I'm good with one orgasm or twenty. Don't stress over it. It's not the destination that matters so much as the route taken to get there."

"Hold up. You'd be fine if you never orgasmed again?" Skepticism colored Dylan's tone.

She poked him in the gut. "Is that what you heard?"

Dylan glanced at Ford. "Isn't that what you heard?"

"I just cleaned my ears last night. I can confirm. That's what I heard."

"Stop!" she insisted on a laugh.

As soon as Ford was done wiping her down with the warm cloth, he warned, "Now that anal sex is easier for you, we're going to fuck you at the same time one day soon."

"Double penetration will be easier thanks to that pretty plug Dylan bought me months ago."

Ford didn't think it would be *that* much easier, but he agreed it would help.

"Maybe you should wear it on our trail ride later," Dylan suggested with a gleam in his eyes.

Erin flicked one of his nipples playfully. "Maybe you two should wear yours, too."

With a laugh, Dylan jerked away and rubbed his nipple.

"Why do I have the feeling we'll be riding each other more than we'll be riding the horses?"

Ford snorted softly. "Because we know it's true."

"We're pros at turning any normal activity into something naughty," Erin said.

"We do have that knack," Dylan agreed. "Now, let's get more sleep. We have a long day of riding ahead of us."

That they did. Checkers wouldn't be the only steed he planned on riding later.

Chapter Twenty-Nine

Erin lifted her face toward the ceiling and took in the mouth-watering scent permeating Dylan's wing of the house. "Smells like breakfast."

Dylan's nostrils flared as he also sniffed. "Sure does."

She pressed a hand to her empty belly. "Do you think Dani would mind us joining her?"

They had an active night. They started in one of the playrooms, where Ford was first tied down. They then moved to the farmhouse where they bound her face-down on Dylan's bed and "tortured" her by flogging and fucking her until she had multiple orgasms.

It was absolute torture.

She smiled softly at the memory.

On a chuckle, Dylan answered, "She should know by now that's expected," drawing her back to the present.

Dylan's sense of humor and joy of life was coming out more and more every day. Back in high school he was normally reserved, and he seemed to be even worse when he first landed back in Fisher Falls.

Formerly uptight and inflexible, he was now a different person. More easy-going. He smiled a lot more. He laughed out loud and with abandon. He cracked jokes. If he spotted Erin, he'd pull her into a nearby closet for privacy and a quick make-out session. He did the same with Ford.

And she knew that because they told her every time they had intimate contact. She didn't demand it, they volunteered that information. One time she even made them do a replay of the quick blowjob Dylan gave Ford so she could watch.

Though, even months later, he and Ford were still trying to outdo each other. They managed to turn an intense competition into more of a playful game between them. One they fed off of to keep the triad's sex life hopping and popping.

She couldn't imagine the desire to one-up each other would ever change since they were both Doms at heart.

Of course, she always benefitted from their silly competitions, so it didn't upset her in the least. In fact, the two men were getting along better than ever. They spent more time with each other than previously, too, and not because of work. If Erin had to guess, they were becoming fast friends in addition to being lovers.

Whenever they had sex together, it was such a turn-on for her. It wasn't only about the physical intimacy, either. It was those moments she'd catch them being emotionally intimate with each other. A brush of fingers. A glimpse. An unspoken message.

Seeing them like that made her heart swell.

When they shared the same touches, looks and messages with her, her heart exploded.

So, yes, she could deal with them occasionally bumping heads as long as their relationship kept developing. Because as long as it did, the bond between the three of them would grow that much stronger.

Her personal opinion was, Dylan loosened up once he agreed to become a switch—albeit reluctantly—instead of strictly being a Dom. While bottoming for Ford, he could lose control without losing who he was at his very core.

After months of being a part of the threesome and learning to share and love each other, he was also allowing more of his kinky desires to surface. A sign he'd been stifling himself.

Maybe in the past he hadn't felt safe enough with anyone to allow himself that. If it wasn't for Ford, Erin might still be in the same boat. Her long-time lover helped slip off her blindfold of restrictive societal norms so she could see the warm and welcoming light of day.

"True," Ford agreed with Dylan. "If it isn't us crashing the kitchen for her cooking, then it's Dayne and whoever he corralled for the night."

"Though," Erin started, "Dani seemed a bit miffed when your brother invited three women he'd had an orgy with to sit and join us at the table one morning."

Ford laughed softly. "That made some interesting breakfast conversation."

"She was only annoyed because they were guests. They could've eaten for free at the lodge," Dylan explained.

"I don't think Dayne was done with them yet," Ford added.

"Apparently, since they didn't even stick around long enough to help clean up." Dylan shook his head. "I have no idea how my bonehead twin satisfies three women at the same time."

"Maybe he doesn't," Ford answered. "It could be they have to satisfy each other while he puts in minimal effort."

"That would be par for the course when it comes to Dayne," Dylan said on a laugh.

Ford warned, "Well, let's go snag some seats before Dayne comes out of his wing like the Pied Piper leading a trail of his conquests and we're then forced to head up to the lodge for breakfast."

Erin wanted to avoid that, if possible. "I'd prefer not to eat at the lodge. While the cooks are great and so is the food, Dani has a culinary touch that's unmatched. That said, I've never heard a single complaint from the guests about the food made by the kitchen staff. Suggestions, yes. Complaints, no."

"That's good and hopefully continues. It wouldn't be good for business if the food sucked since their stay is all-inclusive. If they had to leave the ranch for a decent meal elsewhere, that wouldn't be good."

Erin agreed. They wanted guests to have everything they needed without being forced to leave the resort. At least until their stay was over. They wanted guests to be sad they had to check out, not be happy to escape. Plus, it wasn't like Fisher Falls was a tourist town with a bunch of offerings for non-locals. Hence, the decision to be all-inclusive. "A guest did request later hours for the kitchen, though. For those late-night munchies. With all the resort's activities, they do tend to work up an appetite."

"I know *we* do," Ford said.

Dylan's brow scrunched low. "What do they want, the kitchen open twenty-four hours a day?"

Erin shrugged. "I told them that was impossible due to staffing."

"And a possible waste of food."

Of course, as a good business owner, Dylan would consider the cost of food waste when it came to the resort. He wanted it to make money, not bleed it. Too many local residents and families now relied on the ranch as their main source of income, as well as for benefits.

She glanced at Dylan. That included the Lyons family. "That, too. But we could set up an area where beverages and non-perishable snacks are available at all hours."

"We originally discussed having a little café," Dylan said. "I'll mention it to my sister again as I'm scarfing down her blueberry pancakes."

Erin's ears perked up and her mouth watered. "You smell pancakes?"

Dylan shrugged. "It's either that or waffles."

Erin *mmm*'d. "I hope it's her buttermilk waffles."

"Can we stop guessing and go eat?" Ford asked impatiently. "Talking doesn't fill this empty pit in my stomach."

Dylan shot him a wicked grin. "I could fill it up, if you want."

Ford hooked a thumb at Dylan and dramatically mouthed to Erin, "Who *is* this guy?"

Apparently, he had also noticed the change in Dylan.

She smiled, and with Ford's arm hooked around her neck, they headed through the door between Dylan's residence and the shared kitchen.

By now, their appearance was no longer a shock to his siblings. It had become a normal occurrence for them to all sit down together and share meals. Ford and Erin had quickly become extended family, and nobody blinked twice about it.

"Shit," Dylan muttered in front of them, coming to an abrupt halt and causing Ford and Erin to do the same.

Erin peeked around him expecting to see Dayne with his latest harem.

It was, in fact, not Dylan's very horny twin nor was it Dani preparing breakfast. Her heart did a somersault.

It was Evelyn Lyons.

The matriarch of the family had no idea about the blossoming relationship of one of her sons with two other individuals. One being another man.

"Mrs. Lyons," Ford greeted sheepishly.

Was he actually blushing?

"Ford," Dylan's mother greeted him back, her eyes flicking back and forth between the three of them. She didn't bother to contain the curiosity in her expression. "Fancy meeting you here."

"He works here," Dylan reminded her as he moved farther into the kitchen.

His mother glanced at her watch and raised an eyebrow. "Do you normally start work this early, Ford?"

"It was a special project," Dylan quickly answered before Ford could.

Her eyes, the same hazel as her children's, bore into each of them one-by-one. When his mother reached Erin, she blanked out her thoughts, just in case the older woman had mind-reading skills.

Was she blushing now, too? Erin pressed her palms to her heated cheeks.

Nothing like looking guilty.

Evelyn waved a batter-covered wooden spoon back and forth between the three of them. "What's this about?"

Could this be *déjà vu*?

Dylan attempted to steer the conversation elsewhere. "Why are you here, Mom? Where's Dani?"

"In the shower. I told her to take her time." She planted one hand on a hip and stared at her son. "*Anyhoo*, good morning to you, too. I came over hoping to have breakfast with my offspring. They've been so busy getting the resort up and running, plus smoothing out the rough spots, they've conveniently forgotten their mother lives right... in... town."

Of course, Evelyn was exaggerating. Her children

hadn't abandoned her, but they hadn't visited as much as she'd probably like since they *had* been a bit busy expanding the resort. However, during those visits, Erin was sure neither Dayne nor Dylan were discussing their sex lives.

Ford grabbed Erin's elbow firmly. "How about we get out of your hair and let you enjoy your morning with your family."

Erin mentally groaned. The smell of freshly brewed coffee was too tempting to simply walk away.

Evelyn shook her head. "Oh no. You two aren't going anywhere until I hear *all* about this *special project.*"

The woman raised three children on a dairy farm. No doubt she could smell bullshit a mile away.

"It's boring, Mom, you—" Dylan started.

"Special project?" Dayne snorted as he sauntered into the kitchen from his side of the house. "That's not what they're doing, Mom. Don't let him fool you."

Evelyn turned toward her youngest son. "Then, what are they doing?"

Dylan stumbled over his words as he rushed to say, "It's not Dayne's place to—"

Dayne cut him off with, "They're fucking," as he approached their mother, gave her a quick peck on the cheek, then glanced over her shoulder to see what she was making.

Crazy enough, Evelyn did not appear shocked at Dayne's answer. "Ford and Erin? Some of us already knew that."

What? That was news.

"No—"

"Dayne!" Dylan barked.

"No what? Finish what you were going to say, son, if you want to remain my favorite," Evelyn cooed, patting Dayne's cheek.

Next to them, Dylan groaned under his breath. Out loud, he said, "Mom..."

Dayne's smirk spread into a full-blown grin, and he turned it toward Dylan. "All three of them."

Evelyn's eyebrows stitched together. "All three of them are what?"

"Fucking," Dayne confirmed with a nod.

Dylan closed his eyes on a sigh and when he opened them, he glared at this twin.

Erin and Ford remained frozen in place, not sure how this was all going to shake out. She had no idea how Dylan's mother would take the news. Would she be accepting or just the opposite?

At the same time, bare feet could be heard racing down the steps.

"No running in this house!" Evelyn yelled out. "You'll tumble down the stairs and break your neck!"

Danica took the last step into the kitchen, fighting her own grin. "I'm in one piece, Mom."

"By the grace of God!" Evelyn huffed. "Now..." She turned back to Dayne, opened her mouth, then closed it with a shake of her head before focusing on Dylan, Ford and Erin. "Where were we?"

Dylan purposely misunderstood and reminded his mother where she was. "In *our* kitchen."

"Yes, that's right. Making my children breakfast because apparently, it's too much effort to keep me up to date with their lives, even though I'm only fifteen minutes or a phone call away."

Dylan groaned over the mother's guilt. This time he didn't bother to muffle it.

"Is that bacon I smell, Mrs. Lyons?" Ford's tone was sticky sweet.

Still wearing his shit-eating grin, Dayne reached behind his mother and held up a piece of crispy bacon to show Ford before shoving the whole strip in his mouth.

Evelyn whacked Dayne's arm. "Don't eat that. They're for breakfast." She turned back to Ford. "Call me Evelyn." She pursed her lips as she studied the three of them. "So, you three are in a single relationship."

She sounded far from shocked. In fact, she said it matter-of-factly.

Huh.

"And how does that all work?"

Oh no. Erin's stomach churned.

"Kind of like an outlet, Mom," Dayne explained so help-fully, "where you can plug in two appliances at a time."

Holy shit.

"Oh," Evelyn breathed, then she nodded. "Makes sense."

Makes sense?

Erin glanced over at a pale Dylan who looked like he was waiting for the floor to open up and swallow him. If that happened, she was grabbing Ford and they were escaping down that hole, too.

This conversation was not one she wanted to have this morning. Or any morning. While Dylan's siblings knew about the threesome, no one thought to warn his mother, who used to live on this very ranch and, like she said, now only lived fifteen minutes away.

Truthfully, she was surprised rumors spread by the locals working at the resort weren't floating around town. And if they were, that Evelyn hadn't run smack dab into any. Espe-cially since she got together with groups of ladies on a regular basis who *loved* to gossip.

Erin narrowed her eyes on Dylan's mother.

Holy shit. The woman knew and this was all an act. Erin

would bet money on it. She expected Dylan to tell her without her having to ask.

"A relationship with three people is the same as with two," Dylan said.

"Except with extra body parts and ho—"

"Enough!" Evelyn scolded Dayne sharply. "As long as my children are happy, I don't care how many body parts or *holes* it takes." She turned her gaze to Dylan. "Are you happy?"

Now it was Dylan's turn for heat to creep up into his cheeks. That had to be a first.

No one moved or said a word while they waited for his answer. In fact, Erin didn't think anyone even breathed.

"Yes," he answered. "I am, Mom."

Her eyes softened and so did her smile. "That's all that matters." She clapped her hands. "I guess we should put out two more place settings, then."

Their mother began to buzz around the kitchen.

Was that the end of the discussion?

It couldn't be that easy.

"Danica, put out the extra settings and also some maple syrup on the table. Dylan, can you pile the bacon onto a plate? Dayne..." She shook her head and skipped over him. "Ford, honey, grab the creamer, juice and butter from the fridge. And Erin, sweetie..." She pointed toward the large kitchen table. "Just sit and relax. One stubborn man was enough for me. Dealing with two must be exhausting. One of the boys will grab you a cup of coffee."

Well then...

It was obvious where the Lyons kids got their personalities and their open minds.

Evelyn had always been kind to her. While she and Dylan dated, after her son left Fisher Falls, and even after Erin married Kyle. She was a compassionate woman at her core. If Dayne wasn't Dylan's identical twin, Erin would think he was adopted.

Maybe it was true that one black sheep existed in every family.

After settling at the table, Ford dropped off a cup of coffee for her with a wink, then went to fetch the remaining items from the refrigerator.

Dylan brought the mountain of bacon, more than enough for six people—another hint that Evelyn had already known —over to the table at the same time Ford returned with the creamer and juice.

Dylan glanced over his shoulder before whispering, "I think we need to rethink you two staying over here."

"Privacy would be good," Ford agreed under his breath.

"Privacy from my family would be even better. If I had expected this to happen, I would've either designed the wings differently or scrapped the idea all together."

Erin assumed *this* meant the threesome, not the fact his mother wanted to spend time with her adult children.

"Too late now," Ford muttered.

"We haven't been open about our relationship with any of the employees or with anyone in town. Maybe we need to get in front of this whole thing."

Erin asked Dylan, "By doing what?"

"Not hiding it anymore."

"Would you be okay with that?" Ford asked him, as surprised as Erin.

"Do we have a choice?"

They really didn't. This morning was proof. "Your mom already knew," Erin whispered. "Look how much bacon she made. Look at that stack of pancakes. She's feeding an army, not just herself and her three children."

Dylan stared at his mother fussing over something on the other side of the large kitchen. "You think?"

Erin gave him a nod. "Yes, and she recovered from the news too quickly."

Dylan's brow furrowed. "Maybe."

"No, Dylan, she knew. That means rumors are swirling around town already. So, it might be too late to control them."

"We control them by being open about who we are to each other," Ford told them.

"We haven't sat down and actually discussed where we go from here. I mean, right now we're just living in the moment and not thinking about the future."

"Well, the future is about to smack us upside the head, Dylan. So, like Ford said, we need to be the ones to be honest and open about it. We need to stop pretending."

"I'm not sure I'd call it pretending," Ford whispered. "It was more like burying our heads in the sand. We knew that this would come out, but we hid in our bubble."

Dylan frowned. "Someone burst it."

"No surprise since the resort is now the biggest employer in the area," Erin reminded him. "We're together too much now for anyone not to notice. It only takes one person mentioning it to someone else for it to spread like wildfire. Gossip *is* the most exciting activity in Fisher Falls."

"What are you three whispering about?" asked Dayne. "What your after-breakfast romp will entail?"

"Romp?" Dylan echoed. He tipped his head as he took in his twin. "Funny how you don't have anyone joining you this morning. Were you the one who told Mom?"

Dayne slapped a hand over his chest and gasped dramatically. "Me? No! I wouldn't do that."

"*Mmm hmm.*"

Dayne lifted a hand. "I swear. I didn't say a word."

"Then why isn't whoever you played with last night not here right now?"

Dayne leaned closer to his brother and whispered, "Because I was smart enough to glance out the window this morning after I heard you all talking out here. I snuck last night's companions out the door before she could spot them. Unlike you, I don't have anyone in my life important enough to meet my mother."

Dylan's lips pressed together as he glanced from Ford to Erin and back to Dayne. "Shit."

Were they at the point they were ready to introduce their poly partners to their parents?

Dayne's grin spread wider, and he whacked Dylan on the back. "Congrats."

Apparently so.

Chapter Thirty

Erin sat in the corner of Dylan's bedroom doing one of her favorite activities... Watching her two men have sex with each other. Without her.

Though, right now it was foreplay. Tonight they'd been doing that longer than normal. Dylan was taking his time exploring every inch of Ford's body. That very thorough exploration included fingers, mouth and, of course, tongue.

"You two are so... beautiful."

Dylan paused mid-lick and lifted his dark blond head. "Beautiful?"

"Yes, like art. Your bodies are living, breathing sculptures. The sounds you two make are music. The motion like choreographed dancing. You two are so in sync, it seems you were made for each other. So, yes, *beautiful*. Breathtaking even. I could watch you for hours, days... forever."

She hoped this threesome *would* last forever. She wasn't sure if it would work at first, but now... She couldn't imagine being with anyone but her two Doms.

"You're not here to only watch," Dylan said in his best Dom voice.

But she wasn't his sub right now. "What's wrong with simply appreciating the show?"

"You're supposed to be a part of it."

Not necessarily. It was true that most of the time whoever was watching ended up joining in on the fun, even if that wasn't the initial plan, but it didn't need to be the case.

She repeated something Ford said months ago. "There are no rules. Except for no jealousy and no favoritism." Everyone was equal in the relationship. The only time it wasn't was when they were in a scene. "Plus, I'm perfectly fine over here."

For the moment, anyway. That could easily change. But this evening, that would be completely up to her.

Not Dylan or Ford.

Ford opened his eyes and raised his head from the mattress, where he was splayed out in unrestrained bliss. "You look perfectly fine from here. Maybe I should be watching you instead of the back of my eyelids."

"A show within a show?" Erin teased.

"A double feature," Ford teased back.

"A one woman show," Dylan joined in. "Maybe we need to get re-situated so we can watch her more easily."

"*Ah*, but I don't want you two distracted."

"That could happen," Ford warned Dylan, grabbing his head and pulling him back down for a long, thorough kiss.

That kiss was enough to distract Dylan, and they continued doing their thing while she went back to doing her own.

She currently wore thigh-high stockings and a leather garter belt, along with a matching leather bra with peek-a-boo holes to show off her nipples, high heels and... nothing else.

And what she was doing was fingering her own pussy and clit as she watched the men play with each other.

Even though they weren't performing for her specifically, she liked to think they were.

All it took to push her toward her first climax of the night was the two of them to start playfully wrestling and fighting to be on top.

The whole scene before her went from hot to scorching. The lazy licking, soft touches or light kissing quickly disappeared. A power struggle evolved, involving teeth, nails, grunts and soft curses.

Ford ended up on top, pinning Dylan down by his wrists and straddling his waist.

Both were now out of breath and Erin could confirm neither man cared right now what she was doing in her little corner. At least until she cried out and her body bowed against the chair as an orgasm ripped through her.

When she finally returned to Earth, she glanced over at the bed again.

Oh yes, the men were in their own little world and missed her orgasm because they were working on their own.

Ford had Dylan's knees pinned to his chest and was already lubing up his hole, preparing it.

Ford clearly won that particular battle.

That was all right. Dylan would "win" the next one.

He always did.

———

Dylan climbed back into bed after cleaning up. "You were wrong earlier."

"Who?" Erin asked sleepily. Three intense orgasms in a

row tended to wipe her out, whether they were self-service or given to her by the men.

"You," he informed Erin.

She raised an eyebrow in his direction, which was on the other side of Ford. "About?"

She no longer was always sandwiched in between them. They now switched up their sleeping positions depending on who didn't want to be stuck in the middle. Sometimes she'd woken up in a sweat if both men were crowding her. They tended to emit heat like furnaces cranked on high.

"You said there are no rules," Dylan answered. "That's untrue. Rules exist for every relationship, whether spoken or not. As for sex, we are only limited by our desires and how far we're willing to go to fulfill those desires."

"That last part should be our mission statement." Ford followed that up with a loud yawn, which caused both Erin and Dylan to do the same.

"For the resort?" Dylan stretched out and got comfortable.

Ford rolled into him. "No, for us."

Dylan considered that for a second. "Do we need one?"

"Not necessarily, but it sounded good."

Erin smiled. "We could say the same thing about love."

Dylan tested that concept out. "We're only limited by our love and how far we're willing to go to…"

"Maintain that love?"

Ford rolled onto his back and added his suggestion to Erin's. "Or grow it?"

Dylan rolled to his side, planted his elbow onto the bed and propped his head on his hand. "Well, how far *are* we willing to go for love?"

Erin held her breath. While she and Ford admitted they loved each other a few months ago, Dylan hadn't joined in.

"You're both here more often than not," Dylan stated the obvious.

Where was he going with that?

"Honestly, I'm starting to feel like a stranger in my own home," Ford muttered.

"Same." Erin slowly circled her finger through Ford's dark chest hairs.

Between working five days a week at the resort, then staying over with Dylan almost every night, she hardly went home anymore. Dylan's wing in the farmhouse was starting to feel more like home than her own place.

They even spent weekends together doing planned activities, like trail rides by horseback or four-wheelers, or hiking the many trails that were only accessible by foot. And at least one of those days or nights, they booked a playroom up in "Heaven."

To say the sex was the most satisfying part of their threesome would be wrong. It was the conversations they shared afterward. Those exchanges had certainly evolved as their poly relationship developed. They were now more intimate and personal.

But then, communication was key for any healthy relationship.

On the other hand, the three were also comfortable enough now to be able to simply bask in silence. They no longer needed small talk to fill the quiet between the noise.

"It's crazy how much stuff you two have left here just in the past six months."

Again, where was Dylan going with this? Was he not feeling the same way as Ford and Erin? Was he feeling pressured or smothered?

She and Ford shared a concerned glance.

"We can take it home if it's bothering you," Ford offered

cautiously. He seemed to be just as confused at this sudden change in direction in the conversation.

"It's an observation, not a complaint."

"What's our other option?" Erin asked carefully. "What are you saying, Dylan? Do you want us to spend less time here? Or to leave after sex?"

"No, just the opposite. I want you to move in."

Her eyes went wide.

"My mother knows and approves."

Erin frowned. "Wait. Why do we need our parents' approvals? We're adults."

"It simply makes life easier."

"Maybe. Maybe not," Ford said. "It might make family gatherings and holidays easier, but not our everyday lives."

"What if your parents have a problem with us being in a poly relationship?"

"Then, they have a problem," Ford stated with a shrug. "Again, I'm an adult. I didn't care if they had a problem with me being bi, the same way I won't care if they have a problem with me being polyamorous. Parents should love their children unconditionally."

"Should, but that's not reality."

Dylan was right, unfortunately.

Ford wasn't done. "If my parents aren't accepting of the two people who love and are committed to me, that's a problem for them. Not me."

She liked how Ford slipped in the fact Dylan loved them, too, without it being too obvious.

She and Ford told each other on a regular basis.

As for Dylan...

His actions spoke for him.

However, both Ford and Erin would like to hear him say it out loud. They just wanted him to do it on his own time. When he was comfortable. And one-hundred percent sure.

If he wasn't, they could wait.

Dylan's eyebrows stitched together. "You're okay with alienating your family?"

"No," Ford answered, "but it wouldn't be me alienating them. They'd be alienating me."

Erin understood where Ford was coming from, but she wasn't sure she could be so accepting about losing her family's love, all due to her choice of being with two men. Despite the fact those two men clearly loved her.

Would she give them up if her family disapproved? She wasn't sure if she could, and she hoped it never got to that.

She rubbed her chest over her heart at that painful thought.

She would need to tell them before she agreed to move in with them.

Did she want to move in with them? That wasn't a decision to be made lightly. Or tonight. Since it would also mean either selling her house or renting it out.

Damn, she needed to have a conversation with her parents and let them know what was going on with her life, other than the mundane updates she told them regularly. No doubt that particular conversation would be awkward.

She had no idea how they'd react beyond shocked at first. They didn't even know she'd been in a casual relationship with Ford for years.

"Christmas is coming up soon. We *could* invite our families here for Christmas and New Years. They could see how we live firsthand," Dylan suggested. "And see how happy we are."

Erin thought that might work. They could see in person how happy they were. Not just hear about it over the phone.

"But just what are they going to see?" Ford turned his attention to her. "Do your parents know where you work now?"

"Yes, I mentioned it."

"Do they know what the resort is all about?"

"They're capable of googling," she said simply.

"But have they?"

"My guess? No, because they've never asked more than, 'How's the new job going, honey?'"

"Do they know you're hardly home anymore? That you practically live out of an overnight bag?"

"No," she answered softly.

"My proposal would change that," Dylan said simply.

"Where would we live? Here?" Ford asked skeptically.

"Well—"

"Your place isn't big enough for three adults."

"I can build a bigger place."

Ford sat up and cocked an eyebrow at him. "You can?"

"A crew can. *We* can. You can design it however you'd like."

"You're the architect," Ford reminded him.

"You could help. Both of you. It would be your home, too. The three of us can figure it out. What do you think?"

"You don't think it's too soon?" Erin asked him. "We've only been a committed throuple for a few months."

Dylan continued, "Baby, we missed seventeen years."

"Okay, but—"

"I don't want to miss any more. Doesn't this feel right?"

"Yes, but..." She glanced over at Ford.

Ford picked up from there. "I just want to be clear... If you're only including me to keep Erin..."

Dylan scoffed, "Come on now, you should know by now that's not it."

"Then, what is it?" Ford still sounded skeptical.

But he should. Moving in together would be a big step and it would definitely spur a flurry of rumors in town.

No, it would no longer be rumors but fact. Any rumors about them would finally be proven right.

"Here's the truth..." Dylan pulled in a long, deep breath. "When you two aren't here, I feel something is missing." He patted his bare chest over his heart. "In here. But it hit me the other day, that emptiness disappears whenever I see one of you. Even from a distance."

"I mean, I feel that way, too," Erin said. "I count the minutes until we're all together again. And it has nothing to do with sex."

Ford leaned over to place a kiss on the tip of her nose. "Same. But I also look forward to the sex."

She laughed. "Well, of course, the sex is great. I was a little worried that being with two Doms would be too much for me. But you two work so well together; something else I didn't expect."

"Same," Ford repeated. "I thought Dylan would be too stubborn to bend."

"Over," Erin added on a giggle.

"I wouldn't bend over for anyone but you," Dylan told Ford.

"Or me," Erin said.

"The only way I'd bend over for you is if Ford ordered you to..." His eyebrows rose. "Have you two been making plans?"

Ford laughed. "I'm always planning. I can be out working on a fence line and something for us to try will pop in my head."

"And pop in your pants?" Erin teased.

"Sometimes it's convenient to work alone."

"Oh, then maybe I need to come out to wherever you are to check on your work. Just to make sure it's up to standards so I can head off any complaints before they roll in."

"Anytime. But you don't need that excuse, darlin'."

"If you're going out to check his *work*," Dylan said, "you need to clear it with the boss first."

Erin grinned. "So you can supervise?"

"Of course," he answered in a serious tone. "Okay, so... Thoughts?"

"About sex during the workday? I'm all for it. Sounds like a great job perk," Ford said.

Erin giggled.

Dylan did not. "You know what I'm asking."

"I only see one problem with your plan... Beside your wing being too small for us and a new place will take a bit to build."

"What's the problem?" Dylan asked.

Chapter Thirty-One

"The problem is—" Ford stopped mid-sentence. He didn't want to pressure Dylan to reveal his feelings before he was ready, but moving in together would be a big step. One to be taken seriously. Especially if both he and Erin sold their homes and moved onto the ranch. Ford needed more than simply being involved in an exclusive relationship.

This would be putting down actual roots. Declaring to the world that they were in a committed polyamorous relationship and didn't care what other people thought about it.

It would also be building a "family."

Erin said years ago she would want children someday. Would she want to have them with Dylan and Ford? How would that even work? That would be another serious, but necessary, discussion.

The reality was, children raised in an unconventional relationship could get bullied. Whose last name would they take? Who would be the actual biological father... Would they care who? This was something they needed to figure out before jumping in with both feet. Or three pairs of feet.

He was up for it, and he knew Erin would be, too, but he first needed to hear something from Dylan the man hadn't shared yet.

"What's the problem?" Dylan prodded with a frown.

"The sex is great, right?" Ford asked.

"Of course," both Dylan and Erin said simultaneously.

"It might have been a bit bumpy in the beginning but now everything between us has fallen into place, right?"

Again, Dylan and Erin both answered, "Yes."

Ford focused on Erin. "You love me, darlin', as much as I love you, right?"

She quickly picked up on where he was leading this conversation. "You know I do."

"Do you love Dylan just as much?"

Dylan stared at her with his expression completely blank as he waited for her answer. She met the man's eyes and said with complete confidence, "Of course I do."

"You never said as much," Dylan whispered, his eyes and expression softening.

"I was worried if I told you, you'd feel pressured to say it back, whether true or not."

Dylan scraped a hand through his hair. "I'm sorry, I didn't realize... Shit. Were you two waiting on me?"

"Like Erin said, we didn't want to pressure you. But yes, we were waiting on you," Ford confirmed. *Holy shit*, this felt good to get off his chest.

Dylan appeared floored. "You love me?"

Once this was out, there was no taking it back. He made sure to meet Dylan's gaze head-on when he admitted, "I do."

Dylan closed his eyes and whispered, "Thank fuck."

Ford chuckled. "*That's* your response?"

"Hell yes! You two kept telling each other but neither of

you said it to me. I was beginning to think I was the third wheel, which was my fear in the beginning."

"What?" Erin exclaimed. "Really? Then why would you ask us to move in with you?"

"I was hoping you'd both eventually feel the same way."

"Dylan..." Erin breathed.

"I guess I was wrong," Dylan added with a grin.

"You were. We both love you," Erin revealed. "And yes, I would love to live with both of *my* men. A house we can turn into our very own home would be wonderful."

"One with more privacy," Ford added his stipulation.

He never expected to be in this position. Exclusive. Committed. *In love.* He mentally shook his head. In love with *two* people who loved him back. And planning a future with them.

"We'll build it farther away from the lodge," Dylan assured him. "And my siblings."

"I'll miss Dani's breakfasts, though," Ford complained. That and Dylan's extensive toy collection were the bright spots of staying in the farmhouse. Of course, the toy collection would go with them.

Ford would also add to it with his own extensive collection. *Hell,* they could design their own private dungeon.

Damn. He was suddenly liking the idea of building a home somewhere on the ranch and getting rid of his house in town better and better.

The three of them could work, live and play together on the ranch. Even raise a family if they wanted.

"No one said we can't stop here in the mornings before work," Dylan said. "Problem solved."

"Oh, now *that's* a plan."

"I also have ideas of my own if we build from scratch," Ford told them.

"I can't wait to hear them. I might be the architect, but like I said earlier, I want all three of us involved in the design."

"Look how easy it was to sort out our lives," Erin half-joked, "once we all got on the same page."

"It won't be easy, but we'll make it work," Dylan admitted.

That was the truth. And a little work never hurt anybody, but Ford had no doubt, the end result would be worth it.

———

Erin was splayed out on her back sideways with her head hanging over the edge of the mattress. Dylan had one hand squeezing her breast tightly and the other clutching the front of her arched throat. He couldn't hear her groans but could feel the vibrations as Ford ate her pussy so enthusiastically, he acted like he'd never get that chance again. Despite the fact he would. Often.

Her groans, moans and whimpers were inaudible because Dylan was shoving his cock deep enough, he was practically fucking her throat. The only time they were giving her a break was during the few moments it took for the men to switch places.

They'd done it four times already, during which she came twice.

Both her wrists and ankles were cuffed, and those leather cuffs were attached to a metal bar designed to keep her legs spread wide. Not that she needed it, she would voluntarily keep her legs open for orgasms.

But that wasn't the point.

For her cuffed wrists to reach the spreader bar, she was forced to hold her legs up in the air. And those legs were now trembling so badly, the bed was shaking. She was either getting tired from keeping them up or it was the result of her intense climaxes. Or it could be a combination of the two.

Either way, he was sure Ford was ready to move on, as neither wanted to come yet and Dylan was already teetering dangerously. He could only imagine Ford had been struggling with the same when standing in Dylan's current spot.

Dylan already established his role as Dom tonight, so everything that happened would be up to him.

While he no longer minded bottoming for Ford, he still preferred to be "The Boss." Surprisingly, that title had grown on him, though Erin still called him *Sir* during scenes, despite Dylan now technically being her boss, too.

"Imp." It took a few tries before Dylan came up with a pet name he liked for Ford, but now that he found one, he used it often.

When Ford responded by lifting his head, Dylan's eyes were immediately drawn to his glistening lips and Erin's arousal clinging to his dark beard. He quickly slipped free from Erin's mouth because seeing that amazing sight was almost his downfall. And that wouldn't be such a stellar "boss move."

"Switch, Boss?"

Dylan shook his head. "We're going to change things up."

"Should I remove the spreader?"

Dylan debated silently, trying to figure out the best position for what he planned next. He already knew what they were about to do would be his undoing. As it would be for Erin and Ford. He now knew their bodies and responses almost as well as his own.

Dylan rounded the bed and eyed up Ford's bare ass. "No, leave it on our good girl, but arrange her face down, ass up, with her head at the top of the bed."

The men exchanged glances for a moment before Ford quickly dropped his gaze and nodded. "Yes, Boss."

"You're such a good boy," he whispered as Ford quickly arranged Erin to Dylan's liking. "Show me her pretty pink pussy."

Ford spread her wide, thumbing her clit while he did so. "She's ready for your cock, Boss."

"It's an amazing sight, for sure. However, I'm not fucking her, you are."

"And you will be..."

And there was why the nickname Imp fit him. He still liked to push Dylan to get a reaction.

"Not questioned," Dylan reminded him. "Unless you want to be punished. And if I have to punish you, you won't get to come in that pussy."

Ford's eyes flared at the warning.

"Get on your knees behind her. While you're fucking her doggy style, I'll be doing the same to you."

That spark in his dark brown eyes turned into a full-blown bonfire.

"Make sure your knees are on that spreader bar, too." That would surely be uncomfortable for him.

"Yes, Boss." Ford got into place.

"Do not fuck her until I give you permission," Dylan warned as he grabbed the bottle of lube off the electric warmer kept by the bed. He had spotted it when ordering more toys for the resort and figured they'd give it a try. They loved it, so he bought one for all of the guests' rooms, cabins and the playrooms.

He lubed up his own cock as he headed back to the foot of the bed, carrying the bottle and a hand towel with him.

Erin certainly didn't need any lube, but Ford sure would. "Spread yourself for me."

Already on his knees, Ford pulled his ass cheeks apart and exposed himself.

So damn hot. How did he get so lucky that he ended up with a sexy man like Ford and an amazing woman like Erin? Especially after he thought he lost Erin forever when he left all those years ago. He'd never been so happy to be wrong.

His life might've taken a few wrong turns—Whose didn't?—but all those turns formed a circle, leading him back where he would've been if he hadn't left in the first place. Only, he had no doubt that life ended up a lot better than it would've if he hadn't.

He wasn't a fan of the saying, *"Things happen for a reason,"* but in this case it was true.

After lubing two fingers up generously, he worked them in and out of Ford, making him groan and tip his ass up even more.

Oh yes. Ford no longer minded bottoming for Dylan, either. It was proof they were willing to compromise for the right person.

Ford and Erin were his people. And he was theirs.

He was so damn happy and content, he sometimes worried that everything was too good to be true.

Stop it. Enjoy what you've built here. A very successful, profitable business and a very successful, loving relationship. Both of which he hoped would last forever.

And in case they didn't, he needed to appreciate and enjoy every moment given to him.

A groaned, "Please, Boss," pulled him out of his head and back into the bedroom.

"Steady, Imp." He lined up the blunt head of his cock after sliding it over Ford's slippery hole a few times. Then without any resistance, he entered his lover easily, pausing a second or two to let Ford adjust around him. Also for Dylan to rein himself in. "Good?"

"Yes, Boss."

He sounded perfectly fine. "Then, you know what to do."

Dylan stayed planted deep inside Ford as the other man shifted forward, lining his own cock up with Erin's slick cunt.

"Tell him how much you want him, darlin'," Dylan ordered her. "Beg him to fuck you. I don't want you holding anything back. He needs to hear you. As do I."

She complied. "Please fuck me."

"Louder."

"Please, *please* fuck me, Ford."

"You want his cock in your pussy while I fuck him?"

"I do, Sir." Her breath caught. "I want him to fill me up at the same time you fill him." A shudder ripped through her.

"Are you ready?" Dylan asked next.

"I want him to fill my pussy with his cock and his cum."

Dylan's fingers flexed on Ford's hip. "I think that pretty pussy needs to be spanked first."

She sucked in a breath and released it in a rush. "Yes, please."

It turned out that Erin loved her pussy being punished as much as her ass, so they began to incorporate it on a regular basis. It made her labia swell and become more sensitive, as well as her clit. It was also a sure way to get her sopping wet.

Doing it not only turned both Ford and Dylan on, so did watching her reaction. Sometimes she would actually orgasm solely from it.

They'd tested doing it with various impact toys, starting off gently and increasing the power of each spank until she was edging close to her limit. Tonight, they used no toys other than the spreader bar and cuffs so Ford would have to use his hand.

Dylan heard the first strike instead of seeing it because he was busy drawing a line down the back of Ford's neck with his tongue. "Do it again." At the nape, he sank in his teeth and listened to the next stinging bare-handed slap accompanied by her whimper.

Dylan released Ford's flesh and glanced up in the mirror to get a better view. "Is he doing it how you want it, darlin'?"

"I want it harder, Sir."

Well then... "You heard our good girl. One more time and make it hurt," he murmured into Ford's ear at the same time reaching around him, cupping his balls and squeezing. "Look how shiny her pussy is right now. Smack it hard."

Ford had initially tensed when Dylan grabbed his sack, but after a second, he melted back against Dylan and slapped Erin's pussy so sharply that even Dylan felt it, causing her to cry out, but not in pain.

"Enough, Imp. She got what she wanted. Now I'll take what's mine. Line yourself up."

Since Dylan's cock was still inside him, he shifted with Ford as he quickly got into position, pressing the head of his cock at Erin's entrance.

"Give her your cock."

Dylan didn't need to repeat that order. With a quick thrust, Ford filled her pussy and immediately began to move. He started out slow, like they normally did until they were in sync. Once they were, Dylan stayed in place and let his Imp do the work to get them both off.

Every time Ford pushed forward, Dylan's cock came dangerously close to pulling out completely. When Ford pulled back, Dylan was driven deeper into his ass. Eventually, it got to the point where Ford was slamming into Erin to give her his cock and then slamming back into Dylan to take his.

The movement reminded him of the pendulum desk toy Dayne kept on his desk with the swinging metal balls that smacked together.

Dylan set his jaw and forced himself to stay in place while letting Ford go at his own pace. But surprisingly, his movements were getting more frantic and out of control. So unlike Ford.

Being a Dom, the man was well-versed in keeping tight control, but recently he started to let that control go when taking the submissive role and used his instincts instead.

Beads of sweat appeared at Ford's temple and Dylan licked them away. He had to be close to breaking.

He reached around, snagged both of Ford's nipples and twisted, causing the man's hips to stutter.

"Don't stop," Dylan growled against his skin. "You do, I won't allow you to come. Then you'll disappoint her by not giving her what she begged for. She wants your cum deep inside her and you want to give her that, don't you?"

Ford panted out a ragged, "Yes, Boss."

Goosebumps broke out all over Ford when Dylan whispered, "Good boy." He dragged his lips over Ford's damp shoulder. "So damn good."

"I want to please you both, Boss."

"Of course you do. But to please her, she needs to come before you do. So make sure you don't fuck that up."

Ford was just as much a pro at taking directions as giving them. That made him the perfect switch. Dylan doubted he was as good, but he was working toward it.

I want to please you both. Dylan wanted to do the same. Erin did, too.

He started out being selfish over Erin, jealous of Ford's relationship with her. That had definitely changed. Even so, he still didn't want to share her with strangers. The night they watched a guest have sex with her quickly hammered home the fact that she was theirs and no one else's. And if she didn't want to share Ford and Dylan with anyone else, she only had to say the word and they would respect that wish. She might be a submissive, but she still had a say.

They all did.

Respect. Trust. Communication. All necessary for their success.

Ford continued with his intense and powerful thrusts, pounding into Erin and slamming back into Dylan until finally...

Erin cried out and tensed as an orgasm ripped through her once more.

Ford's knees had to be screaming by now as he knelt on that metal bar. Now that she came, he was fucking her no holds barred at the same time impaling himself on Dylan's cock.

Fuck. Was Ford trying to make him come too soon? Because that was about to happen.

But the hitch in Ford's hips, his labored breathing and his knuckles turning white as he clutched Erin's hips meant one thing...

The man was about to come undone.

Thank fuck.

"Can I come, Boss?" Ford tagged on a desperate, "*Please.*"

"The second you fill her pussy, I'm going to fill your ass," Dylan forced between clenched jaws.

He gave Ford's nipples one last hard tweak, then followed him with the final thrust as Ford drove deep into Erin one more time and came hard with a long, low grunt. His orgasm pulsed around Dylan's cock, causing him to explode, his balls emptying deep inside Ford.

Every time he came inside Ford, it was more than sexual relief. He was possessing Ford, marking him as Dylan's.

That was so damn satisfying.

He pressed a cheek against Ford's back as they both stayed curled over Erin, but Ford was holding his own weight as well as Dylan's. When Ford trembled from the effort to keep from crushing her with their combined weight, Dylan forced himself upright and pulled free, letting Ford do the same.

He wiped himself off with the nearby hand towel and offered it to Ford to do the same. They both worked as a team to unbuckle Erin's leather cuffs and put the spreader bar aside.

Once they were completely cleaned up, they all fell back to the bed and tangled their limbs together to bask in the "afterglow."

The best part? No one had to say a word.

Dylan's eye shifted to Erin to see her eyes closed, a soft smile curving her lips and her features relaxed.

Totally content.

Once again, they made her come undone.

He then glanced at Ford, who gave him a slight chin jerk.

They shared a grin, interlocked their fingers together, then both of them pressed a kiss to her forehead.

His father's death might have ended one chapter in Dylan's life, but it also created a new beginning.

Sign up for Jeanne's newsletter to learn about her upcoming releases, sales and more! https:// www.authorjeannestjames.com/

Welcome to Double D Ranch, the adults-only ranch resort where your fantasies become reality. Unpack, unwind, and get uninhibited...

Librarian Cara Leone fell down a rabbit hole when she began secretly reading very spicy books. They not only piqued her interest in that lifestyle, but made it abundantly clear how much her love life has been lacking in the intimacy department. On a whim, she books a week-long stay at the resort to see if the sweat-inducing romances she reads are more fiction than reality.

Dayne Lyons loves all things dirty. When he and his twin brother partnered to open the all-inclusive resort, he planned on using it as his own personal playground. How convenient was it to have a choice of guests at his fingertips to play out all of his fantasies? One night, when he runs into a very nervous Cara, he can't ignore the obvious... This resort guest is out of her element.

Heath Thompson desperately needs a little getaway. The investment trader has been all work and no play for the last few years while financially recovering from his ugly divorce. However, once he arrives at the resort, things don't go quite as planned. His unexpected attraction to both Cara and Dayne has him teaming up with the resort owner to help open up a whole new world for the innocent Cara.

Only, what starts out as a temporary partnership ends up being so much more.
o help open up a whole new world to the innocent Cara.

Turn the page to read the first chapter of the next book in the series: Unbridled

Unbridled

Double D Ranch, book 2

Cara moved through the thick crowd, bumping into people like a pinball. Her multitude of apologies probably went unheard due to the deep bass thumping from the loud dance music.

She had never been to a nightclub—it had never been her scene—but she could imagine this would be a similar atmosphere.

The volume of *One More Time* by Daft Punk was deafening, to say nothing of the people trying to talk above the din, as well as others singing along with every tune the DJ was spinning onstage to rock down the house.

Or more like event hall.

Colorful lights ricocheted around the inside of the building named The Mane Event Hall. They tinted people different shades and occasionally blinded Cara as she worked her way around the large interior.

Drinks flowed freely. Resort guests danced without reserve: bumping and grinding, twirling and twisting. They laughed and shouted.

While everyone else was having a good time, Cara felt a little out of place.

Some attendees had dressed for tonight's fantasy theme. Glitter, fairy wings, gossamer skirts and body paint. Costumes in vibrant blues, greens, pinks, purples, and every other color a person could imagine.

Others ignored the party's theme by going naked or wearing risqué outfits. She spotted men and women alike wearing leather harnesses that exposed their breasts, as well as other parts.

When her elbow was knocked by two women making out along the wall, half of her lemon drop martini landed on the floor. The other half on her.

"Shit." She looked at the now-empty glass, the wet floor, then down at herself. That was a waste of a good martini.

She could head to the bathroom and try to clean up, or she could go back to her room and call it a night.

Only having checked in a few hours ago, she wasn't quite sure why she decided to attend tonight's special event. Her room looked more inviting by the second. As did the silence.

She had come to Double D Ranch to dip her toes into this unknown world, not to jump in feet first. It might be better to expose herself to this lifestyle in small doses in order to see if she was even interested. To see if it was for her.

She set her empty glass on a nearby tray meant for dirty glassware and continued on her way. If she kept moving, maybe no one would notice how out of place she looked. Or how awkward she felt.

This was not her scene.

She didn't belong here.

Someone would spot her, see she was out of her element, and call her out. She just knew it.

She glanced around to see if anyone was staring. Or pointing fingers.

Of course they weren't. She was being paranoid over nothing. Nobody cared she was here.

She decided to book this trip for that reason. The website stated the guests weren't pressured to do anything they weren't comfortable with. They could do whatever they wanted with anyone willing to do the same. Or guests could do absolutely nothing.

Once she ran across their website, it took her five days until she was brave enough to call. She unreasonably thought they would instantly know this world was not for her. Alarms would go off and red alerts would be sent out via text, phone, and email.

It was silly, she knew.

Eventually, she finally did call because, even after reading their FAQ page on their website—*three* times no less—she still had questions.

But then, she did tend to overthink things.

For some reason, she didn't expect a man with a toe-curling voice to answer. He was not only pleasant to listen to, but patient and helpful. Maybe he picked up on how intimidated and unsure Cara came across.

Her first question had her cheeks burning hot and she was glad it was a phone call instead of a video chat or in-person conversation. "Is this a...BDSM club?"

She had read plenty of erotica and erotic romance novels involving kinky sex clubs at the public library where she worked.

Funny enough, that unquenchable interest started when a regular library patron, to whom Cara normally recommended books, turned around and told her about a book by one of her favorite authors.

At the time, she had no idea a toe-curling, steamy romance about sex clubs would cause her to evaluate her own life. After the first one, she fell down a rabbit hole and couldn't read them fast enough.

Those stories hammered home the fact that her past sex life had been lacking.

Big time.

That simple book recommendation took her down a path she never expected. She began to search for a similar place to those she had read about in those books. But somewhere other than in her hometown. Where she might be recognized. Where she worked. Where she knew *so many* people.

"Not a club. A ranch resort. But it's really whatever you want to make of it. You can simply come for a getaway. Take a relaxing trail ride or a dip in the pool. Soak in the hot tub or get a massage. *Ooooor*...you can get spanked, choked, and fucked by a masked stranger." His tone came off as amused.

Fucked by a masked stranger?

What front desk employee talked like that? Was he messing with her?

He finished with, "The sky's the limit. The only limits will be of your own making."

"Is it a working ranch?" she asked next, then groaned silently and bounced her fist against her forehead.

"Well, it's not like you'll be chasing down and roping wayward cattle on horseback, but we do have livestock here. We have goats and cows for fresh milk and cheese, chickens for eggs, horses for trail rides..."

"Are there a lot of single guests?" She worried it would be painfully awkward if she went and no one interacted with her.

"If you can't find a willing single guest during your stay, plenty of couples are looking for a third. And if three aren't enough, sometimes random orgies break out. Nobody would notice or care if you joined in."

Random orgies? Really? Nobody would care if she just... joined...in?

"We have standalone lakefront cabins that have private hot tubs. We also have guest rooms in the lodge itself. Would you like to make a reservation?"

Her heart was pounding so loudly that she almost missed his question. "*Umm.*"

"Hold on. Our reservationist just returned from break. I'll let her handle it. I look forward to you being our guest. I hope it's everything you're looking for."

She did, too, but she had doubts. "I'm sorry, but before you go...what did you say your name was?"

Something about his low chuckle gave her goosebumps. Not because he was creepy or anything, but because she could imagine herself blindfolded and his warm honeyed voice enveloping her while murmuring naughty suggestions into her ear.

Possibly reenacting a panty-wetting scene from one of her favorite books.

She shook herself mentally.

Even tonight, she still remembered his voice but regretted never getting his name to at least thank him. It was a shame, really, but as an employee, he probably wasn't allowed to fraternize with the guests, anyway. Not that it mattered. Simply trying to make her way through the crowded party proved plenty of actual guests were available to engage with. If they welcomed it, of course.

Another reason she picked this particular resort was how the website clearly stated multiple times that consent was not only important, but required. That alone made her feel more secure about booking since she'd be by herself.

The site also stated that anyone stepping out of line would be dealt with quickly since the management took their guests' safety seriously. All guests also had to electronically sign a legal agreement to that effect, as well as an NDA, when they made a reservation.

Now, here she was. All stemming from a crazy idea that got stuck in her head. She had never been this impulsive in all her thirty-one years.

To make this experience successful, she really needed to lean into the resort's motto: *Unpack, unwind and get uninhibited.* She already unpacked her bags, now she needed to follow through with the rest.

You can do this.

She might need another drink. Or two...

Or twelve.

As she fought her way to the restroom to attempt to dry her blouse, she stopped short when her path was cut off by a man walking on his hands and knees, wearing a tight leather collar around his neck with a chain leash attached.

He was one of the attendees not wearing a costume per se, but a leather harness around his torso. She blinked and as he kept going, Cara followed the line of the leash up to the woman holding the other end. She wore a black leather miniskirt, a matching leather bra with holes exposing her pierced nipples, suede thigh-high, high-heeled boots, and a wicked smile. Every once in a while, she would give the leash a sharp jerk and make the man come to heel. In her other hand, she carried a long thin whip of some sort.

Cara leaned closer to the person standing next her; a woman wearing a red vinyl, form-fitting, one-piece outfit with a matching mask. "Is he supposed to be a dog?"

The dark-haired woman shook her head and shouted over the music, "Slave!"

Slave? Was that term even acceptable? It seemed wrong. But then, maybe it wasn't in this scenario?

"She walks him like a dog." Of course, she just pointed out the obvious like an idiot.

When the woman turned toward her, the eyes behind the mask slowly traveled from Cara's head all the way to her toes and back. "You must be new." Her bright red lips curled. "He has a humiliation kink."

She wasn't sure all the fiction she read had prepared her for this reality. Not even close. "What's that around his..."

"Cock?"

Cara nodded.

"It's a cage."

"It has a lock." She silently groaned. She kept mentioning the obvious!

"Of course."

Cara frowned. "There's not enough room for him to... grow."

"That's exactly the point. He needs to have enough discipline so he doesn't get hard. If he does, then..." She shrugged.

Not that she should be staring, but...the colorful lights were catching something sparkly tucked between his bare ass cheeks. She narrowed her eyes. "Is that a jewel?"

The woman's grin grew into a blinding smile and she laughed softly. "You are definitely new. That's an anal plug."

She knew what an anal plug was. She read about them, she'd just never seen one. In person, anyway.

She should've watched tons of porn before she came. For educational purposes, of course. At least she might have some basics under her belt instead of feeling like such a novice.

With a quick thank you to the very sexy lady in red, she continued toward the sign at the back, and above the crowd, that said *restrooms*.

No telling what she'd find in there.

Damn. She was so out of her element. Once again, her gut was telling her that this "vacation" might have been a mistake. Maybe she *should* check out and drive—

No. She would not wimp out. She spent a fortune on the reservation and the website clearly stated refunds wouldn't be given to guests ending their stay early.

She'd saved up for this and not taking advantage of what she already paid for would be a financial hit. Plus, after what she paid, she certainly couldn't afford to stay anywhere else. She would need to drive back home and take the loss.

You don't have to do anything with anyone, she reminded herself.

She could do what Mr. Sexy Voice said on the phone. Simply relax, take advantage of their spa—since the pampering was included—or lounge by the pool, enjoying a complimentary cocktail.

She could eat until she was as stuffed as a Thanksgiving turkey. Some of the online reviews—which she scoured before making her reservation—mentioned how delicious and fresh the food was since they tried to locally source as much as possible. A few stated that, unlike most resorts, the meals were far from cafeteria or diner quality.

She could also be active and head out on a trail ride. She could hike. Paddle around the serene lake. Sit around the bonfire. Take one of the ATVs out to explore. Feed the goats...

Damn it. None of those activities were the reason she came. *None.*

Once she entered the restroom, she breathed a sigh of relief when she found nothing kinky going on. Only two women chatting while they washed their hands.

After a quick nod in greeting, she stopped in front of the

large mirror to take in the damage. Snagging a few paper towels, she blotted the large wet spot. It wasn't helping.

"Looks like someone got wet," came from the woman remaining at the sink next to her.

"Yes, I..." *Wait.* She blushed. *Damn it*, she needed to stop that! "Someone knocked into my drink."

With a sly smile, her sink mate said, "I promise you, you can get messier than that here. Don't worry about the spot. Unless you're worried about it ruining your blouse?"

"No..." She only wore washable clothes. She leaned toward being more practical, and that included her wardrobe.

"Or you could simply take it off. Going topless is encouraged around here."

Fire licked at her cheeks at the idea of walking around with her breasts hanging out. She was certainly not ready for that, and she might never be. She gnawed on her bottom lip.

The woman squeezed her arm. "Look. Don't stress over it. You won't be judged for anything you do. You could walk completely naked around this ranch for a week and no one will blink an eye. They might give you an appreciative glance, maybe invite you to join them for a session or two, and then move on."

"A session?"

"Yes, in their room or cabin. Out along a riding trail. In one of the paddle boats. Or in one of the playrooms. If you keep yourself open-minded, the opportunities are endless. Do as much or as little as you'd like."

The voice over the phone whispered through her mind. *The only limits will be of your own making.*

"Enjoy your stay."

"Thank you. Same to you."

As the woman met Cara's eyes in the mirror, she purred, "I always do. This is already my third time here. I've visited a lot of clubs and resorts all over the world and I have to say, this place is now my favorite." With a last smile and a tip of her head, she walked out of the bathroom, leaving Cara alone.

Cara stared at the woman in the mirror.

Who are you?

What are you doing here?

Did you really think this was for you?

When have you ever done something so irresponsible?

She sighed. Then, with a last glance at the dark spot on her royal-blue blouse, she pulled in a bolstering breath, gave herself a nod, and headed back out to the party. One more lap around the room and another martini wouldn't hurt.

The second she stepped out of the restroom, the loud music and crazy lights bombarded her again. Was it possible that the crowd managed to swell even more? Where were all these people coming from?

Once her anxiety with the situation began to spike again, she realized it was time to go. It was all too much for her first night.

Like a quality wine, she needed to take small sips instead of guzzling down the whole bottle at once.

Not wanting to fight the crowd to escape, she searched for the closest exit.

Get the rest of the story here: Unbridled (Double D Ranch, book 2)

If You Enjoyed This Book

Thank you for reading Undone. If you enjoyed this polyamory story, please consider leaving a review at your favorite retailer and/or Goodreads to let other readers know. Reviews are always appreciated and just a few words can help an independent author like me tremendously!

Want to read a sample of my work? Download a sampler book here: BookHip.com/MTQQKK

Also by Jeanne St. James

Find my complete reading order here:

https://www.jeannestjames.com/reading-order

<u>Standalone Books:</u>

<u>Made Maleen: A Modern Twist on a Fairy Tale</u>

<u>Damaged</u>

<u>Rip Cord: The Complete Trilogy</u>

Everything About You (A Second Chance Gay Romance)

Reigniting Chase (An M/M Standalone)

<u>Brothers in Blue Series</u>

A four-book series based around three brothers who are small-town
cops and former Marines

<u>The Dare Ménage Series</u>

A six-book MMF, interracial ménage series

<u>The Obsessed Novellas</u>

A collection of five standalone BDSM novellas

<u>Down & Dirty: Dirty Angels MC®</u>

A ten-book motorcycle club series

<u>Guts & Glory: In the Shadows Security</u>

A six-book former special forces series

(A spin-off of the Dirty Angels MC)

<u>**Blood & Bones: Blood Fury MC®**</u>

A twelve-book motorcycle club series

<u>**Motorcycle Club Crossovers:**</u>

<u>Crossing the Line: A DAMC/Blue Avengers MC Crossover</u>

<u>Magnum: A Dark Knights MC/Dirty Angels MC Crossover</u>

Crash: A Dirty Angels MC/Blood Fury MC Crossover

Romeo: A Dark Knights MC/Blood Fury MC Crossover

Beyond the Badge: Blue Avengers MC™

A six-book law enforcement/motorcycle club series

<u>**Double D Ranch**</u>

A six-book MMF ménage series

<u>**COMING SOON!**</u>

Property of Stone (Kings of Anarchy MC: Pennsylvania)

Dirty Angels MC®: The Next Generation

WRITING AS J.J. MASTERS:

The Royal Alpha Series

A five-book gay mpreg shifter series

About the Author

JEANNE ST. JAMES is a USA Today, Amazon and international bestselling romance author who loves writing about strong women and alpha males. She was only thirteen when she first started writing and her first published piece was an erotic short story in Playgirl magazine. She then went on to publish her first romance novel in 2009. She is now an author of almost 70 contemporary romances. She writes M/F, M/M, and M/M/F ménages, including interracial romance. She also writes M/M paranormal romance under the name: J.J. Masters.

Want to read a sample of her work? Download a sampler book here: BookHip.com/MTQQKK

To keep up with her busy release schedule check her website at www.jeannestjames.com or sign up for her newsletter: https://www.authorjeannestjames.com/

www.jeannestjames.com
jeanne@jeannestjames.com

Newsletter: http://www.jeannestjames.com/newsletter signup
Jeanne's Down & Dirty Book Crew: https://www.facebook.com/groups/JeannesReviewCrew/

facebook.com/JeanneStJamesAuthor

instagram.com/JeanneStJames

bookbub.com/authors/jeanne-st-james

goodreads.com/JeanneStJames